One Hot Teddy

Uncle Dorsey was vague about how he'd obtained the Mourning Bear, saying he'd "found" it while on duty somewhere in Germany. Call me suspicious, but I can't tell you the number of thieves I met during my police career that, when arrested for possession of stolen property, claimed that they'd "found" the hot goods.

Once Ashleigh was free to talk, I asked, "Hey sweetheart, do you know who owns the Mourning Bear they're auctioning today? Elizabeth Ewell. Recognize the name?"

Ash's lips tightened slightly. "I know of her. Liz Ewell is very wealthy, so she didn't come into town very much to associate with us rabble. Thinks she can get whatever she wants." Ash's voice became increasingly surly. "Back in 1972, she decided that she wanted some land my daddy owned but didn't want to sell, so she got a Richmond lawyer and went to court. She won only because she had so much money that she could have bankrupted us just by keeping it in the courts."

There was an unholy light in Ash's eyes and a dormant Virginia mountain accent emerged in her voice. "She called my daddy an ignorant hillbilly and said she hoped he'd learned his lesson not to cross his betters."

"Maybe she's changed. After all, she's donating the auction proceeds to charity."

"More likely trying to buy her way into heaven."

"Want to hear something else interesting?" I lowered my voice. "As of about an hour ago, the Mourning Bear wasn't here yet . . ."

Praise for John J. Lamb's *Echoes of the Lost Order*

"Mystery fans, meet John Lamb, a former Southern California homicide detective turned author . . . you're in for a real treat . . . Full of suspense, plot twists, well-crafted characters, and fun."
—Martha C. Lawrence

"[A] compelling mystery by a dazzling new talent." —P. B. Ryan

"Intriguing . . . a rip-roaring, rebel yell of a read."
—Tracy Dunham

P9-DZP-224

The Mournful Teddy

John J. Lamb

BERKLEY PRIME CRIME, NEW YORK

THE BERKLEY PUBLISHING GROUP
Published by the Penguin Group
Penguin Group (USA) Inc.
375 Hudson Street, New York, New York 10014, USA
Penguin Group (Canada), 90 Eglinton Avenue East, Suite 700, Toronto, Ontario M4P 2Y3, Canada
(a division of Pearson Penguin Canada Inc.)
Penguin Books Ltd., 80 Strand, London WC2R 0RL, England
Penguin Group Ireland, 25 St. Stephen's Green, Dublin 2, Ireland (a division of Penguin Books Ltd.)
Penguin Group (Australia), 250 Camberwell Road, Camberwell, Victoria 3124, Australia
(a division of Pearson Australia Group Pty. Ltd.)
Penguin Books India Pvt. Ltd., 11 Community Centre, Panchsheel Park, New Delhi—110 017, India
Penguin Group (NZ), Cnr. Airborne and Rosedale Roads, Albany, Auckland 1310, New Zealand
(a division of Pearson New Zealand Ltd.)
Penguin Books (South Africa) (Pty.) Ltd., 24 Sturdee Avenue, Rosebank, Johannesburg 2196, South Africa

Penguin Books Ltd., Registered Offices: 80 Strand, London WC2R 0RL, England

THE MOURNFUL TEDDY

A Berkley Prime Crime Book / published by arrangement with the author

PRINTING HISTORY
Berkley Prime Crime mass-market edition / August 2006

Copyright © 2006 by John J. Lamb.
Interior text design by Stacy Irwin.

ISBN: 0-425-21112-6

BERKLEY® PRIME CRIME
Berkley Prime Crime Books are published by The Berkley Publishing Group,
a division of Penguin Group (USA) Inc.,
375 Hudson Street, New York, New York 10014.
BERKLEY PRIME CRIME and the BERKLEY PRIME CRIME design are trademarks belonging to Penguin Group (USA) Inc.

PRINTED IN THE UNITED STATES OF AMERICA

10 9 8 7 6 5 4 3 2 1

Dedicated with love, to our dear friend
Frankie Uchimura.
We treasure her unfailing friendship and
support, are inspired by her strength and
cheerfulness in the face of adversity,
and thank her for bringing sweet Bear into our lives.

Chapter 1

It was just before dawn on Saturday morning, the first day of October, and I again awoke to find myself in a strange bedroom . . . only this time my wife, Ashleigh, was gone. The background racket of Bay Area suburbia was also conspicuously missing: no omnipresent hum of vehicle traffic, no clatter of police or air ambulance helicopters, no sirens, and no popping sounds that left you wondering whether they were a backfiring truck or someone resolving a thorny personal problem with a gun. Instead, I heard a meadowlark trilling "hello–good-bye" and the robust rushing hiss of the South Fork of the Shenandoah River as it flowed past the front of our new home. The serenity was more than a little disturbing. Even though we'd lived in Remmelkemp Mill, Virginia for three-and-a-half months, the house and the region still felt alien to me, which I suppose, was to be expected since I'd spent the bulk of my life in San Francisco—the world's largest unfenced lunatic asylum.

I wasn't surprised that Ash had gotten up so early. Today was a big day for her because in a few hours we'd be driving halfway across the valley to the Rockingham County fairgrounds in Harrisonburg to exhibit her menagerie of stuffed bears, tigers, and lions at the Shenandoah Valley Teddy Bear Extravaganza. And, by this afternoon, we'd know whether her Miss Susannah S. Seraphim—a twenty-four-inch-tall pink German Schulte–mohair bear wearing a handsewn Victorian dress, straw hat, and wire-framed glasses—would be awarded the first prize in the artisan bear category.

Ash had collected and made teddy bears for years, but it wasn't until we moved from California that she'd grown confident enough in her work to exhibit them for sale and enter them in a professional competition. I'm beginning to become somewhat of an expert on teddy bears myself and I think hers are appealing. More important, I'm damn proud of her for being brave enough to submit her work for critical inspection. Most people go through their entire lives fearfully dodging that sort of opportunity. It's just one of the nine hundred or so reasons I'm madly in love with her.

I rolled over onto my back and considered trying to catch another hour of sleep, but then I smelled the delicious aroma of hot chocolate and my left shin began to throb as if someone was playing the *boom-boom-boom* rhythm that opens Queen's "We Are the Champions" on my rebuilt bones with a ball-peen hammer. Half a dozen doctors have assured me that—after over a year—the pain is psychosomatic. Maybe they're right, but that doesn't make it any less real. Considering that Ashleigh and I have been married twenty-six years—and she knows me better than I know myself—I think I've done an excellent job of keeping my painful reaction to the scent of all things cocoa a secret from her. She loves her morning hot chocolate and I won't be the one to take that pleasure away from her.

My name is Bradley Lyon and I spent twenty-five years with the San Francisco Police Department, the last fourteen as an Inspector in Robbery/Homicide. I'll be forty-eight years old in July and, considering I had one of the most stressful careers in the world and we've just undergone one of the toughest years of our lives, I look about as well as can be expected. I'm a shade under six-feet tall, could lose about twenty pounds, and up until recently my hair was auburn. Now it's mostly silvery gray—so much so that I'm often asked if I want the senior discount when Ash and I go shopping. I suspect the person who originated the myth that gray hair on men looks distinguished was a middle-aged guy whistling in the dark.

As I mentioned a moment ago, Ashleigh and I have been married for over a quarter century. That's a geological epoch by today's standards of matrimonial duration. We met back in 1977 in Northern Virginia. She was a student at George Mason University in Fairfax, and I was finishing up my three-year army enlistment as a battlefield intelligence analyst at Fort Belvoir. We fell in love, and although she's smarter than almost anyone I know, she left school and followed me to the West Coast when I began to pursue my lifelong dream of being a San Francisco cop. Our marriage produced two children, both now grown and doing well. Christopher got his degree in viticulture and enology from UC Davis and works at a winery, in of all places, Missouri. Our daughter, Heather, continued the family tradition and is a patrol officer with SFPD, assigned to the Mission district.

The story behind why the odor of chocolate makes my leg ache is brief: Back in the early spring of 2003 my partner, Gregg Mauel, and I chased a murder suspect into

Ghirardelli Square, a reasonably pleasant tourist trap featuring a large ice cream parlor and candy shop operated by the chocolate conglomerate. The plaza was crowded and we didn't dare risk taking a shot at the guy, but he wasn't real worried about where his bullets were going. His second shot pretty much obliterated an inch of my fibula and tibia as it tore through my left calf. I crashed to the pavement and Gregg did the right thing—he kept chasing the crook and eventually ten-ringed him. Meanwhile, I waited for the paramedics and writhed in agony while sucking down huge gulps of obscenely rich chocolate-laced air.

From that instant forward, I couldn't endure the aroma of chocolate. I don't care whether it's a stale Hershey's Kiss left over from last Halloween or a four-dollar Godiva truffle—one whiff of the stuff and I'm transported back in time to that moment when a bullet shattered my shinbones like pretzel sticks. The ironic postscript is that the Ghirardelli Chocolate Company feels so bad about my being shot and crippled in front of their store that they send me a five-pound sampler box of their merchandise every month. Ash loves the hot cocoa mix.

Realizing that I'd never go back to sleep now, I climbed out of bed and got dressed in sweatpants, a plaid flannel shirt that Ash repeatedly threatens to throw away because it's so threadbare, and tennis shoes. I glanced at my Irish blackthorn cane leaning against the wall in the corner of the bedroom and decided I'd leave it there for now. Then I stumped toward the stairway and began a slow descent down the steps.

Our new home was built in 1899, but it's in excellent shape. It used to belong to Ash's paternal great-grandparents and it stands about twenty yards west of the river at the bottom of a wooded ridge. The house is constructed of brick painted white, is two-storied, and has a tin roof that, when it rains hard, makes a sound like the tap dance recital from hell. Upstairs, there's our bedroom, bathroom, a sewing room, and what someday may be a guest room once we clear it of the boxes that we still haven't unpacked. Downstairs is composed of a snug kitchen, dining nook, and living room. The house sits on the east edge of a 700-acre expanse of farm and pastureland jointly owned and worked by various elements of the Remmelkemp family, who've occupied this portion of the Shenandoah Valley since shortly after the Revolutionary War. And, as you'll have deduced by now, the town is named after my wife's family.

Our home looks like a teddy bear museum—not that I'm complaining, because I think it creates an atmosphere of warmth and welcome. Maybe I appreciate those things more than most men since twenty-five years of police work had taken me inside some pretty dreadful homes. Anyway, we own about 500 bears and at any given time about 300 are on display throughout the house.

Ash was so absorbed in her work that she didn't hear me clump downstairs. She was wearing my flannel robe and sitting at the dinner table fiddling with a knotted blue fabric bow that adorned a brown bear togged out in an old-fashioned sailor's uniform. As I scanned the living room, I could see she'd been busy. When we'd gone to bed last night, the thirty or so bears we were taking to the show were carefully packed in plastic crates, but now they were scattered on every horizontal surface in the living room and dining nook, evidence that Ashleigh had taken each stuffed animal out for yet another final inspection.

Even after being with Ash all these years, she's still so lovely that sometimes the mere sight of her is enough to make me catch my breath. Yeah, I know that sounds like overripe dialogue from a romantic movie that ought to be accompanied by a rising swell of violins, but it also happens to be true. In her youth, Ashleigh was a knockout and she still draws ill-concealed and admiring stares from men. Her strawberry blonde hair is long and wavy; her skin is flawless, like a porcelain doll's, and her eyes are an almost incandescent bluish-green that reminds me of the Pacific Ocean on a sunny summer afternoon. She's got a Junoesque figure, which, as far as I'm concerned, is how a real woman looks. Those anorexic TV actresses and fashion models that are supposed to be the epitome of modern feminine beauty look like androgynous famine victims to me.

Finally I said, "Good morning, my love."

Ashleigh looked up and showed her sweet smile that never fails to make my heart skip a beat. "Morning, sweetheart. How are you?"

"Wonderful." I hobbled over, kissed her on the forehead, and did my best not to inhale the steam rising from her mug of cocoa. "How long have you been down here?"

"Since about three-fifteen. I woke up and just couldn't go back to sleep."

"Excited?"

"Nervous. Almost every major teddy bear collector and manufacturer in the world is going to be there today."

"For the auction of that *Titanic* bear, right?"

"The Mourning Bear." Ash made a frustrated sound and untied the fabric bow.

I remembered her telling me about the Mourning Bear almost a month earlier when the news first broke that one was going to be auctioned for charity at the teddy bear show. The black mohair bear was produced in 1912 by the German toymaker Steiff to commemorate the sinking of the *Titanic* and there were only 655 ever made. It was one of the most rare and valuable stuffed animals on the globe and that meant collectors from all over the world would be at the bear show.

"And they really think the thing is going to go for over one-hundred-and-fifty-thousand?"

"Oh, easily more." Ash carefully retied the bow. "Three years ago, a Mourning Bear was auctioned in England and sold for ninety-four thousand pounds."

"That's . . ." I tried to do the math in my head. The last time I looked at the newspaper, the exchange rate was right around a dollar seventy-nine to the British pound. Then I gave it up and pulled the calculator from a kitchen drawer. A moment later I whistled and said, "That's over one-hundred-and-sixty-eight-thousand dollars. Honey, you just keep right on making those teddy bears."

She smiled and held up the bear so that I could examine the bow tie. "Does this look okay?"

I peered at the knot and decided it looked fine and told her so—but then again, I thought the first bow had looked fine too. However, I also knew that, regardless of my answer, she was going to keep retying the bow until she was completely satisfied that it was perfect.

Ash put the bear down and went into the kitchen. "Can I make you some coffee?"

"That'd be nice. Where's Kitchener?" I asked, referring to our Old English sheepdog.

"Outside exploring."

"You mean outside searching for something dead to eat. The Shenandoah Valley has turned our dog into a ghoul."

This was new behavior for our dog—not that he'd ever encountered any carrion in our boxing ring–size backyard in San Francisco. But now Kitch had three acres to wander in a place teeming with wildlife. Two weeks earlier, I'd interrupted him before he could dine *al fresco* on a dead groundhog and a few days after that he'd proudly trotted into the kitchen with a headless goldfinch in his mouth. Ash was horrified and I—the hard-boiled former homicide detective—was queasy over handling a dead bird.

Once the coffee was brewing, Ash asked, "You need some ibuprofen?"

"No. Sometimes it's just a little tweaky in the morning. Maybe it's the dampness."

"Are you going to be okay today? I mean, if you want to stay here, I'll understand."

"Are you kidding me?" I took her hand. "I wouldn't miss our first teddy bear show for the world. Besides, if I don't go, who's going to take the pictures of you when Miss Susannah wins first prize?"

"You really think we have a chance?" Ash sounded cautiously hopeful.

"Better than just a chance. That bear is flat out the best thing you've ever done and it's not just because it's technically perfect . . . there's something about her that looks as if you had the time of your life creating her."

"It wasn't just me. You helped make her."

"Honey, ramming polyester stuffing inside Susannah hardly constitutes helping."

"I disagree. And you were also right about her eyes. They *were* too close to each other at first." The coffeemaker began to gurgle and Ash opened the cupboard to get a mug. "In fact, you had some pretty good ideas. Maybe I'll let you make the next one."

"Thanks for the vote of confidence, but I'm not ready for that. I'm afraid any bears that I made would look like furry mutants," I said dismissively. Yet I had to silently admit I was more than a little intrigued at the thought of making a teddy bear. I hadn't done anything really creative in nearly thirty years and I was surprised that the bears fired my imagination. But in order to make one, I'd have to learn to operate Ash's high-tech sewing machine, a task I dreaded. With its LED display, glowing lights, and touch-pad controls, the machine looked only slightly less difficult to run than a nuclear accelerator.

Ash poured the coffee. "Oh, I think you're selling yourself a little short."

I took the mug and raised it high. "I'd like to offer a toast to Susannah, the cutest teddy bear in the Western Hemisphere."

Ash grabbed her cup of cocoa and tapped it against the mug. "To Susannah. She *is* perfect, isn't she?"

"Just like her maker," I said and kissed her on the cheek. "I'm going to take my coffee outside. Want to join me?"

Ash glanced at the bears and then turned imploring eyes on me. "I just need to double-check them one more time and then I'll be right out."

"Take your time."

"Thank you, honey."

I grabbed a ragged old towel from the mudroom and went outside. The sky was growing brighter as the fog began to dissipate, but the forested ramparts of the Blue Ridge Mountains were still invisible, although they were less than three miles away. A thick mist persisted just above the swiftly flowing river, which was about sixty yards wide and as muddy as a candidate's answer at a presidential debate. Although the water had receded somewhat overnight, the Shenandoah was still well above its normal level. The remnants of Hurricane Jeanne had rumbled through Virginia two days earlier, dropping over four inches of rain in less than twenty-four hours. We'd had a few tense hours when the river briefly overflowed its banks, but our house was never in any danger.

I wiped down the wooden slats of the bench in our front yard, sat down, and took a sip of coffee. The air seemed to be full of swallows gracefully dipping and soaring through the sky in search of insects. An enormous century-old Chinquapin oak stood between our house and the river and from its upper branches I heard the harsh challenging call of a blue jay. I looked for Kitchener and finally located him near the riverbank beneath a sycamore tree. When he saw me, he ambled over for his morning scratch behind the ears and when he discovered I didn't have any dog biscuits he wandered back to his original position near the water.

Sipping my coffee, I found myself once more reflecting on the painful odyssey that eventually led us to this rural village in Virginia. The orthopedic surgeons operated on my shin twice after the shooting but the damage was just too severe. I should have been overjoyed with what the doctors accomplished because I could walk with the assistance of a cane long before anyone anticipated, but that wasn't enough. My police career was on the line because I knew what would happen if my doctor categorized my injury as "permanent and stable"—the city would medically retire me, something I dreaded.

But as the weeks passed it became clear that no matter how skilled the surgeons were and how hard I rehabbed, I was going to be crippled for the rest of my life. The city medically retired me and I'm not proud of what happened next. For several months I wallowed in bitter anger and depression. If Ash hadn't been there, I don't know what might have happened. All I can say is: Thank God she possessed the patience to endure my Mardi Gras of self-pity until I finally pulled my head out of my fundament.

To make a long story short, Ash wanted to move back to the Shenandoah Valley to be close to her family and I was excited with the idea of the change of scenery. We'd visited her folks several times on vacation and I'd always liked the central Shenandoah Valley. The region was primarily rural; yet there were decent-size towns nearby like Harrisonburg, Staunton, and Charlottesville with shopping centers and cultural activities. The pace of life was slow, people still had manners, and best of all, there wasn't a Starbucks coffee shop on every street corner. Country folks are often portrayed as being little better than cretins, but they're smart enough not to pay three-ninety-five for a cup of coffee.

When I finally came out of my reverie I noticed Kitch was still there by the river, looking down at something that I couldn't see. I decided it might be a good idea to investigate, because the last thing we needed this morning was to have to bathe a hundred-pound sheepdog after he went swimming in the muddy river. So, I got up, walked over to Kitch, and looked down into the torrent of brown water. Our dog had shown a remarkable ability to locate dead critters, but this time he'd completely outdone himself.

A man was floating face down in the river about twenty yards from the shore. His hips and legs were snagged on the thick branches of a huge fallen log. He rose and fell on the surging waters, yet I could see his arms bobbed lifelessly. Over the years I'd seen enough corpses fished from San Francisco Bay to know for a certainty he was dead.

For a second, I found myself wondering if this was a really bad joke. I'd retired from cop work, moved 2,700 miles, and was just beginning to enjoy the fact that stiffs were no longer an integral part of my life and what happens? One washes up in my front yard. What are the odds?

Then I looked down at Kitchener and asked, "Nice catch. What kind of bait were you using?"

Kitch just panted and looked proud. I took him by the collar and led him toward the house because things were about to get hectic in our front yard. Going into the house,

I called to Ash, who was worrying over another teddy bear. "Sweetheart, can you get me the phone?"

"Sure. Why?"

"Because we've got some guy named "Bob" out there in the river and he's dead."

My wife looked up in shock. "Oh, my God! Are you sure he's dead? And how do you know his name is Bob?"

"Well, the two questions are kind of connected. I know his name and his condition because he's *bob*-bing face down in the water."

She grabbed the cordless phone, pressed 9-1-1, handed it to me, and then galloped up the stairs.

Realizing I was going to be on my feet for some time, I called upstairs, "Honey, please bring my cane when you come down."

By the time I'd told the volunteer fire department dispatcher about the body and given my address, Ash was back downstairs, dressed in jeans, a long-sleeved tee-shirt, and tennis shoes. She handed me my cane and headed for the door at a dead run. I followed her across the yard and joined her a minute later on the riverbank.

Ashleigh peered at the body and then raised her hands in entreaty, palms upward. "What do we do?"

"Nothing. Even if he were alive we couldn't risk going into that water. We don't have the training or equipment."

A moment or two later, we heard a siren start up from the direction of town and begin moving north on Cupp Road toward the gravel lane that led to our house. Then the Volunteer Fire Company River Rescue Team's Ford F-350 appeared, its red lightbar flashing. The truck skidded to a halt and two firefighters jumped from the truck. As they jogged toward us, I realized that this day was swiftly going from bad to worse because one of the volunteer firemen was Marcus Poole, the effervescent pastor of the Remmelkemp Mill Apostolic Assembly.

Although everyone else in town adored him, I was inclined to dislike Reverend Poole. He'd been a high-school classmate of Ashleigh's that I suspected had never quite gotten over having a huge and unrequited crush on her. The first time he'd visited our new home, shortly after we'd moved in, Poole gave Ash a hug that—at least in my mind—didn't look entirely as if it was an innocent expression of Christian love. Add the facts that he was three inches taller than me, not crippled, in superb physical condition, and his hair wasn't the color of brushed aluminum, and—oh, all right—I'm a little bit jealous, which is ridiculous because I know Ash views Poole as nothing more than an old friend. But even if he hadn't embraced my wife a little tighter than I thought appropriate, I would have been wary of the pastor because on some intangible level my inspector senses detected the submerged aroma of fraud. Poole was so perpetually cheerful, energetic, compassionate, and painfully earnest that the saintly behavior impressed me as a superb performance. I'm sorry, call me a cynic, but nobody is *that* consistently perfect and it left me wondering why he was playacting.

Poole was wearing heavy rubber boots, baggy yellow firefighting turnout pants with canvas-colored suspenders, and, despite the cool temperature a skintight white tee-shirt to show off his well-developed chest and abs and muscular arms. *Jeez, he looks pretty good,* I thought, with more than a trace of envy. He and his partner—a plump guy I'd seen around town but didn't know by name—stood and looked at the body for a moment while quietly conversing. Then, while the other fireman went to the back of the truck and began to screw the pieces of a long metal gaffing hook together, Poole came over to us and intoned:

"Dear Lord, what a tragedy. Sister Ashleigh, are you all right?"

"I'm fine, Pastor Marc. Just a little upset."

"Still, it must have been a horrible shock. Is there anything at all I can do to provide some spiritual comfort?"

"Getting the body out of the river would be a good start," I muttered under my breath and resisted adding: *And don't even think about hugging my wife.*

Poole turned his empathetic gaze on me. "And Brother Bradley, how are you dealing with this terrible occurrence?"

"Oh, I think I'm holding up pretty well under the circumstances."

If Poole noticed the dry tone in my voice, he chose to ignore it. However, Ashleigh recognized the sarcasm and shot me a look that said: *He's harmless, behave.*

Off to the northwest—over on U.S. Route 33, if I judged correctly—a new siren began to wail. Poole glanced in that direction and said, "That'll be the Sheriff's Department. Our dispatcher called them." Then he made a big production out of squaring his brawny shoulders. "Well, it's time to get to work."

"Please, be careful," said Ash.

And God help me if Poole didn't sound exactly like Buzz Lightyear from *Toy Story* when he replied, "Don't worry. Recovering a body from the river can be very dangerous, but we're experts."

As Poole returned to the fire truck and began to pull on a pair of hip-waders, Ash whispered, "Honey, I know he's a little full of himself . . ."

"Oh, you think?"

"But I truly don't believe he meant anything by that hug."

"If you say so, love."

"And I think it's really sweet that even after being married all these years, you still act like a high-school kid ready to fight behind the gym because he thinks someone

is making a move on his girlfriend." She took my hand.
"But you don't have to worry because I wouldn't trade
you for anyone or anything."

"Thanks, Ash, and I'll try to behave."

Poole had finished putting on the waders and was now
adjusting the straps of a sturdy nylon harness that fit over
his shoulders and around his waist. Two long and thick
ropes were attached to the back of the harness and the
chubby firefighter carefully tied them to the trunk of a
sycamore tree. Poole smiled, gave us a thumbs-up, and
took the twelve-foot-long gaff pole in hand. Then both
firefighters went to the river's edge and Poole proceeded
cautiously into the murky water. The pastor moved very
deliberately, using a fallen tree for a handhold as he moved
farther into the rushing stream. You could see the water
pushing against his legs and I'll give the guy this: going out
into that river took some real *cojones*. I wouldn't have
wanted to attempt it, even with two good legs.

Down at the end of the lane, I heard the approaching
siren shut off and a few seconds later a white and gold
Massanutten County Sheriff's car pulled up behind the
fire truck. The female deputy was tall—right around six
feet—with black curly hair and a round, sweet face that
belonged on one of Ash's teddies. She paused to speak
briefly with the firefighter on the riverbank and then she
joined us.

"Hi, folks. I'm Deputy Tina Barron. Can I get some information from you?"

"Sure."

"Who found him?" The deputy pulled a pen and notepad from her breast pocket.

"That'd be me," I replied.

After I'd provided our names, address, and phone
number, Barron asked, "So, Mr. Lyon, when did you first
see the body?"

"I don't know—call it six-forty."

"Any idea of who he is?"

Ash knew what I was thinking and squeezed my hand. "Well, I know it's definitely not Bob."

Barron gave me a searching glance and I thought I saw a brief, suppressed smile. Then we turned our attention to Poole. The pastor now stood hip-deep in the cascading water and had gotten to within a few yards of the body. Gradually and carefully, he extended the metal pole toward the corpse and expertly slipped the large metal hook inside the back of the dead man's jacket collar. Poole twisted the hook slightly and then began to pull the body free from the tree branches. A few seconds later, he was towing the corpse to shore.

Barron helped Poole and the other firefighter drag the body up the riverbank and lay the dead man on our front lawn. Poole checked the guy for vitals, but it was a waste of effort.

"No wallet or ID," said Barron, checking the victim's pockets.

I could tell the dead man hadn't been in the water for very long because his skin hadn't yet begun to turn adipose—that is, looking waxy and fatty. He was a runty little white guy—maybe five-foot-five and 150 pounds soaking wet, which—come to think of it—he was. I estimated his age at about thirty-five years and saw that he'd tried to compensate for his diminutive physique by shaving his head and growing a fierce moustache and goatee combination. His clothing consisted of an orange University of Virginia tee-shirt, a leather jacket, a relatively new pair of jeans, and some battered Nikes.

"Our Heavenly Lord, please bless this poor sinner that's come home to you." Poole's head was tilted skyward and his eyelids were shut. "And, please, dear Jesus, guide your noble servant, Deputy Tina, that she might discover this man's name so that his family won't spend the rest of their days worrying over his fate. All this we ask thee with humble and loving hearts, amen."

There was a moment or two of silence and then Barron said, "Well, I guess I'll call the coroner and get started on my accidental drowning report before he gets here. Would you folks mind if I used your kitchen table to write on?"

I cleared my throat. "You know, Deputy, I'm not trying to tell you your job, but you might want to hold off on your accidental death report for a little while. In fact you probably should call out a detective."

"Why's that?"

"Because this guy has petechial hemorrhaging in both eyes. You see those little bloodstains on the whites of his eyes?"

"Yeah, now that you mention it. What does that mean?"

"It tells us he didn't drown. The only way you get that sort of bloodstain is if the victim's been strangled or suffocated." I shifted my gaze to the dead man's neck and pointed. "You see that faint red line?"

"Right there?" There was a flicker of excitement in Barron's voice.

"Yeah. It's a narrow ligature mark. Ten-to-one the autopsy will show his hyaline cartilage has been fractured— classic evidence of manual strangulation. You've got a murder victim here."

Chapter 2

"You're sure?" Barron asked.

"Absolutely certain," I replied.

"You mind telling me how you know so much about people who've been strangled?"

"Because he was one of the top homicide inspectors on the San Francisco Police force," Ash said proudly.

"The city of Satan, sin, sodomites . . ." Poole struggled to think of another alliterative bad thing to say about my old hometown.

"Shameless strumpets?" I offered and pretended not to notice Ash's eyes rolling upward.

"Thank you, Brother Bradley."

Barron stood up. "So, what you're saying is that somebody murdered this guy and then threw him in the river, hoping he'd drift downstream all the way to Chesapeake Bay while the water was high."

"That's one scenario," I replied. "Here's another: The victim was killed and tossed into the river because the suspect hoped by the time the body was recovered it'd be in such bad shape that it would be easy to misidentify the cause of death."

"Any idea of how long he's been dead?"

"I'd just be guessing, but it probably happened some-time last night. His skin hasn't begun to become adipose yet, which means he hasn't been in the river all that long." I lifted up the man's arm by the sleeve of his leather jacket and then released the limb. It struck the ground with a squishy thump. "And it looks as if he's already been in and out of rigor."

"Well, I guess I'd better call the sheriff," Barron said dolefully.

"Will you need us for anything else?" Poole began to remove the hip-waders. "Our shift is about over and I've got to get over to the church. Today is our monthly char-ity flea market and things just get out of control unless I'm there."

"I can't think of any reason for you to stay. Thanks for pulling him out of the water," said Barron. "Oh, and will you make a copy of your rescue report and drop it by the Sheriff's Department?"

"I'll get it done this afternoon." Poole stepped out of the waders and turned to us. "And I just want to tell you Ashleigh, that I thank our loving Savior you married this fine man and brought him home because if he hadn't been here today, a great evil would have gone unnoticed."

"Why, thank you, Pastor Marc." She gave me a be-seeching look that said I should acknowledge Poole's olive branch.

"Thanks for the compliment." I offered my hand to Poole and he gripped it tightly.

Ash gave an almost imperceptible sigh of relief and said, "And maybe if we get the chance we'll try to stop for a few minutes at the flea market before we head into Harrisonburg."

"Oh, I don't imagine there's anything there you'd find the least bit interesting. Truth is, it's mostly junk, but it's all for a good cause," Poole said in a self-effacing noble voice. Then he threw his arm around the other firefighter's shoulder. "Hey, Brother Tony, it's quitting time. Let's head for the barn."

Barron watched the pastor climb into the rescue truck and muttered something I don't think she intended us to hear: "Junk, my butt." Then she pulled the portable radio from her gun belt and told the dispatcher that she needed Sheriff Holcombe to respond to the scene. I wondered what *that* comment meant.

Once the fire truck was gone, I checked my watch. "We have to be at the fairgrounds at ten, love?"

"Are we running out of time?"

"Well, it's seven-fifteen now and we'll have to leave here by nine-thirty at the latest. Why don't you go in and shower? I'll hang loose out here until the sheriff arrives."

"Okay, but I want you to sit down. Your leg is beginning to ache, isn't it?" Ash had noticed I was leaning heavily on my cane.

"A little."

"You sit down on the bench and I'll bring you some fresh coffee. Deputy Barron, can I get you some coffee too?"

Barron's radio squawked. She listened to the message, acknowledged the transmission, and gritted her teeth. "No thanks. I've been ordered to get back on patrol. Sheriff Holcombe will be here in about ten minutes."

"Whoa! What about our soggy friend here? Who's going to secure the crime scene?"

"You'll have to ask the sheriff that. He told me to clear out."

"That doesn't make any sense. Why would he do that?"

"You don't keep up on local news, do you?"

"Been too busy putting the house together."

"I'm in the doghouse because I'm running against him in the upcoming election. He can't stand the sight of me. And I took a big risk by telling you that, because if he found out, he'd claim I was campaigning on duty and suspend me without pay." Barron snapped the portable radio back into the metal holder on her gun belt with a little more force than necessary. I could see that she was furious, but too professional to articulate her anger.

Ash had been married to me long enough to know the sheriff's instructions made no sense. "But you can't just go away and leave a homicide victim unattended."

"Homicide victim?" Barron made no effort to conceal the disdain in her voice. "Sheriff Holcombe has already closed the case as either a suicide or an accidental drowning. Apparently he forgot to tell me about a call the department got last night reporting that a man was seen jumping from the Island Ford Bridge into the river."

"And he hung himself at some point during the two seconds it took to hit the water?" I struggled to control my growing agitation. "This guy didn't drown—he was strangled."

"I believe you."

"So, did you tell the sheriff about the trauma on the body?"

"Of course, and he told me that the victim must have gotten caught on debris in the river and that's what caused the marks."

"That's amazing. Without coming to the scene or looking at the body, he can tell precisely how this poor son-of-a-bitch died. How long has your sheriff possessed clairvoyant powers?"

Barron grimaced. "You'll have to ask him."

"And you're going to just go along with this charade?"

Ash touched my shoulder. "I don't think she has any choice, sweetheart."

"You're right, Mrs. Lyon, there isn't anything I can do. Maybe if I'm elected next month . . ." She looked away from us and toward the river. She sighed and continued, "Look, I'm truly sorry, but if I rock the boat . . . well, I'm a single mom with three kids at home and I need the paycheck."

"What if we rock the boat?" I asked.

"Then I'd offer you a little advice: Be very careful. Welcome to Massanutten County." Shoulders drooping, Barron returned to her patrol car. A few moments later she was gone.

I sagged onto the bench. "Honey, what do you know about Holcombe?"

"Not much. He was a couple of grades behind me in high school and I think I remember hearing Daddy say that he'd been a cop down in Elkton before coming back home and being elected sheriff."

"How would you like to do me a favor? Go give your folks a call. If we're going to lock horns with this guy, I'd like a little intel."

"Still want a fresh cup of coffee?"

"Please."

After refilling my mug, Ash returned to the house to telephone her parents. I sipped my coffee and waited for the sheriff. The sun began to burn the fog off and the sky gradually began to turn blue. To the east, Hanse Mountain started to emerge from the dense mist and the outline of the Blue Ridge was visible beyond. Other than the fact that I had a murdered man lying on my front lawn and was about to bump heads with the sheriff, it was shaping up to be a lovely day.

Ash came out again a few minutes later carrying an old lavender-colored blanket that she spread over the corpse. Sitting down beside me, she said, "It just isn't right to leave him laying there like that."

"Sorry, that never occurred to me. What did your dad say?"

"He was surprised when I told him what happened. He said that Holcombe was elected back in eighty-eight and—all in all—he's done a pretty good job. As a matter of fact, he was going to vote for him next month."

"If that's the case, why is he trying to pull a stunt like this?"

"Daddy didn't know, but he told me a couple of other things. About a year ago, Holcombe promoted his son, Trent, to sergeant. Trent was apparently promoted over a bunch of more senior deputies and that made everybody unhappy. Then one of the cops complained and Holcombe fired the guy for insubordination."

"So, our honest lawman isn't above nepotism and persecuting any employee bold enough to say that what he's doing is unethical. Guess some things are the same no matter which coast and what size the department."

"It also means Deputy Barron had an excellent reason for being concerned for her job." Ash's tone was gently chiding and I realized she felt I'd been excessively harsh on the deputy, which, in light of the new information, I had to admit I was.

"You're right. Guess I owe her an apology. Did your dad say anything else?"

"Only that Holcombe's wife, Pauline, is very sick with some sort of cancer. He has to take her over to the UVA Medical Center in Charlottesville every few weeks for treatment."

"Okay, Holcombe just won some major sympathy points from me because that is my worst nightmare."

Ash touched my cheek. "Mine too."

I checked my watch. "Honey, we're cutting it pretty close for time. Why don't you go up and get ready? I'll deal with the sheriff."

"You're sure?"

"Absolutely."

"And you won't try to goad him? We'll miss most of the teddy bear show if I have to bail you out of jail," Ash said with a half-hearted chuckle that told me she wasn't entirely joking.

I raised my right hand. "Scout's honor."

"Besides, maybe once he sees the body, he'll understand."

"We'll see."

She kissed me on the forehead and went into the house. After about five minutes, I heard the crackle of a motor vehicle rolling along gravel and then a sheriff's patrol car appeared down the lane. The car stopped and Sheriff Eugene Holcombe got out. He wasn't what I expected. Like most urbanites I had a bigoted view of Southern rural cops—they were all fat rednecks who wore Ray-Ban mirrored aviator sunglasses, smoked cheap cigars or perhaps chewed on a toothpick, and drawled cornpone expressions such as "y'all in heap 'o trouble, boy."

Instead, he was roughly the same height as me, but much thinner, with a marathon runner's carriage and elastic gait. His tan uniform trousers and brown shirt bore sharp creases that you could have cut your fingers on, and his gun belt was made of gleaming patent leather. Holcombe's silver-flecked brown hair was cut short, but not severely so, he was clean-shaven and there was a certain gauntness to an otherwise cheerful face that hinted at prolonged fatigue.

"I expect you're Mr. Lyon. Good morning, I'm Sheriff Holcombe." The sheriff's voice bore just a musical trace of a Virginia mountain accent.

I pushed myself to my feet and we shook hands. "Pleased to meet you."

"So, you're Ashleigh Remmelkemp's husband. You're a lucky man."

"Thanks. I know."

"I hear you were a homicide detective in San Francisco."

"That's true."

"Man, you must have seen some awful things."

"Yeah, sometimes it was pretty bad."

"And I also heard about what happened to your leg." Holcombe's gaze flicked toward my cane. "That's a darn shame."

"You seem to know quite a bit about me."

Holcombe chuckled, but I thought the laugh sounded forced. "There aren't too many real secrets out here in the country. People get to know each other in a small town and the main source of entertainment for folks is talking about their neighbors."

"If that's so, I guess we'll know what everyone will be talking about for the next week."

"Yep, *this* dad-blasted fool." He turned toward the body.

He actually said "dad-blasted," I thought in amazement.

Holcombe continued: "We got a report about this fella last night around eleven—anonymous call, unfortunately. They said they saw him take a header off the Island Ford Bridge. You know where that is, don't you?"

"Yeah, a few miles upstream." I pointed to the south.

"So this could be either an accidental drowning or a suicide. We may never know which it was."

And there was the Gospel according to St. Holcombe—
I wondered how he was going to react to my display of
heresy. "Sheriff, pardon me if this looks as if I'm trying
to interfere with your business, but that man did not
drown. He was strangled."

"You're absolutely sure of that?" Holcombe didn't
sound offended and I relaxed a little.

"Yeah, I've seen this before—it's textbook strangulation trauma. He's got petechial hemorrhaging in both
eyes and an obvious ligature mark across the front of his
throat . . . but your deputy already told you that."

"Yes, she did."

"So, why did you tell her that it was an accidental
drowning?"

Holcombe's soft smile remained fixed but his tone began to grow a little frosty. "Mr. Lyon, I don't have any
doubt that you were a first-class homicide detective, but
you don't really have any experience with what a river
like the Shenandoah can do to a man."

"How do you mean?"

"White people have been living beside this river for
over two hundred years and during that time all sorts of
junk and rubbish has ended up in the riverbed." He pointed
to the opposite shore. "You see that wire fence over there?"

"Yeah."

"That's the third fence Donnie Tate's had to put up
since I began working as a deputy back in nineteen-
eighty—the other two were washed away by floods.
There's all sorts of stuff in the river that can choke a
man—fencing wire, old rope, metal cables, even honey-
suckle vines are strong enough to do the job."

"And your point is?"

"The point is, knowing those facts, let me ask you a
question: Isn't it *possible* this man fell or jumped into the

river and while still alive caught his neck on something that choked him?"

"I'll allow it's possible, but not the least bit probable."

"In *your* opinion, which means absolutely nothing. Mr. Lyon, I take no pleasure in this, but I must tell you exactly how I feel about your well-intentioned meddling." Holcombe sounded sad but resolute.

"My what?"

"Please, don't interrupt. I'm very sorry you were . . . handicapped and can no longer be a police officer." Now there was a pitying tone in his voice that enraged me. "Sometimes former cops feel as if the entire purpose of their life is gone and that just eats at their insides. And maybe they do things to show that they're still . . . men. Who knows? I might feel that way in your place. But that does not entitle you to willfully insert yourself into a sheriff's investigation or to mislead my personnel so that you can demonstrate your personal worth."

I was gripping my cane so tightly my knuckles were white. "Finished?"

Holcombe shifted his hands so that they rested on his gun belt. "No. I want to remind you of two very important facts. First, you aren't a peace officer in the Commonwealth of Virginia. Therefore you have no legal authority whatsoever to participate in an investigation into anyone's death. Second, if you persist in interfering in my official duties I will be forced to take you into custody. Do I make myself clear?"

"Utterly."

"For your benefit, I hope so. Now, I would appreciate it very much if you would go back into your house and wait there until the ambulance arrives and removes the body."

Chapter 3

I hobbled into the house and withstood the almost overwhelming urge to hurl my cane against the wall. Kitchener ran to the door and began to bark, so I looked out the living room window. A white ambulance van had just arrived and two young women climbed out of the vehicle. One was wearing dark blue trousers and a uniform shirt while the other wore a calf-length black dress, a blue Windbreaker with fire department patches on the shoulders, and a small white gauzy cap on her head that marked her as a member of the Mennonite faith. Sheriff Holcombe pulled the blanket aside and stood by as the women deftly shoved the dead man into a zippered vinyl body bag. They loaded the corpse onto a gurney and soon the ambulance was rolling back down the driveway, presumably en route to the Massanutten County Morgue. The entire body pick-up procedure had lasted less than five minutes.

Holcombe watched the ambulance depart and tossed the blanket onto the bench. He looked at the river for a few moments and then turned toward our house and noticed me watching from the window. The sheriff grimaced, gave me a curt nod, and climbed into his patrol car.

As the cruiser rolled down the driveway and out of sight my anger was slowly replaced by a nebulous feeling of puzzled disquiet. I couldn't quite put my finger on it, but there was something about Holcombe's behavior during the collection of the body that was all wrong. Playing the scene over again in my head, it suddenly hit me—he hadn't so much as glanced at the dead man's face. As a veteran lawman, it wasn't likely Holcombe was squeamish, so why had he studiously avoided looking at the corpse—particularly when the man was thus far unidentified?

Kitchener shoved his head beneath my hand and I scratched his muzzle. "It doesn't make any sense, Kitch. But, you know what? Solving murders isn't my job any more. Remind me of that the next time I want to play Sherlock Holmes."

I went upstairs and found Ash in the bathroom, wrapped in a blue cotton bath sheet and staring into the mirror as she blow-dried her damp hair. As I told the story, she clenched her jaw and her eyes narrowed.

"He said *what*?"

"You heard right. I'm intruding because I have a desperate need to prove my manhood."

"That little creep. What did you say to him?"

"Nothing. I was too mad and I could tell he wasn't bluffing about arresting me. Besides, what if he's right?"

"You don't actually believe him?"

"I don't know, sweetheart. Maybe I *was* trying to impress everyone." I looked at the floor. "I was a cop most of my adult life and what am I now?"

"You're my partner in our new business and the man I love more than life. And I have absolutely no questions about your manhood." She lifted my chin and leaned close to give me a long, slow kiss.

When I caught my breath, I said, "I don't know if I'm entirely convinced. Maybe there's something else we could do to bolster my fragile male ego."

Ash chuckled and stroked my cheek with the back of her hand. "I'd love to, but we're running out of time, honey. Tonight?"

"Okay, but in the meantime I'm going to need a cold shower."

Later, as I was shaving and Ash was getting dressed, she said, "You know, I thought of a new name for our teddy bear business last night."

"I thought you liked Ashleigh's Menagerie."

"It's okay, but I told you, I don't want it to be just my name."

"Sweetheart, you are the gifted teddy bear artist and I'm the happy and somewhat dimwitted sidekick. It *should* be just your name."

"How about, Lyon's Tigers and Bears?"

"Oh, my," I added and looked from the mirror to Ash. "Hey, that's inspired. In fact, it's so good . . ."

"That some other teddy bear artisan must already have it as a business name?" Ash began tucking a cream-colored turtleneck pullover into her russet-colored slacks. "That's what I thought too, so I searched on the Internet last night. It doesn't look as if anyone else is using it."

"I like it a lot. It's cute, clever, and easy to remember."

"And it's both of our names."

"We've still got some card stock. Would you like me to make some business cards before we go?"

"I already did it last night." Ash put on a navy blue woolen sweater decorated with brightly colored embroidered autumn leaves. "Honey, I'm going to go bring the truck around to the front door and start loading the crates. Thank goodness we packed the tables and chairs last night because it's getting a little late."

"I'll be down in a second to help."

As I got dressed, I heard Ash drive our Nissan Xterra from the detached garage to the front door. Back in San Francisco we'd never owned a SUV nor had wanted one, but we definitely needed a four-wheel-drive truck here in the country. Downstairs, the front door opened and I heard Ash tell Kitchener to move out of the way as she carried a plastic crate containing the bears out to the Xterra.

Going down to the living room, I grabbed the Fuji digital camera and turned it on. The battery icon indicated half-strength, which from experience I knew meant I might be able to take two flash photos before the camera shut down. Ash came in the house and I asked, "Do we have any more double-A batteries?"

"No, is there time enough to stop at the Wal-Mart in Harrisonburg?"

"It's Saturday—glaciers move faster than the traffic at that shopping center and it's out of the way. Let's hit Garber's," I said, referring to the combination grocery and general store on the main road in Remmelkemp Mill.

"They cost twice as much there, but I suppose we'll have to."

Once the crates were loaded, we secured Kitchener inside his large plastic pet crate and turned the television on. Our dog suffers from separation anxiety and he chews furniture and teddy bears when he gets upset—which is pretty much whenever we're gone for more than five minutes. The crate is his safe haven and we'd discovered that the background noise from the TV seemed to further calm him. Most people would imagine he'd enjoy watching the

Animal Planet Network, but Kitch is actually a huge fan of QVC—especially when they're selling New York–cut steaks.

"Do you want to drive?" Ash asked as she locked the front door.

"Thanks, I'd like that."

I drove down the driveway, made a right onto Cupp Road and after traveling about a quarter-mile arrived at the T intersection with Coggins Spring Road where we made another right turn. The fog had burned off entirely while we were in the house and it was a gorgeous and pleasantly warm autumn morning. We rolled down the windows and savored the fresh air.

Emerging from the river valley, I slowed the truck to admire the breathtaking view. We live in a picture postcard and if the day ever comes when I cease being utterly spellbound by it, I sincerely hope Ash borrows my cane and smacks me right between the running lights. The land is composed of rolling hills carpeted with emerald grass and capped with oak, maple, and loblolly pine trees. Five miles to the west and towering above the verdant farmland is Massanutten Peak, the southernmost crest of a forest-covered mountain range that runs down the middle of the Shenandoah Valley for fifty miles. Up near the summit—where the nighttime weather was cooler—the foliage was beginning to show traces of crimson, yellow, and orange.

I rounded a bend in the road, stepped on the brakes, and slowed the Nissan to a crawl. Just ahead, a column of about thirty musket-toting Confederate infantrymen was marching down the hill and into town. A horse-mounted officer and a billowing red Rebel battle flag led the troops. It was the Massanutten Rangers, a local Civil War reenactment group that often camped across the river in William Pouncey's pasture. On Saturday mornings, they came into town to salute the monument honoring the skirmish at Remmelkemp Mill and afterwards load up on fresh bottles of hard liquor for the nighttime revelries around the campfire. I knew this because Ashleigh's "baby" brother, Joshua, was the Rangers' First Sergeant.

Seeing the oncoming lane was clear in front of us, I pulled out and began to creep past the troops. "Want me to slow down so you can say hi?"

"You know how he hates to be teased when he's playing soldier."

"So, you want me to slow down."

"Of course."

Ashleigh is without question the sweetest human being I know and I don't just say that because I adore her. She truly is kind, caring, and compassionate. That said, she and Josh have apparently always enjoyed deviling each other whenever they get the chance. Ash assures me that they really do love each other, but it seems to me they have a strange way of showing it.

We drew abreast of a short and stern-faced soldier at the front of the column. His butternut-colored uniform coat bore the light blue chevrons of a sergeant. Ash called out sweetly, "Hey, Josh, isn't it a little early for Halloween?"

Joshua kept his eyes riveted on the road and growled, "Knock it off, Trashley."

"And you being so short, I thought mama was sending you out as Frodo this year!"

Some of the troops started to chuckle and Joshua shouted, "Quiet in the ranks!"

Ash laughed and I stepped on the gas to prevent a further escalation of verbal hostilities. I said, "Well, that was a new experience—wheelman in a drive-by taunting. And this is normal healthy brother-sister teasing, right?"

"We're just having fun." My wife's eyes were bright with merriment.

"I'll remind you of that when he gets even with you—and you know he will."

The first thing you see when coming into town from the east is the monument I mentioned a moment ago. It stands on a small traffic island in the middle of the road and is one of the most peculiar things I've ever seen—and that's the opinion of someone who spent his adult life as a cop in San Francisco. The base of the monument is a stark four-foot cube of white marble upon which is mounted a full-size bronze sculpture of a Civil War musket, with its muzzle pointing skyward, closely flanked by two water buckets. A plaque says the statue commemorates a minor victory gained by local soldiers in 1864 when they drove off some Union troops who'd torched the mill, and after that, extinguished the fire set by the Yankees. But as far as I'm concerned, the thing looks an awful lot like the magical marching broomstick with the water pails from Disney's *Fantasia* and I can't help but begin to hum "The Sorcerer's Apprentice" whenever we pass the monument.

Although Remmelkemp Mill is the governmental seat of Massanutten County, it's just about the same size as a football field with a population of maybe one hundred. The most impressive building in town is the County Courthouse and Administrative Center, which was built in 1908 and stands on the south side of Coggins Spring Road. It's a handsome two-storied Greek Revival structure, constructed of dark-red local brick, fronted by six tall Ionic pillars, and crowned by a whitewashed cupola. Dogwood trees surround the courthouse and the only jarring element to the picture is the new Sheriff's Department and County Jail—a cheerless and oversized cement shoebox—attached to the rear of the complex.

Other than the government buildings, "downtown" Remmelkemp Mill consists of six small businesses, the volunteer fire station, and Poole's church. Garber's grocery store is directly across the road from the courthouse and I turned into the parking lot, which, to my surprise, was crowded with vehicles. Fortunately, a car backed out of a space just as we were pulling in and I grabbed the spot.

"I've never seen it this crowded before. What do you suppose is going on?" Ash asked.

"Overflow parking for the flea market." I pointed to a couple returning to their truck from the Apostolic Assembly, which was next door to the market.

The man was carrying a DVD player and the smiling woman was fastidiously examining a brown suede-leather jacket that appeared brand new. I now understood why Deputy Barron had made the sarcastic response to Poole's claim that the merchandise sold at his charity bazaar was junk. That, and the fact that there had to be about a hundred busy shoppers gathered around the sales tables in the church parking lot, made me very curious as to why he'd tried to discourage us from visiting the flea market.

"Sweetheart, how much would a jacket like that cost at the Belk department store?" I nodded in the direction of the couple.

Ash peered at the coat. "I don't know, maybe two-hundred dollars—two-fifty tops for that one."

The man was now close enough for me to see the label on the front of the device. I said, "And a new Sony DVD player. Not bad for a yard sale."

"That *is* strange, now that you mention it. But I can't believe that Pastor Marc would be up to anything dishonest."

"You're probably right. But can you humor me and get the batteries while I take a quick look at the moneychangers in the temple?"

"Okay, but I'll be right back."

"Give me a shout."

As we got out of the truck, the Rangers marched into town and came to a halt in front of Garber's, which housed a tiny State Alcoholic Beverage Control shop. The officer on horseback ordered the troops to break ranks and I saw Josh Remmelkemp start toward Ash with fire in his eyes.

"Here comes your loving brother. You need any back-up?"

"For him?" Ash made a dismissive sound.

Josh gave me a congenial hello, the expected argument erupted, and I limped as fast as I could toward the church parking lot. Soon, my left leg was aching and I was thinking: *What the hell do you think you're doing? They could be selling Iraq's weapons of mass destruction at that freaking flea market and it's none of your business because you aren't a cop any more.*

Viewed from the air, the Apostolic Assembly is shaped like an inverted L with the main church as the vertical line and the congregation's community center as the horizontal bar. The church is sheathed in white vinyl siding, there's an ugly truncated steeple that looks like it was added as an afterthought, and the two front doors are painted the same color as a stop sign. Although it wasn't visible from my location, I knew that Poole's small house was behind the community center and next to the church cemetery.

As I limped along, I was passed by two Confederate soldiers also on their way to the flea market and I overheard a brief snatch of a conversation:

"I still can't believe you didn't hear them arguing last night. They were loud enough to wake the dead."

"That last cup of tangle-foot flat knocked me on my ass . . . head *still* hurts."

"Oh, you shoulda heard it, Fred. She was callin' him

vile names." The soldier leaned close to his friend and apparently whispered what was said.

The other man whooped and laughed. "Hell, I'm sorry I missed it. Wake me up if it happens again tonight."

"Count on it, pard."

Once I got to the parking lot, a quick scan of the first few tables caused me to wonder if I'd jumped to conclusions. Most were loaded with mismatched sets of discount glassware, collections of Avon novelty perfume bottles, strands of archaic Christmas lights, used toys, empty cigar boxes, chipped knickknacks, and old paperbacks—junk, to be precise. However, most of the bargain hunters were clustered around two tables nearest the community center and I gently pushed my way through the crowd to see what had attracted them.

I'd finally hit pay dirt and I'll admit I was shocked. On the tables were CD and DVD players, boom boxes, video game units, digital video cameras, car stereos, and even a laptop computer—pretty much everything you'd expect a professional burglar would steal from your auto or home. Furthermore, the stuff was priced to sell and the tables were being emptied faster than a box of free samples of Viagra at an AARP convention. A smiling church lady stood at the end of the table collecting cash from the joyful buyers.

I picked up a Pioneer CD player, turned it over and was anything but surprised to see that the serial numbers were removed. Glancing to my right, I noticed a guy of about my age examining an Xbox video game system. I asked in what I hoped was a casually disinterested voice, "Hey, this is kind of unusual merchandise for a flea market, isn't it?"

"Sure is."

"Do they have this kind of stuff every month?"

"Yep."

"You worried that any of it might be stolen?"

The man squinted at me. "Now what makes you say that?"

"Because it looks as if the serial numbers have been removed from a lot of the electronic items."

"For your information, mister, Pastor Marc gets this stuff from the monthly police auctions in Richmond."

"Oh, well that explains everything." Actually, it didn't, but it was the perfect cover story—so long as you didn't know that most law enforcement agencies auction unclaimed property once a year.

As I stood there watching the nice people paw at the loot, several questions occurred to me. First, how was it possible that a stolen-goods bazaar of this scope could be convened monthly across the street from the Sheriff's Office? It was now obvious that Deputy Barron suspected Poole was selling booty from burglaries and it was just as clear she felt powerless to intervene. That could only mean Sheriff Holcombe had commanded his deputies to ignore the monthly church plunder festivals. And, of course, that made me wonder why? Was Holcombe getting a kickback from the pastor or was he fearful of crippling his chances for reelection if he jailed the local minister and then couldn't get a grand jury indictment? Finally, since it was impossible for me to imagine Poole breaking into homes and vehicles, I wondered who was funneling this bonanza of hot goods to the church?

Ash called and I turned to go back to the Xterra. Stumping past the tables, I saw a sleek, new, tobacco brown Jaguar XJ-8 with tinted windows appear from behind the opposite side of the church and speed down the west driveway toward the road. The Jag turned right onto Coggins Spring Road and accelerated so quickly that the vehicle briefly lost traction and slewed into the oncoming lane. As the car shot off westward in the direction of Massanutten Mountain, I noticed that it bore a red, white, and blue license plate, but I couldn't quite make out the state or numbers and letters. Add deteriorating eyesight to the bliss of middle age.

As I neared the SUV, Ash saw the pensive look on my face and asked, "What's wrong?"

Once behind the wheel, I told her what I'd seen.

"You're kidding."

"Nope. If that stuff were any hotter, those shoppers would need potholders." I started the truck and backed out from the parking lot and onto the road.

"Is it possible Pastor Marc doesn't know?"

"There's a greater possibility that I'm going to throw this cane away and learn to dance flamenco."

Chapter 4

We drove through rolling farmland, headed for the intersection with U.S. Route 33, which was about two miles away. Ash silently watched the passing scenery and I knew she was mulling over my accusation against Poole.

Finally, I said, "Look, I know it's hard to believe and you may think I'm naturally prejudiced against the guy—which I'll admit I am—but Poole is selling stolen property."

Ash put a reassuring hand on my knee. "No, honey, you may be irrationally jealous of Pastor Marc, but I absolutely believe you."

"Thanks, I think."

"I'm just trying to figure out why he would do such a thing."

"No way of telling. Maybe he just figures that it isn't up to him to sit in judgment of how the Good Lord provides for a 'good cause'—whatever he meant by that."

"You don't believe he's keeping the money for himself?"

"Oddly enough, no. My read on Poole is that he cares more about being loved and admired by everyone than wealth."

Ash nodded in silent agreement. "So, where do you suppose he's getting all the stolen property?"

"Not from around here, that's for certain. All it would take is for one person to see his or her DVD player on one of those tables—and go to the State Police instead of Honest Gene Holcombe—and the sacred stolen-goods bazaar would be finished faster than you can say, 'Thou shalt not steal.' "

"So, who's supplying the stuff?"

"Whoever he is, he's got a sweet deal going, and as a bonus, he won't do any real time in jail if he's ever arrested."

"How do you mean?"

"When this guy is finally popped for housebreaking he's going to offer to tell everything he knows about Poole and Sheriff Holcombe—for a price," I explained. "And there isn't a prosecuting attorney on this planet that won't play let's make a deal to get a felony conviction on a prominent clergyman and a corrupt sheriff—if only for the good publicity."

Ash patted my knee. "Darling, have I ever told you that you have a very cynical attitude about the human race?"

"Well, it's the first time today."

We arrived at the intersection with U.S. Route 33 and turned west. The highway has an actual name—Spotswood Trail, but I don't think I've ever heard anyone use it. It's a four-lane road posted with fifty-five-mile-an-hour speed limit signs that are completely ineffective because everyone is driving way too fast to see them—including me.

Okay, there's no point in denying it. Unless I'm going someplace fun like to the dentist for a root canal, I operate a motor vehicle as if I'm still behind the wheel of a black-and-white, which means that I don't drive so much as fly at a very low altitude. Fortunately, it appears as if everyone from around here has also driven a cop car at some point in their lives, so I blend right in.

I drove through the small community of McGaheysville and then the road swung to the southwest as it looped around the base of Massanutten Peak. We crossed into Rockingham County and after traveling another few miles I turned left onto Cross Keys Road. The Rockingham County Fairgrounds were south of Harrisonburg, and rather than fight the weekend traffic in town, I intended to cut cross-country on secondary roads.

Besides, the drive was much prettier. At first, the winding road was hemmed by dying cornfields, the tall, bronzed stalks trembling in the morning breeze. Then came verdant pastureland studded with low outcroppings of gray rock and dotted with milky-white Charolais cattle. Cresting a hill, we found ourselves between a distant pair of cobalt-colored waves with the Blue Ridge to our left and the Appalachian Mountains farther away to our right. If there is a heaven, I'm convinced it must look like this part of the Shenandoah Valley because I can't imagine any improvement on this astonishing beauty. At any rate, I hope it's a long, long time before I find out for sure.

Fifteen minutes later, we were southbound on Valley Pike, approaching the fairgrounds, which stand on a low flat hill on the west side of the highway, hidden from view by a dense wall of tall evergreens. Although Ash had told me the Mourning Bear auction was going to attract a large number of potential buyers, I was nonetheless stunned by the traffic jam of high-priced vehicles all making their way up the long driveway leading to the grassy parking lot. There were Cadillacs, Infinitis, BMWs, battle cruiser-size Lincoln Navigators, and Mercedes—most with out-of-state license plates. Yet I shouldn't have been surprised at the parade of automotive affluence. Anyone that can spend one-hundred-and-seventy grand on a twenty-inch teddy bear doesn't drive a rusty AMC Gremlin to the sale.

We joined the procession, but didn't follow the other vehicles to the parking lot. As exhibitors, we had permission to temporarily park at the hall's back door to unload our truck. I followed a small cardboard directional sign and turned onto a gravel lane that led to the rear of the building. There, we found maybe eight vehicles parked at various angles from which women were removing chairs, folding tables, and box upon box of teddy bears. Swinging the SUV around, I slowly backed into an empty spot near the double doors.

"Okay, sweetheart, I'll unload the stuff and carry it to our spot." I handed Ash the truck keys and continued in a mortified voice, "And I'm sorry, but you're going to have to park the truck. It's too far for me to walk unless you don't mind me arriving sometime much later this afternoon."

"I already knew that, honey." Ash rubbed my cheek. "And there's no need to apologize."

"If you say so. We're space fifty-one, right?"

"Right, and the map they mailed us last week shows that we're in about the middle of the building." She opened my old leather briefcase and retrieved a flimsy cardboard card with my name printed on it and encased in a clear plastic sheath. "Oh, and here's your nametag, otherwise they won't let you in."

We got out of the truck and had everything unloaded in a couple of minutes. As Ash drove off, I moved the seven crates of teddy bears to a spot inside the door and then lugged the first six-foot-long aluminum folding table toward our assigned space. The exhibit hall is about the size of a small high-school gymnasium and constructed of cement cinderblocks painted light green—the overall effect being that you feel as if you've stepped inside a gargantuan and empty carton of mint-chocolate-chip ice cream. Inside, I saw that a large, rectangular canvas tent had been erected directly in front of the hall, effectively doubling the amount of floor space.

We were among the last exhibitors to arrive and the place was already beginning to fill with hundreds of teddy bear aficionados. The assigned spaces were marked out on the floor with blue masking tape and I quickly found our allotted place. By the time Ash appeared, I had both of our tables set up, the chairs unfolded, and the crates of bears ready for her to arrange for display. I was also sweating like an Enron executive testifying before Congress.

"You should see the crowd out there; there's even a camera crew from Channel Three," said Ash, referring to Harrisonburg's NBC Television affiliate.

"Did you see the judges' tables on the way in? I want to get a picture of Susannah."

She pointed toward the tent. "They're in there next to where they're going to hold the auction."

"Why don't I go and take some pictures now before things get busy?"

"Good idea, honey. I'll get set up while you're gone."

Ash began to remove the bears from the boxes and place them on the table with the same caution and care that I would have employed to defuse a neutron bomb. Mind you, I'm not making fun. She's got a natural talent for arranging and posing the bears in eye-pleasing combinations. I grabbed the camera, kissed Ash on the forehead, and stumped toward the tent.

If you've never been to a teddy bear show you really should go to one, even if you're firmly convinced that stuffed animals are just for kids or—even worse—adults suffering from terminal immaturity. Yet in a world brimming with sorrow, strife, and mindless brutality, a room full of teddy bears, artisans, and collectors is good medicine for your soul. As a general rule, the people in the hobby are cheerful, mannerly, and laugh often. If that's the contemporary definition of childish behavior, I'll take immaturity any day, thank you.

There looked to be about seventy teddy bear exhibitors in attendance and even though I've been to several shows, I never cease to be amazed at the number and sheer variety of stuffed animals on display. On our aisle alone I saw reproductions of old-fashioned hump-backed bears, whimsical magenta and lime-colored bears with long arms and comically oversized feet, luxurious bears made from recycled fur coats, and realistic-looking black bears climbing up small artificial pine trees. In addition, there were many bears dressed in exquisitely handsewn costumes as nurses, barnstorming pilots, scarecrows, firefighters, witches, angels, ballerinas, Santa Claus, and even a Queen Elizabeth I, complete with a miniature white pleated neck ruff.

Another thing I noticed was the relaxed and congenial atmosphere as collectors swarmed the tables, often greeting artisans and other fans they'd met at previous shows. Even though it was crowded, no one was pushing, complaining, or copping an aggressive attitude. Part of this might be because women dominate the hobby, but having seen the "fairer sex" ruthlessly battling over bargain merchandise at department-store holiday sales, I think it has far more to do with the teddy bears themselves. While I don't believe in magic, I'm firmly convinced there is something almost supernatural about the bears' soothing effect on people.

I passed through the doors and into the adjoining canvas tent. The left half of the tent was fenced off with lightweight white vinyl railing, and within the enclosure were perhaps a hundred folding chairs facing a polished wooden podium. Although the auction was set for 3 P.M., there were thirty or forty people already in the VIP corral, and they loitered near a long table packed with baked goods, fresh fruit, and champagne bottles. Standing guard at the entry gate was a young guy—definitely out of place with his sour face—dressed in a gray suit and holding a thick stack of tri-fold color brochures. I assumed the fliers contained information on the Mourning Bear and since I'm becoming a dedicated student of the history of teddy bears, I decided to grab one.

I smiled and asked, "Hi, could I have one of those?"

The kid gave me the once over, sniffed, and obviously concluded I didn't look wealthy enough to be a bidder. "I'm sorry, sir, but it's our policy to reserve all literature for certified participants."

"It's not literature—it's a seventeen-cent brochure."

"And what part of 'you can't have one' don't you understand?"

"Lighten up, my friend. This is a teddy bear show, not an anger management seminar." I used the empathetic Father Flanagan voice that had secured more suspect confessions than I could remember. "You look unhappy. What's the matter?"

The kid blinked in surprise. People are almost always stunned when you don't react aggressively to overt rudeness. Looking back and forth to make sure he wasn't overheard, he said, "Sorry, man, it's just that my boss is busting my ass because the Mourning Bear isn't here yet."

"Is that your fault?"

"No, it's his for not checking with the owner when it wasn't delivered last night. But he's never wrong, so I get smacked."

"Sounds like a real jerk."

"Look up the word in the dictionary and you'll find a picture of him."

"Well, good luck and just a word of advice from someone who's worked for more than his share of jerks: Don't ever let him see he's gotten you angry. That's how he controls you."

"Thanks, man, and here." He handed me a brochure.

Tucking the brochure into the pocket of my leather jacket, I went to the opposite side of the tent where a crowd was gathered around the tables displaying the teddy bears to be judged later that afternoon. Susannah stood in the group of five finalists from the "Artisan, Large Dressed" category. The others were cute—a pirate, a Renaissance princess, a fairy, and a toy soldier—but I truly believed Ash's bear was the best. My only hope was that the judges agreed with my utterly unbiased opinion. I took a couple of photographs of Susannah and then headed back to our table.

By the time I arrived, Ash was in the process of selling her very first teddy bear. A woman was bent over the table writing a check while my wife smoothed out the blue ribbon around a cinnamon-colored bear's neck and quietly told the toy that it was going to a good home. I was surprised to see that Ash's eyes were moist as she lovingly wrapped the bear in white tissue paper and put it into a plastic bag. Then she took the check and handed the bag to the woman.

As soon as we were alone, I asked, "Honey, are you okay? I thought you'd be overjoyed to sell a bear."

"I am. I'm thrilled, but it's kind of hard to give a bear up after you've spent so much time making it absolutely perfect." She pulled a tissue from the briefcase and dabbed at her eyes. She gave me an embarrassed smile. "I guess that sounds kind of stupid, huh?"

"Not at all. However, I do think you're going to get plenty of practice on giving up your bears today," I said as three women approached our table.

I sat down and let Ash do the talking and with good reason. She's the artist who translates her wonderful visions into plush and mohair reality. I'm the guy that shoves polyester foam into the bears and hopes to someday graduate to pouring beans into their bottoms. Be honest: If you were buying an artisan teddy bear, which of us would you rather talk to?

After awhile, I got bored with watching people and I pulled out the brochure. There was a color photograph of the Steiff Mourning Bear on the inside—and aside from the fact that it's one of the most rare and valuable stuffed animals in the world—there wasn't anything too remarkable about it. The bear was made from black curly mohair with a shaved snout, black embroidered nose and mouth, yellowish-taupe paw pads, hockey stick-shaped arms, and glistening eyes the color of anthracite.

I already knew the basic tale of how the Mourning Bear came to be created after the sinking of the *Titanic*, but the brochure contained some mildly interesting additional information. Apparently, the bears were produced in two separate groups, with the first 494 made shortly after the disaster in 1912 and another 161 produced between 1917 and 1919 for a total of 655.

Under the heading "Provenance" there were some generic personal facts about the soon-to-be former owner, Elizabeth Ewell, and how she'd come to own the bear. The lady was eighty-six years old and had spent her entire life on a large farm bordering the South Fork of the Shenandoah River in an area known as Caisson Hill. With a start, I realized that Miss Ewell lived approximately three miles upstream from us and I wondered if Ash knew her.

I read on and was surprised to learn that there was no connection between the *Titanic* sinking and the Ewell family. Rather, Ewell's Uncle Dorsey came home from World War One with the bear as a gift for his newly born niece. Uncle Dorsey was vague as to how he'd obtained the bear, telling the family only that he'd "found" it while on occupation duty somewhere in Germany. Call me suspicious, but I can't tell you the number of thieves I'd met during my police career that, when arrested for possession of stolen property, claimed that they'd "found" the hot goods.

Once Ash was free to talk, I asked, "Hey sweetheart, do you know who owns the Mourning Bear they're auctioning today?"

"No. Who?"

"A neighbor. Elizabeth Ewell. Recognize the name?"

Ash's lips tightened slightly. "I know of her. Liz Ewell is very wealthy, so she didn't come into town very much to associate with us rabble."

"Yow. I believe that's the first time I've ever heard you say anything bad about the people around here."

"She's different—thinks she can get whatever she wants just because she has money." Ash's voice became increasingly surly. "Back in nineteen-seventy-two, she decided that she wanted some bottomland next to her property that my daddy owned. She offered to buy it, but daddy didn't want to sell, so she got a Richmond lawyer and went to court and claimed that the survey was wrong."

"What happened?"

"She won—not because she was right, but because she had so much money that she could have bankrupted us just by keeping it in the courts."

"That stinks."

"Tell me. And you know what she told my daddy when they were done?"

"What?"

There was an unholy light in Ash's eyes and a dormant Virginia mountain accent emerged in her voice. "She called my daddy an ignorant hillbilly and said she hoped he'd learned his lesson not to cross his betters."

I exhaled slowly. Calling somebody a "hillbilly" and meaning it around here elicits the same violent response as standing on a South-Central Los Angeles street corner and screaming the "N" word. After a moment, I said, "Well, maybe she's changed. After all, she's donating the auction proceeds to charity."

"More likely trying to buy her way into heaven."

I chuckled. "And *I'm* the one with the cynical view of humanity. Want to hear something else interesting?"

"What's that?"

I lowered my voice. "As of about an hour ago, the Mourning Bear wasn't here yet."

"Now, how do you know that?"

I held up the brochure. "The kid from the auction company told me when I got this. The bear was supposed to have been delivered last night and the auction company owner is apparently in shake factor five."

"Well, you know what I think? Liz Ewell would steal the pennies from a dead man's eyes, so it's impossible for me to believe she'd give anything to charity. I'll bet that greedy old witch decided not to sell and is having a big laugh over all the fuss she's caused."

Chapter 5

During the next hour or so, a constant stream of collectors stopped to admire our bears and Ash sold another one— Gloria Excelsius, a white-winged bear dressed as an angel, with sparkling highlights woven into her plush ivory fur and holding a tiny brass French horn. Based on the envious and admiring comments of our neighbors, our business was brisk by teddy bear show standards.

After awhile, I noticed something sad but not particularly surprising. Although most of the women I saw wore wedding rings, men were about as scarce as lawyers in heaven and I wondered why. Yes, I realize teddy bear collecting is primarily a women's hobby and I'm undoubtedly very different from most guys since I actually like bears, and, more importantly, want to be with Ash all the time. Still, how much effort would it have taken for all those absent husbands to turn off the college football or

NASCAR race for just one Saturday and go to a teddy bear show with their wives?

Right around noon, a woman walked up to our table, picked up Joey, a honey-colored bear dressed in periwinkle baby's corduroy overalls and oversized white baby shoes, and began to carefully examine him. I paid attention to the newcomer because unlike the other collectors that had thus far visited our table, she wasn't chatty or even very cheerful. Her demeanor was businesslike, bordering on taciturn, and her only response to Ash's greeting was a distracted but firm, "Just looking."

The woman was forty-something, of medium height with a willowy frame, had straight collar-length reddish-brown hair and stunning green eyes. Another distinctive thing about her was her clothing. Most women attending teddy bear shows dress for both comfort and to advertise their beloved pastime, which usually means blue jeans and a blouse or pullover shirt decorated with teddy bears. Yet, our visitor was wearing gray woolen slacks, a burgundy-colored turtleneck cashmere sweater, and matching blazer—and I know enough about women's clothes to be certain that nothing in that ensemble was purchased off the rack. She also had a briefcase, and once she put Joey down she reached into it and produced a Nikon digital camera.

"Do you mind if I take a picture of him?"

"Not at all. His name is Joey," Ash said.

"Yes, I saw that from the tag." She crouched, aimed the camera, and the strobe flashed. As she turned Joey for a profile shot, she continued, "You've got a bear in the finals for artisan-dressed. The pink girl in the Victorian costume, right?"

"Yes. Susannah."

"Original design?"

"Of course."

"Do you have a business card?" The camera strobe flashed again.

Ash handed her one.

The woman looked at the card. "Lyon's Tigers and Bears. Cute name. Don't you have a web site?"

"Not yet. We've been kind of—"

"Get one. Good luck with the judging." The woman stuck the business card into her briefcase and she disappeared into the crowd.

"Charming conversationalist. Did she graduate magna cum laude from the Donald Trump School of Etiquette?" I asked.

Before Ash could reply, one of our neighbors leaned over in her chair and said, "Oh my God! Do you know who that was?"

"No. Who?"

"Lorraine Cleland."

Ash's eyes widened. "From the Boston Bear Company?"

"Uh-huh. I'd give my left arm for her to stop and look at my things."

"Why? Isn't she exclusively mass-market plush?"

"Not any more. She's about to expand her line of bears with some licensed artisan, limited-edition designs. It was in last month's *Teddy Bear and Friends*."

"It's the first I've heard. We just moved here and in between unpacking and getting ready for the show, I haven't been able to look at any of the magazines."

"I have mine here." The woman produced a copy of a teddy bear magazine, flipped through the pages and then handed it to Ash, while pointing to a color photograph of the woman who'd just been at our table. "Read this."

I looked over Ash's shoulder. The article was a one-page question-and-answer profile on Lorraine Cleland, who'd established the Boston Bear Company back in 1993.

Although the business was only eleven years old, the BBC, as it was called, was already number seven on the list of top ten American teddy bear manufacturers and preparing to make a move into the top ranks. Moreover, following the lead of bear-making giants, Gund and Boyds, the BBC was about to launch it's own premium line of artisan bears, which would be called the Beacon Hill Platinum Collection.

Ash glanced up at me. "You don't actually think she might be interested in our bears for the new artisan line, do you?"

"Why not? She sure didn't stop to chat."

"But, that's crazy. This place is filled with great designers."

"And even though this is your first show, you're one of them."

"Do you think she'll be back if we win?"

"If *you* win and we'll know in about ninety minutes, my love."

We had a lunch of pulled pork sandwiches from the snack bar and Ash talked to more collectors, but we didn't sell any more bears. She began to fidget as one-thirty approached. Finally, a woman's voice echoed from the public address system requesting that all finalists go to the judging area. We spread a sheet over the teddy bears and our neighbors said they'd keep an eye on the table while we were away. Then, holding hands we followed the crowd into the tent. I guess it was a slow news day in the Shenandoah Valley, because the Channel 3 news camera crew was still there.

There was a two-foot-tall wooden platform beside the judging tables and on it stood a plump middle-aged woman who wore more make-up than a Kabuki dancer. Speaking too loudly into the microphone, she launched into a long tale of how much time and effort it took to organize the annual Teddy Bear Extravaganza, which just seemed to be a clumsy way of patting herself on the back.

I whispered, "Wake me when she actually starts handing out awards."

Ash gently elbowed me. "Be nice. She worked hard."

At last, the woman finished her speech and began to read off the winners. There were six categories and Large Dressed was the very last to be awarded, so we had to wait for about another five minutes as each of the winners from the five other groups were photographed receiving their trophies. Then it was our turn and I noticed my breath had become rapid and shallow.

The woman opened the envelope and removed a sheet of paper. She cleared her throat and read, "And finally, the first-place award for Large Dressed goes to Susannah S. Seraphim, created by Ashleigh Lyon."

All right, I'll admit it: I was shocked and not because I didn't objectively think that Ash deserved the award. She did—hands down. But in a skewed universe where Paris Hilton is a cultural icon, and a software company can turn a profit on a computer video game of the JFK assassination where the player is Lee Harvey Oswald, I always figure it's wise to expect that the right thing will never ever happen.

Ash looked stunned and I had to nudge her toward the platform. There was only a smattering of applause because we were new to the hobby and largely unknown to the other artisans, but I made up for it by clapping until my hands ached. Then I slipped through the crowd and took a picture of her receiving the trophy—a handsome plaque made from frosted glass cut in the silhouette of a teddy bear and mounted on a round oak base. Ash was beaming and I was so happy for her that my cheeks were sore from smiling.

Once the final speechmaking was finished and the group photos were taken, Ash stepped from the platform to join me. She had Susannah under one arm and the trophy under the other and she wore a look of dazed joy. I was giving her a huge hug when Lorraine Cleland appeared from the milling crowd.

"Congratulations, Ashleigh!"

"This is an excellent sign. You have a name now," I whispered and released Ash so she could talk with the teddy bear mogul.

"Thank you, Ms. Cleland. I'm very sorry I didn't recognize you earlier."

"Yeah, we weren't expecting someone looking so young to be the head of a major company," I said, injecting just the right amounts of earnestness and mild surprise. Like most veteran homicide cops, I'm a very accomplished liar when the situation demands.

Cleland blushed. "Please, call me Lorraine."

"This is my husband, Brad. He helped make Susannah."

"Hi, I'm the unskilled labor. Ashleigh is the brains of the operation."

"I'm pleased to meet you both and I'd like to set some time aside tomorrow so that we can meet and talk."

"About what?"

"As you may know, I'm preparing to produce a select line of limited-edition bears and I'm still in the process of identifying those I'm interested in reproducing. However, I like Susannah a great deal."

"Oh my God! That's wonderful!"

Cleland held up her hand to signal a halt. "Please understand, I'm not making any sort of formal offer right now, but I would like to at least discuss the basic elements of our licensing agreement. Are you interested?"

"Very much." Ash shot me a look that said: *I can't believe this is happening.*

"Excellent. I understand you live near here. That's convenient."

I perked up at that. Since Ash's business card just listed our home telephone number, the only way Cleland could know where we lived was if she'd already contacted the show organizers and obtained our address from the registration form. That meant she'd either checked a local map or asked someone about our obscure hometown because there are folks that have lived their entire life in the Shenandoah Valley and are vague as to the location of our Remmelkemp Mill. It also signified that Cleland was more than just a little interested in Susannah.

"That's right. Over in Remmelkemp Mill, across the valley," Ash said.

"And I'm staying at the Massanutten Crest Lodge."

"Why, that's just a few miles from where we live."

I wasn't surprised with Cleland's choice of lodgings. The Massanutten Crest Lodge is without a doubt the finest and most luxurious hotel in the central Shenandoah Valley. It stands on the southeast side of the mountain and I've been told it's supposed to be modeled after King Ludwig II of Bavaria's famous fairytale Neuschwanstein Castle. However, I think it actually resembles Cinderella's Castle from Disneyland—so much so, that the one time Ash and I went up there for Sunday brunch, I half expected the concierge to be dressed in a Mickey Mouse costume. Rooms routinely go for 700 dollars a night, and while I'm told you get a free breakfast for those seven bills, that still seems a little exorbitant to me.

When I tuned back into the conversation, Cleland was saying, "I'll be tied up the rest of this afternoon and evening. Could we meet sometime tomorrow afternoon?"

"Certainly. When and where?" Ash asked.

"How does three o'clock work for you?"

"Three o'clock is fine. Where do you want to meet?"

"Since you live nearby, how about your home? I'd like to see where you work and it'll give me the chance to look at some more of your bears without you having to pack them up again and bring them to the hotel."

"Thanks. We appreciate that."

"Look, I'd love to chat, but I want to get a seat before they're all gone." Cleland pointed in the direction of the auction enclosure. "Could you write your address down for me?"

"Absolutely." I took one of her business cards. "So, you're here for the Mourning Bear auction too?"

"Actually, it's the main reason I came down here. Finding your wife's work was an unexpected bonus."

"Thanks and good luck."

I finished writing down our address and handed the card back to Cleland. A moment later, she was slicing her way through the crowd toward the auction enclosure, which was rapidly filling with people. However, I noticed that although the scheduled start of bidding was only a few minutes away, there was still no sign of the Mourning Bear.

I turned to Ash and stroked her golden hair. "Mrs. Lyon, I'm damned proud of you."

"I can't believe it. Brad, I won first prize! This kind of thing only happens on sappy Hallmark Channel shows." Ash was glowing with happiness.

"I'm not surprised one bit. And I'll tell you something else: She'll make an offer on the licensing rights for Susannah tomorrow afternoon. Otherwise, she wouldn't be coming out to our house."

"If you'd told me that an hour ago, I'd have said, 'Brad, honey, you've completely lost your marbles,' but I think you're probably right." Ash paused to exchange pleasantries with a woman who'd stopped to congratulate her. Once the lady moved on, Ash said, "From what some of the other designers have told me, we shouldn't expect her to offer much money."

"Which is no problem because you don't look at the teddy bears as a business."

"But God, wouldn't it be amazing to walk in and see Susannah in a gift shop?"

"Yeah, but it still might not be a bad idea to give Scotty a call when we get home, just to run it past him." Scott Shueford was a former neighbor from San Francisco and a very skilled corporate attorney.

"That's a good idea. Well, I guess Susannah and I'd better get back to the table."

"Yeah, what with the award, we've probably got some customers." I held up the camera. "I'll be with you in a minute, but I want to go out in front and get a picture of the tent and the teddy bear show sign for the photo album."

Ash leaned over to give me a warm kiss on the cheek. "Thank you for having faith in me, Brad."

"My pleasure, honey."

As I went outside, I saw the young man from the auction company who'd given me the brochure. He was getting out of an Acura sedan and wore a preoccupied expression. I said, "Hi, there. It doesn't look like your day's improved."

He blinked, recognized me, and replied, "Not by a long shot."

"What's wrong? Didn't the bear ever arrive?"

"No, so my boss sent me to Miss Ewell's house over there by the mountains." He pointed vaguely to the east.

"What did she say?"

"Well, I didn't actually get to talk to her. She has this live-in nurse or something and she said that Miss Ewell was asleep and couldn't be disturbed. But the nurse told me that Miss Ewell's nephew picked up the bear last night around nine-thirty and was supposed to deliver it to our motel here in Harrisonburg."

"And that's the last anyone saw of him?"

"Basically."

"Didn't the nurse think that was strange?"

"Oh yeah. She was getting all frantic and wanted me to go and wake up the old lady and tell her that her nephew ripped her off." The young man laughed nervously. "So, I'm like: 'No way. *You* break the bad news to her. I'm outta here.'"

"But you do have to break the bad news to your boss. That won't be pretty."

"No, it won't."

"Hey, just to satisfy my curiosity, what is the nephew's name?"

"I think she said it was Robert Thayer."

"Thanks, man, and best of luck dealing with your boss."

I took a couple of photos of the sign that would forever commemorate the location of Ash's first teddy bear competition victory and then heard an announcement over the public address system that due to unforeseen circumstances, the Mourning Bear auction was being postponed. The speaker added that everyone would be notified by mail when a new auction date was set.

And don't hold your breath waiting for that letter, I thought, because I was suddenly and irrationally certain that the Mourning Bear was long gone.

A moment later, Cleland blasted out of the tent like a Minuteman ICBM being launched from its missile silo and headed for what obviously was the VIP parking area. She didn't see me, but I watched her get into a tobacco brown Jaguar XJ-8 that bore red, white, and blue Massachusetts license plates. The engine roared to life and she flew from the lot, sending loose gravel flying.

I watched the departing vehicle and thought: *In a day*

already chock full of riddles, here's another real puzzler. Unless she was in the market for a hot DVD player— which seemed real unlikely—what possible reason could there be for Lorraine Cleland to have been at Pastor Poole's flea market earlier this morning?

Chapter 6

Two hours later, we loaded up the truck and headed home. Exhausted from being up all night tinkering with the bears and the long emotionally fulfilling yet draining day, Ash reclined the Xterra's passenger seat. However, she couldn't relax because she was still trying to make some sense of the news that I'd seen Cleland's Jaguar at the Remmelkemp Mill Apostolic Assembly that morning. "You're absolutely sure it was the same car?"

"Not a doubt in my mind. And even though I didn't see her behind the wheel at the church, I still know it was her in the Jag."

"How?"

"Because she's got a lead foot—accelerates like she's at a drag strip."

"Unlike you."

"That goes without saying."

Ash snorted and I did my best to look surprised and offended. We were driving eastward on Pleasant Valley Road headed home and I want to make it absolutely clear that I wasn't speeding. However, I will admit that the only reason for this was because we were behind a slow farm tractor pulling a large trailer loaded with hay bales and there was no safe place to pass.

"Maybe it was just a coincidence. She could have been doing some sightseeing, got lost, and turned around in the church parking lot. Think of how many times we had lost tourists come down our driveway this past summer," Ash said.

"I hadn't thought about that. You're probably right," I said, wanting to accept Ash's very plausible explanation. Aside from the fact that it really wasn't any of my business why Cleland was at the church, I'm trying to break this awful habit of always expecting deceit from everyone but my wife and a few close and proven friends.

"But you aren't buying that."

"I didn't say that."

"No, but you were thinking it."

Remember what I said a little earlier about being an accomplished liar? That's true except when it comes to Ash. She unfailingly knows when I'm withholding the truth. I said, "Do you have any idea of how spooky it is to be married to a mind-reader? Okay, I don't think she was sightseeing."

"I can think of lots of times when you've positively enjoyed the fact I could read your mind." Ash gave me a coquettish smile. "So, why would she be at the church?"

"To pick up background information on you."

"How do you mean?"

"There was a picture of Susannah on the Teddy Bear Extravaganza web site along with the other finalists, right?"

"Yes."

"And we can assume Cleland saw that picture. What if she knew before coming down from Boston that she was interested in buying licensing rights?"

"That doesn't explain why she went to the church."

"It does if she wanted to collect some background information on you before the show. That's what I did before interviewing a possible suspect—I talked to his friends and neighbors."

"What kind of background information?"

"Something as simple as our income. If we were poor, she could drive a harder bargain because we would need the money."

"But I can't imagine Pastor Marc telling her anything and I'm certain he'd have called us."

I thought for a second and recognized that—despite my dislike for Poole—Ash was correct. Poole would have told us, if only to score points with Ash. "You're right, which shoots my cunning theory down in flames. Okay, she was sightseeing and I promise that tomorrow I'll be a little less paranoid."

We turned left onto Cross Keys Road, finally losing the lumbering tractor, but I didn't speed up because there was a spot just ahead where the Rockingham County Sheriff's deputies ran radar. A few minutes later we turned onto Highway 33 and headed eastward.

"Hungry?" I asked.

"Starved."

"How about we celebrate your victory by picking up some ribs and chicken from Pinckney's Brick Pit?"

"Ooh, and some cole slaw too?"

"Absolutely."

As we approached the intersection with Coggins Spring Road, I was startled to see bright blue lights and wigwagging headlights flashing in my rearview mirror. We were being pulled over by a Massanutten County

Sheriff's cruiser. Now, I swear to God, I wasn't speeding—traffic was too heavy and I was slowing down to make the right-hand turn onto Coggins Spring Road.

"We're being pulled over?"

"Yeah, and I can't think of why."

Not wanting to stop in the intersection, I completed the right turn, pulled over to the side of the road, and shut the engine off. Watching in the side mirror, I saw a large deputy get out of the patrol car and make a slow, swaggering approach to my window. The cop was built like Hercules, with the sort of massive chiseled muscles that can only be created by diligent daily work with free weights and the occasional injection of anabolic steroids. If I had any doubts about that they vanished when I got a closer look at the deputy's face. Although he appeared to be only in his late twenties, he was suffering from acne and was also beginning to lose his hair—classic symptoms of long-term steroid use. With all the fanatical bodybuilders in San Francisco, I saw this sort of thing all the time.

"I want your driver's license, vehicle registration, and proof of insurance." The cop leaned over to look in the window

"Certainly, Deputy," I said, trying not to inhale. His breath was bad enough to asphyxiate trash barge seagulls. Severe halitosis is one of the other wonderful side effects of steroids.

"Sergeant." He flexed his brawny left shoulder to signal the fact he wore three gold chevrons on his shirtsleeve.

"My apologies, *Sergeant*. Do you mind telling me why I've been stopped?"

"You ran the red light and I'm gonna issue you a citation." He pointed back to the intersection of Highway 33 and Coggins Spring Road.

I struggled to keep my voice serene. "I don't understand how that's possible. You turned your emergency lights on to stop me about fifty yards *before* we got to the intersection and, besides, the light was green."

"Why don't you shut up—or I might just decide that you're interfering with my duties. Now, gimme your license, registration, and insurance card and don't make me tell you again."

Then I noticed the cop's nametag above the pocket on his uniform shirt. Removing my license and car insurance card from my wallet, I said to Ash, "Honey, I'd like you to meet one of Massanutten County's finest, Sergeant Trent Holcombe."

Ash, who was already simmering, leaned over to look out the driver's window. "Imagine trash like that wearing a badge."

"I'd watch my mouth if I were you, ma'am."

"I've always believed that you can tell how brave a man is by the way he threatens an unarmed woman." I handed Trent the license and insurance card. "My vehicle registration is in the glove box. Can I reach for it or are you going to claim you thought I was reaching for a weapon so you can stick your gun in my ear?"

"If I wanted to point a gun at you, I wouldn't need any excuses."

I grabbed the registration form and gave it to Trent. "So just to satisfy my curiosity, did your daddy send you out on this errand or is this just a routine psychotic episode caused by your steroid addiction?"

For a moment I thought I'd gone too far. Trent's jaw got so tight you could actually hear his teeth gritting and his hands balled up into enormous fists. Then he seemed to regain some control over his emotions. Taking a deep breath, he said, "Shut up, you goddamn cripple."

Trent went back to his car and I watched in the mirror as he stood and wrote out the ticket. He came back a couple of minutes later and stuck the leather-bound ticket book under my nose. I took the book and examined the citation, amazed at Trent's awful penmanship. Not only had he charged me with running the light, he'd also cited me for having a brake light out. Of course, my brake lights were in perfect working condition, but I knew that if I said anything to Trent, he'd break out a taillight with his nightstick. I'd occasionally run into badge-heavy thugs like Trent back in San Francisco and knew how they operated.

"Sign here."

I took the pen and signed the ticket—there was no point in disputing the false charges here because all that would do was land me in jail. Handing the citation book back to Trent, I asked, "So, what did I do to annoy your dad? I thought I was properly respectful earlier this morning."

Trent snatched the ticket book away, tore out my copy of the citation, and flipped it through the window. "This was all my idea. I just wanted to introduce myself and to make sure you understood to mind your own damn business and watch that wise-ass mouth of yours."

"And if I don't, I might get pulled over and ticketed a lot, right?"

Trent chuckled. "I'm just enforcing the laws. It's not my fault if you're a bad driver."

I held up the ticket. "Any point in fighting this in court?"

"Not unless you want to really piss me off."

"Thanks for the guidance."

"Y'all drive safe now."

Ash was quivering with rage, but managed to suppress it until Trent returned to his patrol car. However, once the sheriff's cruiser drove off, Mount Saint Ashleigh erupted. Volcanoes are fascinating to watch—so long as you're not in the zone of destruction, so I allowed her to vent. Finally, she looked at me incredulously and demanded, "Why aren't you mad?"

"Oh, I'm mad, sweetheart, but I'm also pondering the most vicious way to get even with that bullying steroid junkie and his sanctimonious father. Nobody threatens you and gets away with it."

"So, what are you going to do?"

"The thing they're most frightened of—investigate the murder that Holcombe decided to hush up this morning."

"Brad honey, that's crazy." Ash didn't sound angry anymore, but there was a tremor of anxiety in her voice.

"Could be, my love, but I'll be damned if I'm going to let maggots like that intimidate us, even if they are wearing badges."

"But how are you going to investigate? You don't even know the man's name."

"We can talk about that later. Let's get some dinner and *then* plot."

We arrived in town a couple of minutes later and I pulled into the parking lot of Pinckney's Brick Pit. It's the only restaurant in Remmelkemp Mill and—unlike so many alleged "genuine" barbecue joints that have switched to gas ovens—the meat is still cooked the old-fashioned way over hardwood charcoal. In fact, the only thing that isn't authentically Southern about Pinckney's is the owner. His name is Sergei Zubatov and although he is an emigré Russian, the man flat out knows how to cook North Carolina–style barbecue. Ash's dad told me that Zubatov arrived in Remmelkemp Mill not long after the collapse of the Soviet Union and shortly thereafter bought the restaurant and it's name.

"Do you want to come in?" I asked

Ash tried to stifle a yawn. "I'm suddenly so tired, I can barely keep my eyes open. If you don't mind, I'll just stay here."

"Not a problem. Be back in a minute."

Pinckney's isn't a fancy place, which is just fine by me. As a lifelong resident of San Francisco, I'd occasionally had a "dining experience" at an upscale eatery. This usually meant paying a king's ransom for tiny portions of fusion cuisine of what might have been broiled mice in papaya-wasabi sauce, enduring a surly attitude from a server, and trying to ignore the sappy New Age zither music playing in the background. At Pinckney's the food is hearty and unpretentious—pork ribs, barbecued chicken, cole slaw, and baked beans. The dining room furniture consists of redwood picnic tables covered with red-and-white checkerboard plastic tablecloths and there isn't a server as such—unless you count yourself.

It being suppertime, the restaurant was crowded, yet despite the noisy buzz of conversation, I heard the superb jazz piano of Theolonius Monk playing "In Walked Bud" coming from a pair of old Bose 901 speakers suspended from the ceiling behind the counter. Sergei was behind the counter, slicing a rack of ribs with a large carving knife. He's a distinguished looking man in his mid-fifties with a head of lush curly silver hair and an iron-gray handlebar moustache.

He put two cardboard plates sagging under the weight of food on the counter and yelled, "Twenty-eight, your order's ready!"

"How're you doing tonight, Sergei?"

"I'm doing very well, Brad. Business is excellent. Where's your lovely wife?" It's a curious fact, but Sergei sounds more British than he does Russian. He didn't pick up that cultured Oxbridge accent here in the Shenandoah Valley and that leads me to suspect he spent a good portion of his adult life outside the Soviet Union. There were only two kinds of people allowed that sort of freedom under the former Communist regime: professional diplomats and spies—different names for the same profession. But that was a long time ago and regardless of any unsavory secrets he might be concealing about his past, I liked him.

"She's in the truck. It's been a long day," I said.

Number twenty-eight came up to claim his food and Sergei waited until the guy was gone before quietly continuing, "You'd better watch yourself. Sergeant Holcombe was in here a little while ago talking about how he was going to take care of you for being disrespectful to his father."

"We met and I now have a ticket for running a red light that was green."

"I see. What did you do to make yourself so popular?"

"You heard about the dead man they pulled from the river at our house this morning?"

"Of course."

I hesitated before continuing because the last thing I needed if I was going to pursue my own private investigation was the word being circulated that I was still in disagreement with the official cause of death. Yet my instincts told me I could trust Sergei. I told him the story of finding the body and what had happened afterwards. At the conclusion of the tale, I said, "All I did was object to the fact that Holcombe is covering up a murder. The man they pulled out of the river this morning has obvious ligature strangulation trauma, yet the sheriff insists it's an accidental drowning."

"This man . . . could you describe him?" I did and Sergei raised his eyebrows in mild surprise. "And you say that nobody recognized him?"

"No. But it sounds like you think someone *should* have

known him, which means you have an idea of who he is. What the hell is going on here?"

He glanced toward the window and I turned to look also. Outside a sheriff's cruiser slowly rolled past the restaurant. Sergei answered, "Nothing that I'd care to become involved in, my friend. Now what can I get you for dinner?"

Chapter 7

At first, I was so disgusted and disappointed over Sergei's display of arrant cowardice that I had to bite my lip to avoid suggesting—in graphic detail—where he could put his barbecued ribs and cole slaw. Then I reined in my temper and ruefully acknowledged that I had no right to be angry merely because he was demonstrating good sense. While it was true that Sergei and I were quickly becoming friends and he'd recently visited our home to enjoy drams of single-malt Scotch whiskey and classic jazz CDs, that didn't mean he was obligated to join in a crusade that was almost certainly destined to land me in the Massanutten County Jail or worse.

I ordered our food to go, paid, and a couple of minutes later Sergei pushed two brown paper bags across the counter toward me. "Here you go, Brad. Enjoy. Oh, and last week Ashleigh asked for my chocolate cake recipe, so I put a copy in the bag. Give my best to her."

The words jerked me from my funk because the day that Ash goes in search of a new chocolate cake recipe you can also look for the U.S. Olympic Committee to show up at our house asking me to be the anchorman in the 440-relay. My wife learned how to bake when she was six-years-old and makes a delectable chocolate fudge layer cake so rich with butter—there's a full pound of it—that every slice should be accompanied with a voucher for a free angioplasty. Sergei knew this because he'd sampled the cake during his visit to our home and pestered Ash for the recipe.

Grabbing the bags, I said, "Am I going to like it?"

"Quite possibly. Let me know."

Once I was back in the Xterra, I handed the bags to Ash. "Do me a favor, sweetheart, and check inside the bags."

"For what?"

"I don't know . . . maybe a note."

"And why is Sergei writing you notes?" She opened one of the bags.

"Because he knows something about the dead guy from this morning, but he couldn't say anything."

Ash unfolded a thick stack of napkins. "Okay. Here it is. He wrote something on a napkin. Let me see . . . it says, 'You'd make a bloody awful spy. Call me tonight after I close.' Then it's got his telephone number. What happened in there?"

"Apparently Trent was in the restaurant earlier today running his mouth about how he was going to take care of us, and Sergei asked me why. I told him about what happened this morning and he reacted as if someone that came to our house should have known the victim."

"Then wouldn't that also mean Sergei has an idea of who the victim is?"

"Yeah. Interesting, huh?" I backed out of the parking space and—since the sheriff's station was just around the corner—I made a driving test-quality left turn onto Coggins Spring Road and headed for home.

"So, who do you think knew the dead man?"

"Holcombe was the only one that acted strangely this morning. If he already knew the victim, it would explain why he never once bothered to look underneath the blanket at the body."

Ash tightened her grip on the paper sacks. "But wouldn't that also mean the sheriff was connected with the man's death?"

"Not necessarily. More than likely, Deputy Barron described the guy when she radioed Holcombe."

"That still doesn't explain why he's covering up a murder."

"There could be any number of reasons. Maybe the guy was a crook and Holcombe can't see any point in investigating something he considers equivalent to the unlawful dumping of rubbish into a public waterway."

"But that's so wrong."

"You won't get an argument from me. Unfortunately, it happens more often than I'd care to admit."

"Brad honey, the moment any of this begins to make the least amount of sense to me, I'll be sure to let you know."

"I'd appreciate it. Until then, let's table any further conversation about murder and properly celebrate your victory today."

"That would be very nice."

We arrived home and while Ash stayed inside to begin putting dinner on plates, I released Kitch from his crate and took him outside to go to the bathroom. As I waited for Kitch to sniff every square inch of the front yard in order to find the perfect spot to lift his leg, I examined the river. Although the water was still the color of Ash's morning hot cocoa, the level had receded between two and three feet during the day and it was far less turbulent than this morning. When Kitch finished, we came back into the kitchen and I fed him his dinner. As Kitch gobbled down the dry kibble, I went to the refrigerator and pulled the vegetable drawer open.

"What are you looking for?" Ash asked.

"Something I picked up yesterday in anticipation of Samantha's win." I held up the dark green bottle of Domaine Chandon Napa Brut I'd hidden beneath a mass of fresh vegetables.

"Brad, that's so sweet, but you know what champagne does to me."

"Yes and that was the other reason I bought it."

Ash giggled and kissed me on the neck. "It's still nice outside. Do you want to eat on the picnic table?"

"I'll get the glasses and meet you out there."

I like to think of our meals outside as a dinner and a show, and I'm really going to miss it when the cold weather finally drives us indoors. The redwood picnic table stands on a low grassy knoll with an eastward view that encompasses the river, an expanse of Currier and Ives farmland, and the mountains. And the lovely landscape isn't the only attraction. Over the past few months we've seen flapping Vs of Canadian geese making more useless noise than both houses of Congress combined, a Cirque du Soleil troupe of squirrels, deer ghosting through the underbrush, the inky spectral form of an osprey gliding through the air just inches above the river waters, and—a couple of weeks earlier—a large black bear lumbering along the opposite side of the river. I've never seen such an amazing profusion of wildlife— unless you count the three days I once spent in LA looking for a murder suspect in that alternate universe called Hollywood Boulevard.

I opened the champagne, grabbed a couple of fluted crystal glasses from the china hutch, and joined Ash at the picnic table. It was twilight now, yet still pleasantly warm. Kitch gazed longingly at the ribs and then lay down beneath the table until he was needed. We no longer have an automatic dishwasher, so our dog is responsible for the prewash cycle. It's a big job, but Kitch is happy to help.

Pouring the wine, I handed her one of the glasses, elevated my own, and said, "I offer a toast to the beautiful woman who created Susannah S. Seraphim. If your prize-winning teddy bears can provide people with so much as one-one-thousandth of the joy you've given me, then the world will be a much happier place."

We touched glasses and Ash whispered, "Thank you, my love."

Dinner was wonderful. The combination of good food, fine wine, superb scenery, and cheerful conversation with Ash about the teddy bear show helped me to temporarily forget the ugly business that had occurred here in the yard earlier that morning.

When we were finished, Ash said, "God, that was good, but I'm stuffed."

"There's a little more champagne."

"I couldn't. I've already had too much and it's hard to clean house when you're half drunk."

"Honey, the Teddy Bear Empress won't be here until three o'clock tomorrow afternoon. I think the chores can wait for a few minutes."

"But . . . well, I guess you're right."

"I know I'm right. So relax, have some more champagne and help me figure something out." I emptied the remainder of the bottle into her glass.

"What's that?"

"If I'm going to investigate this murder, the first task is to go upriver and check out both banks."

"To find where he was put into the river."

"Correct. The story about some 'anonymous' witness seeing him jump from the Island Ford Bridge is just like me."

"Huh?"

"Lame. When guys jump from a bridge to commit suicide they do it from a *real* bridge—"

"Like the Golden Gate."

"Exactly. The Island Ford Bridge is what—twenty feet above the water? He couldn't hurt himself falling that distance and it isn't real likely he intended to drown himself. People just don't commit suicide that way."

"Unless . . ." Ash said and took a sip of champagne. "Unless, it's James Mason in *A Star is Born*. He killed himself that way—walked into the ocean and drowned himself."

"You've definitely had too much to drink. I love it."

"Thank you, my darling. So, your question is: How do we search the riverbanks for clues?"

"Right. If I recall correctly, isn't there a little store near the river up in Port Republic where we can rent a canoe?"

Ash lowered her champagne glass. Although it was nearly dark I could see her peering at me in utter disbelief. "A canoe? Brad, honey, when was the last time you paddled a canoe? Or, for that matter, when was the *first* time you paddled one?"

"When we took the kids on that trip to Disneyland in . . ."

"Nineteen-eighty-eight? Sweetheart, that was sixteen years ago and the river in Frontierland is not real."

"I know that, but I can't think of any other way."

"Well, I can. Why don't I call Daddy and ask to borrow his aluminum boat and outboard motor?"

"That'd be great."

"When do we want it?"

I gave her my best example of imploring puppy dog eyes.

"Tomorrow?" she asked.

"The clock is ticking. The longer we wait the more likely we'll lose any evidence that might be out there."

"But, we've got Lorraine Cleland coming at three."

"If we leave first thing in the morning, we'll be back in plenty of time."

"And what happens if Sheriff Holcombe or Trent sees us and puts us in jail?"

I flicked my hand dismissively. "Oh, I wouldn't worry about that. They can't take the risk of enraging your family—too many prospective voters and it's too close to the election—so they'd only arrest *me*. You'd be free to make the appointment."

"Honey, have you completely lost your mind?"

"I prefer to think of myself as reality-challenged. How about I take care of the dishes while you go in and call your dad?"

Ash stood up and kissed me on the forehead. "I can't believe I'm letting you talk me into this."

"Sweetheart, who do you think you're kidding? I've never once 'talked' you into anything that you didn't want to do."

She paused and gave me a wry smile. "That's true. I'll call Daddy and then I think I'll give Scotty a call and fill him in on the possibility of this teddy bear contract. I'd like to get some input from him before we talk to Lorraine tomorrow."

"Good idea."

I grabbed the plates and followed Ash into the house. While she telephoned her parents' house I went back outside to finish clearing the table. Then Kitch began to bark and I heard the approaching crackle of vehicle tires on gravel. An older model bronze colored Dodge minivan appeared and came to a stop in front of our house a few seconds later. Deputy Barron got out and knelt to pet Kitch, who'd ambled over to greet her. She was dressed in black denim pants and a white pinstriped jersey bearing the stylized purple and turquoise capital "A" of the Arizona Diamondbacks.

"Hi, Deputy Barron. Aren't you taking a real big chance being seen here?"

"Hi, Mr. Lyon and, yeah, I guess I am."

"Please, call me Brad."

"If you'll call me Tina?"

"Deal. And before I say anything else, I owe you an apology. The fact is that I shot my mouth off this morning without having all the facts and I'm truly sorry."

Tina looked at the ground. "That really isn't necessary."

"Yes, it is. Now that I'm beginning to understand how things operate in Massanutten County, I realize what you're up against."

"Well, I accept your apology."

"Thank you. So, to what do we owe the pleasure?"

"Two things. I wanted to talk to you about that dead man this morning and I also came to congratulate Mrs. Lyon—"

"Ashleigh."

"Okay, Ashleigh—for winning that prize for her teddy bear earlier today. I saw it on the news."

"Yeah, we were just celebrating." I held up the empty champagne bottle.

"I'm not interrupting anything, am I?"

"Not at all." I motioned toward the picnic table. "Let's sit down. So, has the dead man been identified yet?"

"Not that I've heard. The autopsy isn't till tomorrow and then someone will have to take his fingerprints to the state crime lab in Roanoke." Tina sat down, arched her back, and emitted a tiny groan. "Sorry, eight hours of wearing that ballistic vest really kinks up my back. Anyway, it could be several days before we get a response from the fingerprint examiners."

"Nobody's been reported missing?"

"Not since I ended my shift at four-thirty. Why do you ask?"

"Because a little earlier today I got some information that could mean the guy was a local."

"Who told you that?"

"I'm not prepared to divulge the name yet."

Tina's lips tightened. "Oh. I suppose I can't blame you for not trusting me."

"It isn't that I don't trust you, but the question is: How deeply are you willing to get involved?"

"In what?"

"My unauthorized and probably illegal homicide investigation. Tina, I'm going to investigate that man's murder and if Holcombe or that goon son of his learns you're even aware of what I'm doing, I think the very least of your concerns will be losing your job."

"And you want to know if I'm willing to help?"

"Exactly."

Tina looked down at the tabletop. "Mr. Lyon—Brad, when you got angry at me this morning, it caused me to do a lot of thinking about the compromises I've been forced to make to keep my job as a deputy. Meanwhile, I'm trying to teach my kids that they should always do the right thing, no matter what, and I wonder how they'd feel about their mom if they knew I was a fraud."

"A fraud doesn't try to get herself elected sheriff to clean things up."

"Maybe." Her eyes met mine. "Anyway, I realized that I couldn't play the game anymore—not when they're trying to cover up a murder—and so I came over here to ask if you'd help me by looking into the homicide. I'm a good solid patrol deputy, but I've never investigated a murder."

"You're sure you want to do this?"

"I've given it a lot of thought—I'm sure."

"It has the real potential to turn ugly."

"I know."

Although it had been a long day and I was tired, I could feel myself growing excited. "Okay then, let's discuss the mechanics of the investigation. For starters, if I come up with a suspect and probable cause to arrest, you're going to have to be the one to present the evidence to the Commonwealth's Attorney. I have no peace-officer authority in Virginia . . . or anywhere else anymore, come to think of it."

"I understand."

"And I need access to the law enforcement computer database, so I'll call you when I need to run a vehicle or a person for wants and warrants. When we go inside, we'll exchange wireless phone numbers. Then, as far as paper is concerned, I'll write investigative follow-ups that you can incorporate directly into your crime report. I'm assuming you have a computer with Internet access at home?"

"Yes, but with three kids I don't get much of a chance to use it."

"Any problems with your kids opening your email and reading the report? The last thing we need is for them to talk about what we're doing. It'll get back to Holcombe in no time."

"I don't see that as a problem."

"Good. The reports will be in the standard Microsoft Word 2003 document format and I'll e-mail you copies as I finish them. That way you can keep up with the investigation without us being seen together. Oh, and I'll also e-mail copies of the files to my old partner back at SFPD just in case . . ."

"Anything happens to our computers?"

"Or us. Still in?"

"Absolutely. Thanks, Brad; I'd forgotten how good it feels to be a cop."

"My pleasure. Let's go in the house and you can say hi to Ash."

It being late in the day, my shin was stiff and achy as I limped toward the front door. I held the door open for Tina and Kitch and, not seeing Ash in the living room or kitchen, called out, "Sweetheart, we have company."

Ash appeared at the top of the stairs with the portable phone in her hand. "I just got off the phone with Daddy and—oh, I thought I heard someone drive up. Hi, Deputy—"

Tina held up a hand in greeting. "Hi, just call me Tina."

"She came by to congratulate you on your victory today."

"And to ask your husband to help me investigate that man's murder."

"So, did we get the boat?" I asked.

"He'll bring it by first thing tomorrow morning." Ash came downstairs and put the phone back in its base station.

"The boat?" said Tina.

"It's a long shot, but we're going to take a little cruise upriver to see if we can locate where the victim was thrown into the river."

But Tina's attention was now riveted on the multitude of teddy bears that stood behind glass-faced cabinets and oaken shelves that lined the far wall of the living room. "Oh my God, look at all the bears."

"And that's only part of the collection," I said.

Tina turned to Ash. "They're amazing. Did you make them all?"

"I wish. A couple of them are mine, but the rest are either one-of-a-kind artisan bears or limited-edition collectibles from manufacturers like Boyds or Hermann. Do you want to look at them?"

"I'd love to. I've always wanted to try my hand at making a teddy bear, but between work and being a single mom there isn't much time for crafts."

They walked over to the shelves and Ash picked up an ivory-colored bear with puffy paw pads. Handing the bear to Tina, she said, "Now, this is an interesting one. Susan Arnot makes these out of recycled fur coats and this little girl is made from mink. I got her when we went to the big teddy bear show in San Diego back in . . . honey, do you remember what year that was?"

"August, two-thousand-and-one."

"But, I thought you guys lived in San Francisco."

"We did, but Brad had to go down to San Diego to testify on a case where he'd helped SDPD. It just so happened that the teddy bear show was that weekend, so I went there with him and we spent all day Saturday and some of Sunday at the show."

"You *like* going to teddy bear shows?" Tina gaped at me and made no effort to conceal the incredulity in her voice.

"Yeah, is that so strange?"

"Around here, it is. Most men don't do that sort of thing."

"Well, I think teddy bear shows are wonderful. Not to mention the fact that they're great places to meet women," I said with all the earnestness I could muster.

"Excuse me?" Ash gave me a faux withering look while Tina giggled.

"And on that note, I'll bid you ladies adieu for the evening. I have to go and start on my report."

"Bradley Aaron Lyon, you are a total brat."

"Yup. And your point?"

I clumped upstairs and went into the guestroom where the computer stood on a small wooden desk. From downstairs I could hear muted cheerful conversation and an occasional laugh from Ash and Tina—the warm and unmistakable sounds of a new friendship being born. I was glad because between moving into the new house and preparing for the teddy bear show, there'd been little time for Ash to make any friends.

Turning on a CD of an old Wes Montgomery album, I sat down to write as the funky and dolorous strains of "Willow Weep for Me" played by the greatest jazz guitarist of all time filled the room. It had been over a year since I'd written an investigative narrative and at first the going was maddeningly slow because technical writing, as with any other acquired skill, suffers if you don't stay in practice. Yet despite the frustrations, on a deeper level I was enjoying myself. Most cops loathe paperwork and therefore don't invest any real effort in mastering it, which is just plain stupid because ninety percent of detective work is writing. However, I'd always prided myself on the quality of my reports and—this is going to sound arrogant—they were some of the best ever produced by SFPD. One of the finest compliments I ever received during my law-enforcement career was from a defense attorney who once told me that when he saw my name on the police report, he knew it was time to plea-bargain his client's case.

The guestroom door opened and Ash came in. I suddenly realized the house was quiet and asked, "Did Tina go home already?"

"Sweetie, it's nearly eleven. She told me to tell you good night."

"Eleven? I guess I lost track of the time," I said, also noting that at some point over the past hour the CD had ended, yet I'd been so focused on report writing that I hadn't noticed it.

"She's nice. I like her."

"Yeah, and she's got some *cojones*—so to speak."

"And after she left, I called Scotty."

"What did he say?"

"Congratulations, he misses us, and that I shouldn't sign anything until we've faxed the paperwork to him. He'll be home all day tomorrow." Ash rested her head on my shoulder and looked at the screen. "So, how's it coming?"

"Slow at first, better now."

"Well, it's late and I think you need to come to bed." She kissed me on the earlobe.

I groaned. "And *I* think I need my head examined for telling you that I have to call Sergei before I can do that."

"Oh. I suppose if you'd *rather* talk to Sergei than—"

"Five minutes. I promise." I dug the wireless phone and Sergei's message from my pants' pocket and started pressing the number.

He picked up on the second ring. "Bradley?"

"Evening, Sergei. I hope you had a good laugh." Then trying to mimic his cultured English accent, I added, "Nothing I'd care to become involved in, my friend. You fraud."

"You should have seen your face. It was priceless."

"And how would you know whether I'd be a bloody awful spy? Is that your professional opinion as a former spook?"

Sergei chuckled. "Oh, I'm certain I don't know what you mean by that, Brad."

"And I'm certain you do, but I'd prefer to save that discussion for some evening when I can get enough eighteen-year-old Glenfiddich into you."

"I'm looking forward to it." I heard a match strike in the background, and Sergei began making smacking sounds, and I knew he was firing up a Cuban cigar.

"So, what about that guy I described? You know him, right?"

"Not by name, and I only saw him once. It was Wednesday morning, shortly after six A.M. I'd come in early to repair the exhaust duct behind the restaurant and I was up on a ladder, which gave me an unobstructed view of Reverend Poole's house."

As Sergei spoke, I grabbed a pen and began taking notes. There was a pause and I said, "And?"

"I saw this fellow with the shaved head and goatee that you described. He was unloading all sorts of appliances and electronic equipment from his truck and taking them inside the house."

"Can you remember what kind of truck?"

"A metallic red Chevrolet S-10 with an extended cab. It looked brand new."

I jotted down the description. "Was Poole there?"

"Absolutely, in fact he was helping the man carry the things into the house." Sergei took a long pull from the cigar and added. "And here's something else you might want to know: When the bald-headed fellow got ready to drive away, Poole became quite angry and yelled at him."

"What did he say?"

"That if he tried to double-cross him again, he'd be sorry."

Chapter 8

I turned off the phone and went into the bedroom, wondering how I was going to break the news to Ash. Actually—and I know this is going to sound insensitive, but I'm sorry, that's just the way guys are hard-wired—my big question was *when* to tell her, since there are few topics of discussion that will dampen a warm romantic atmosphere more quickly than telling your wife that her childhood friend was now "a person of interest" in a homicide investigation. Look at it from my point of view: Why should I lose out on an evening of bliss with Ash simply because Poole threatened his stolen goods supplier a mere three days before the crook turned up dead? And the most aggravating part was that I only had myself to blame. If I hadn't been so damned diligent and insisted on calling Sergei this wouldn't be a problem . . . and it was a problem, because I couldn't lie to her.

Ash was in bed, her head propped up on a couple of pillows, reading a mystery novel about an amateur sleuth and her talking Pomeranian dog. My wife is a big fan of mysteries, but I've never cared for them. In fact, they drive me nuts, because the cops are almost always portrayed as endowed with the brainpower of gravel—and not high-grade gravel—the killer is invariably brilliant and erudite, and the perfect murder is solved by a canny layperson with the assistance of psychic intuition, magic, or an anthropomorphic house pet, for God's sake.

Ash lowered the book and said, "So, what was the cloak-and-dagger message that Sergei wanted to convey?"

I put the wireless phone on the dresser and started to undress. "He told me that he saw someone matching the victim's description at Marc Poole's house early Wednesday morning. I guess Poole was absent the day they covered the eighth commandment at Bible college because they were both unloading stolen goods from the guy's pickup truck and taking them inside the house."

Ash sat up in bed. "What?"

"Wait, it gets better. Poole was also flamed at the guy and told him he'd be sorry if he double-crossed him again."

"But this morning he acted like he didn't know that man."

"Yeah, the heartfelt prayer asking the Lord to help Tina identify the poor sinner was a masterful touch." I tossed my clothes into the laundry hamper and pulled my nightshirt over my head.

"So, how was Pastor Marc double-crossed?"

"Sergei didn't hear that, but it probably had something to do with how they were dividing up the profits from the flea market. Maybe our victim was holding some of the property back or wanted a bigger cut. Whatever it was, Poole was mad."

There was an interval of uncomfortable silence. Then Ash said, "Brad, are you seriously suggesting that Pastor Marc had something to do with that man's murder?"

I shrugged wearily and said, "Honey, I know you like him, but we can't ignore the facts. Poole knew the victim and lied about it, which you'll have to admit doesn't look very good."

"I agree that he's covering something up. I just find it impossible to believe he could murder anybody."

"And I respect that because you're an excellent judge of character. Still, he's the closest thing we have to a suspect so far."

"What are you going to do? Are you going to talk to him?"

"I don't know. The problem is that once I do, it probably won't be much more than five minutes before Holcombe knows what I'm up to."

"How so?"

"That monthly stolen goods carnival couldn't exist without the tacit approval of the sheriff—who is undoubtedly getting a cut from the action."

Ash closed her eyes and rubbed her temple. "Okay then . . . so, it's in the sheriff's best interest to make sure there isn't a murder investigation, otherwise Pastor Marc would tell a grand jury about the graft he's been paying to Holcombe."

"Precisely. Remember that old acronym from the cold war, MAD—'Mutual Assured Destruction'? That's what we have here. It explains why the sheriff never looked under the blanket, because the faster the death is ruled accidental and the guy is shoved into some pauper's grave, the better for the spiritual and legal leaders of Remmelkemp Mill."

I went into the bathroom to wash my face and brush my teeth. When I returned a couple of minutes later, Ash was still sitting up in bed. "Just for the sake of argument, couldn't Sheriff Holcombe have killed the man?"

"I'm always ready to believe the worst about him. Tell me more," I said, climbing into bed.

"Well, what if the double-cross that Pastor Marc was talking about was directed at the sheriff? Remember earlier today, when you were talking about how whoever was providing the stolen property to the flea market would never do a day in jail because he'd roll over on Poole and Holcombe?"

"Yeah."

"Maybe that's what happened. Maybe the dead guy was arrested someplace, bailed out, and came back to blackmail them. They pay him off or he tells everything he knows to a prosecutor."

"It's a plausible scenario except for one thing: Holcombe is an intelligent and experienced cop, so if he was going to kill someone, he wouldn't just throw the body into the river and hope for the best. Either he'd bury the victim somewhere in the Alleghenies or . . ." I hesitated because I didn't want to frighten her.

But we'd been together too many years and Ash had already guessed my thoughts. "Or he'd kill them, ostensibly in the line of duty, and claim he was acting in self-defense."

"Yeah, and make sure there was a stolen throw-down gun next to the victim when the other cops arrived."

"I see what you mean about the sheriff, but what about Trent? *He* isn't that smart, is he?"

"No, but then again, if he killed the guy, I'd have expected to see trauma from a beating. Trent impresses me as the sort of vicious cretin that'd get off on pounding someone until they begged for mercy. Still . . ."

"This is beginning to get scary."

"Beginning?" I hesitated before continuing. "Would you be more comfortable if we just dropped this entire investigation idea?"

"And let somebody get away with murder?" She doesn't do it often, but Ash has a way of lowering her head, staring, and opening her mouth in surprise that never fails to make me feel as if I've said something irredeemably foolish.

"I'm not thrilled with the notion either, but it's an option. After all, I'm not a homicide inspector anymore, so it isn't my duty to right the wrongs of Massanutten County—especially if there's the chance that I'd be putting you in danger."

"Honey, how long have we been married?"

"Twenty-six years."

"And how long were you a cop?"

"The same amount of time."

"And did I ever once wimp out while you were working a murder?"

"No."

"So, what makes you think I'm going to start now?"

"Maybe I'm the one that wants to wimp out."

"Brad, you are so full of it, your eyes are brown. Don't worry about me, we'll get through this together, just like we always have."

"Thanks, sweetheart. Well, I guess it's time we got some sleep." I turned the bedside lamp off and leaned over, intending to give Ash an innocent goodnight kiss, but discovered that she was interested in much more than a chaste peck on the cheek. This may sound unbelievable, but when Ash kisses me, the effect is exactly the same as the very first time we kissed twenty-six years ago—total sensory overload.

* * *

I awakened to the sound of the shower running and the rich aroma of the cinnamon bun–scented soap Ash was currently using. One of the things I love about her is the fact that she always smells so good. She always uses lotions and bath products that smell warm and soft. Most guys don't pay any attention to that, but it's important to me.

Rolling from the bed, I went over to the window and checked the river. The water looked relatively calm and the level had gone down another foot or so overnight. It was a beautiful morning with clear blue skies, a gentle and balmy breeze blowing out of the southwest, and excellent prospects for another unseasonably warm day. Although autumn was officially over a week old, we'd yet to see anything approaching cool weather, but Ash assured me that it was coming.

We had breakfast and afterwards, while waiting for Ash's dad to arrive, I took Kitchener outside to play. I've been trying to teach him to chase a tennis ball, but he's real vague on the concept of retrieving. Every time I throw the ball and yell for him to chase it, he cocks his head and looks at me in a puzzled and slightly offended manner as if I've asked him to do something completely unreasonable, such as name the capital of Mauritania. I haven't given up hope yet, but I'm starting to believe there's a greater likelihood that someday he'll say, "Hey, just in case you didn't know, Nouakchott is the capital of Mauritania" before he brings that tennis ball back to me.

Shortly after 9 A.M., Lolly Remmelkemp arrived. His actual Christian name is Laurence, but nobody in the area has called him that since before Franklin D. Roosevelt was elected to his fourth term as president. The nickname originated with his younger brother, who couldn't pronounce "Laurence" as a toddler. Lolly was driving his battered blue Dodge pickup and towing a trailer with an aluminum rowboat on it.

I really like Ash's parents. Her mom's name is Irene and with her milky complexion, silvery hair, and buxom figure, she looks like a slightly older version of her daughter. She is also a wonderful cook and her pan-fried chicken and mashed potatoes with cream gravy are famous throughout the region.

Besides being a sweet and genteel lady, Irene knows her Bible like a personal injury attorney knows the back-end of an ambulance. She lives by Jesus' admonition to turn the other cheek and forgive your enemies . . . except when it comes to offenses against her family. I learned this the first time Ash brought me home to introduce me to her parents. Irene waited until we were alone and then tranquilly told me that if I ever hurt her daughter she'd hunt me down and skin me. We were in the kitchen when she made this announcement and pointed out the large wooden-handled carving knife she'd use. Of course, regarding the emotional protection of my own daughter, I have a far more progressive attitude. I never once considered threatening Heather's first serious boyfriend with an old-fashioned edged weapon if he didn't treat her with perfect respect—I would've used a semi-automatic handgun with a laser sight.

Lolly doesn't look sixty-eight years old. He's got a barrel chest, a full head of white hair, and a round, cheerful face highlighted by blue eyes that glint with the sheer joy of being alive. And not surprisingly, his behavior isn't that of a senior citizen. He's a full-time farmer, manages a herd of Texas longhorn cattle, goes hunting for bear and deer with a single-shot black powder musket, and when the ladies aren't around, tells some of the most extraordinarily dirty jokes I've ever heard—jokes that you'd never expect a lay church deacon would even be aware of, much less tell with consummate skill.

Lolly also owns every power tool known to the human race and can fix absolutely anything. If he'd been one of the astronauts on *Apollo 13*, he'd have repaired the damage and the mission would have been a success. As an added bonus, the expression "Houston, we have a problem" would never have made its way into popular language, to be used by a generation of dullards who know more about the Olsen twins than they do about the amazing program that put human beings on the moon.

I limped over to the truck as he climbed from the cab. "Good morning, Lolly. Thanks for letting us borrow your boat."

"Anytime, son. Hey, I heard about that BS Trent Holcombe pulled yesterday afternoon. Anything you want me to do about it?"

"What do you mean?"

"I know Mike Cribbs, the traffic-ticket magistrate. If I asked, he'd dismiss the ticket."

"Thanks, but let's hold off on that for now. If what I'm working on pans out, bogus traffic cites will be the least of Trent's concerns."

"Well, there must be something I can do."

"There is—vote for Tina Barron next month. Trent's just a symptom of a much bigger problem. We need a new county sheriff."

"Already a step ahead of you. Check this out." Lolly led me to the rear of his pickup truck where a rectangular piece of plywood was wired to the tailgate. It bore a message in bright red spray-paint: BARRON 4 SHERIFF.

"Very nice, but when Trent sees that he's going to go into low-earth orbit."

"Let him. That boy had no call to behave that way." There was an uncomfortable pause. "Son, Ash told me what you're up to and I have to ask you a question."

"Am I going to keep your daughter safe?"

"Yeah."

"I'll do everything in my power, but she insisted on coming and you know what happens when she sets her mind to do something."

"Don't I just." Lolly chuckled.

"And all we're going to do is take a little cruise up-river, so please don't worry."

"Okay, I won't. So, where is Ash?"

"Upstairs, I think."

"Good. You'll love this one." Lolly leaned closer and continued in a conspiratorial tone, "This fella wearing a clown suit goes into this proctologist's office and says—"

"Good morning, Daddy!" Ash emerged from the front door carrying my cane and a lightweight knapsack.

Without missing a beat, Lolly turned and said, "Hi, honey. Brad and I were just talking about your trip."

"I love the sign on your truck," said Ash, giving her dad a hug.

"Hey, congratulations! We saw you on the television last night and I expect you'll be in tomorrow's paper."

"Thank you. How's Momma?"

"Just fine. She's getting ready for church, which I should be too. I'll get the boat off the trailer and into the water."

"Thank you, Daddy."

Ash handed me the cane. "Sweetheart, you're going to need this."

I sighed in what was now conditioned disgust. "My cane. Can't leave home without it. God, I'm a gimp—like Lionel Barrymore in *Key Largo*."

"He was in a wheelchair and you are not a gimp." She kissed me on the cheek and gave me the knapsack.

I looked inside. "Camera, spare batteries for the camera, binoculars, Massanutten County map, notepad, two bottles of water—don't drink from mine because I don't want girl cooties—"

"I'll try to remember that."

"Ibuprofen and pens. Great, honey. Looks like we have everything we need."

"Not everything." Ash pulled something from her pants pocket and pushed it into my hand. "I think you might want this."

It was my black leather case that contained the SFPD retiree badge and ID card I received when the city showed me the door. Since that day, I hadn't so much as looked at the badge; I'd hidden it away in a box because the last thing I needed was something to remind me of how much I missed being a homicide detective. Unfolding the case, I gazed down at the gold seven-pointed star with the word "Inspector" inscribed on it in royal blue letters. I was surprised to find there was a lump in my throat. Without looking up, I asked, "Where did you find it?"

"I've always known where it was." She wrapped her arms around my shoulders. "And I figured that as long as you're back in the investigations business, even if it's only temporarily, you'd better have your badge."

"Thank you, my love," I said, slipping the badge case into my back pants pocket.

A few minutes later, the boat was bobbing in the river, secured to a sycamore tree with a rope. As Lolly began to give Ash a quick refresher course on operating the Evinrude outboard motor, I took Kitch inside the house and secured him in his crate. It wasn't necessary for me to know the intricacies of the motor because the job of piloting the small craft belonged solely to my wife. She'd grown up along the banks of the Shenandoah and was learning to steer a boat on the river when I was still riding a bike with training wheels. My assignment was to be the JAFO, which in the police helicopter service stands for

"Just A Freaking Observer" . . . except cops use a slightly more colorful term than "freaking."

I put the knapsack on, clambered into the boat, and sat down on an aluminum bench near the bow. Ash gave her dad a hug and then got into the boat and took a seat on the bench at the rear near the outboard motor. She gave the engine some gas and we began to slowly churn our way upriver. We both waved to Lolly and a few seconds later he was invisible behind an emerald wall of trees and foliage.

At first, there wasn't much to see. The west side of the river was hemmed right down to the water's edge with forest while a low bluff blocked our view to the east. Peering into the shallow water, I caught a glimpse of a largish fish that might have been a trout, and a few moments after that I saw a very chubby raccoon scramble along a fallen log and disappear into the underbrush. It all seemed so pristine and idyllic, yet I knew the South Fork of the Shenandoah is still badly polluted with toxic chemicals such as mercury, even though the factory waste was dumped into the river decades ago. Ordinarily, I'm not a proponent of capital punishment, but if we could ever find some of those scumbag industrialists who fouled this river because it meant a bigger profit margin . . . well, lethal injection is *way* too good for them, if you ask me.

Ash scanned the west bank. "So, honey, what exactly are we looking for?"

"A miracle."

"Huh?"

"I was hoping we'd find some signs of a struggle that would tell us the actual place our victim was thrown into the river, but now that we're out here, I can see that may not have been a realistic goal."

"Be patient. We've just started."

After about a half-mile, we came to "the island," which

was actually an overgrown sandbar, slightly more than a half-acre in size and shaped like an inverted teardrop, studded with maybe a couple of dozen morose-looking cedar trees. In the summer, you can leap across the meandering western channel to the island, and even in the wake of a hurricane, the water wasn't much wider than a residential driveway.

Keeping to the eastern channel, Ash soon pointed to a crumbling stone foundation that was overgrown with brush and vines and said in a voice loud enough to be heard over the engine, "The mill."

I'd heard about the place but never seen it. Invisible and all but forgotten, this quadrangle of stones was all that remained of the original Remmelkemp Mill—the building rescued from Yankee arson by brave Southern soldiers. The ironic postscript to the story, which isn't mentioned on the peculiar-looking monument, is that about a week after the heroic episode, sparks from a Confederate sentry's campfire set the mill's wooden shingles ablaze and the building burned to the ground.

A moment later, we motored past the south end of the island and then under the Coggins Spring Road overpass. The river ahead looped lazily to the right and widened slightly. About a mile ahead, on the east side of the river, I saw Caisson Hill jutting just above the tree line. It's a small and sparsely wooded knoll that got its name because it was an overnight home for one of Thomas "Stonewall" Jackson's artillery batteries just before the Battle of Port Republic in 1862.

That tiny geographic fact illustrates something amazing about life in the Shenandoah Valley. It's so permeated with the past that it's like taking up residence in an American history book. The roads are full of historical markers and they don't merely record episodes from the Civil War. Just a few miles to the east is Swift Run Gap, the place where English settlers first entered the Shenandoah Valley in 1716. Go north to Winchester and you can visit George Washington's office during the French and Indian Wars or travel south and you'll find Cyrus McCormick's farm where the mechanical harvester that changed agriculture forever was invented. The sheer volume of history is just mind-boggling.

The river continued to loop to the west for about 200 yards and then gradually curved back toward the east. For the first time, I noticed a sturdy diamond-mesh galvanized steel fence running along the water's edge to our left. The barrier was six-feet tall, topped with rusted strands of barbed wire, and every few feet bore a rectangular metal placard that read NO TRESPASSING in red letters. I wasn't surprised to see many of the warning signs were pitted and dented as a consequence of being used for target practice. The vandalism was forgivable—perhaps even admirable—because there was something very arrogant and intrinsically wrong about this prison fence standing next to a waterway so beautiful that the original Native American inhabitants christened it Shenandoah—Daughter of the Stars.

I hooked a thumb at the east shore. "Whose land is that?"

"Liz Ewell's. She put that fence up shortly after she stole the land from us. I wonder if it's still electric."

"The more I hear about this woman, the more I want to meet her."

"Better you than me, if I see her I'm liable to slap her."

As we rounded the bend, Ash leaned closer to me and pointed to a rolling grassy meadow behind the fence and at the base of Caisson Hill. The field looked as if it'd once been cultivated but was long since given over to the weeds. In an icy tone, Ash said, "That's the piece of land Liz Ewell stole from us."

We were traveling almost due east and at last that

damned fence turned inland and away from the river. Caisson Hill was now directly to our left, and ahead, the upper ramparts of the Blue Ridge Mountains were visible above a dying cornfield that adjoined the river. Then the Shenandoah curled southward again, and as Ash guided the boat through the turn, we both saw something that definitely qualified as a clue.

On the east side of the river, a metallic red Chevy S-10 pickup truck was parked behind a colossal pick-up-sticks jumble of fallen tree trunks.

Chapter 9

"Well, isn't that interesting." I got the binoculars out and scanned the terrain surrounding the S-10 for any signs of other people, but soon saw that we were alone. "Honey, just how much farther upriver is the Island Ford Bridge?"

Ash peered southward. "A couple of miles."

"Okay, let me get this straight: In order to buy the sheriff's theory, we're supposed to believe that the dead guy parked his—"

"He wasn't dead yet."

"You know what I meant, my love, and please don't interrupt—I'm a soliloquizing detective just like in those silly mystery novels of yours, and if life were like fiction, Kitch could talk with a voice like Sebastian Cabot's and he'd tell us how the guy really died. Anyway, we're supposed to be stupid enough to believe that the soon-to-be-dead guy—"

"Much better." Ash tried to suppress a giggle.

"Parked his truck here in the middle of nowhere and then hiked a couple of miles to the bridge—"

"In the dark and through muddy fields."

"Correct. And then jumped from the bridge to drown himself."

"Yet, you don't sound as if you believe that."

"Oh, you think? So, can we land over there and take a closer look?"

"Sure, but not right next to the truck. The bank is too steep."

"That's just as well because I wouldn't want to risk destroying any shoe impressions we might find in the mud."

A couple of minutes later, we'd tied the boat to a tree and were picking our way through the dense undergrowth toward the truck. Actually, Ash wasn't having any problems and she was carrying the knapsack. However, I was finding the going increasingly tough and was relying more and more on my cane as my leg began to ache. Gnats and large flies buzzed around our heads and I swatted uselessly at them. Finally, we came to the clearing and saw that the Chevy had been abandoned at the end of a dirt lane that was invisible from the river. The road led up the low bluff and into the cornfield. The truck was exactly as Sergei described it, with the exception of a pair of two-inch rounded scars on the driver's side of the windshield that I knew were caused by bullets striking, but not penetrating, the sloped safety glass.

I glanced into the cab and cargo deck and was immensely relieved not to find a bullet-riddled body beginning to turn into corpse pudding in the warm weather. You haven't lived until you encounter the cloying stench of a dead body that's been inside a car for a couple of days in the summer sun. It permeates everything. You can smell it on your clothes, on your skin, and in your hair.

It's one of the few things about being a homicide inspector I definitely don't miss.

"I take it I'm not supposed to touch anything," said Ash.

"Not until we get Tina to process the truck for latent fingerprints."

Since the passenger window was open about five inches, I decided to take a closer look inside the cab. The first thing I noticed was a handheld Uniden Bearcat police radio scanner lying on the front passenger seat—standard equipment for a professional burglar. Other than that, there wasn't much to see. The glove box was closed, there were no vehicle keys visible, and the ignition system hadn't been punched or hotwired.

"It's got to be the victim's truck. There's a scanner on the seat."

"And who goes out without one of those?" Ash nodded in the direction of the windshield. "Are those marks what I think they are?"

"Yup, somebody capped a couple of rounds at the truck. Probably with a pistol or revolver."

"How can you tell?"

"Your average handgun bullet doesn't have the mass or enough velocity to puncture safety glass—which is pretty tough stuff. What usually happens is that the projectile gouges the glass and ricochets off."

"But I don't understand. If the killer had a gun, why did he strangle the guy?"

"I don't know . . . maybe he was a practical choker."

Ash laughed and rolled her eyes. "Brad, that's terrible."

"Thank you. It's a relief to know I haven't lost my talent for gallows humor. And by the way, you asked a damn good question. The gunfire doesn't make any sense. Why crank off a couple rounds and run the risk of drawing attention to yourself when you intend to quietly strangle your victim?"

"So, what do we do now?"

"First, we find out who the registered owner is." I dug the phone from my pants' pocket and pressed the number for Tina. The phone rang and rang and then switched over to her voice mail. I listened to the salutation, waited for the beep, and then said, "Tina, this is Brad and I need you to run a vehicle plate for me ASAP. It's Virginia license three-William-Lincoln-Mary-six-one-five and should come back to a late model Chevy pickup. We're on the east side of the river about—I don't know—maybe a mile south of Caisson Hill. Call me and I'll explain the rest."

"I wonder why she didn't answer."

"Probably out on a call and couldn't pick up. At least, I hope that's the reason."

Ash pointed toward the ground near the front of the truck. "I noticed these while you were on the phone and I think you'll find them very interesting."

I joined her and nodded in agreement. The marks in the muddy soil pretty much told the entire story of what had happened here. It was like a connect-the-dot puzzle or one of those dreadfully unfunny "Family Circus" Sunday comic strips where you can follow Jeffy's path on a black dotted line as he meanders through his neighborhood.

The trail began at the ground beneath the driver's door. There were prints from what looked like maybe a man's size ten boots, and they led to the rear of the truck where the person wearing those boots had undoubtedly pulled the dead man from the cargo bed. I knew this because the segment of boot impressions that led away from the tailgate clearly indicated the person was walking backwards, since the boot heels had made much deeper impressions in the mud. Running between the boot prints now, and sometimes obscuring them, were two shallow grooves in the dirt, a trail made by the dead man's tennis shoes as he was dragged past the barricade of fallen trees and toward the river. We walked a parallel course, careful not to obliterate the physical evidence. The path led to the edge of the river where the drag marks abruptly stopped and the boot marks turned back toward the gravel lane and the cornfield beyond.

Ash also understood the cuneiform tale etched in the dirt and said, "So, he was killed someplace else, brought here in the back of the truck, and dumped in the river. But why here?"

"Excellent. You're beginning to think like a homicide inspector. You tell *me* why."

"I suppose because the killer was familiar with how to get here."

"Correct. And we also know the killer is in good physical shape because he moved the dead man by himself."

"Trent's got those kind of muscles."

"I hate to remind you of this, but so does Pastor Marc, and for that matter, Sheriff Holcombe looks wiry enough to have done it."

"That's true," Ash said grudgingly.

The phone rang and I answered it. "This is Brad."

"Hi, it's Tina. Sorry I didn't get your call, but I was up in Thermopylae."

That explained her being unable to receive the wireless call. Thermopylae is a collection of farms and cabins hidden in a narrow gap between Hanse Mountain and the Blue Ridge. I said, "That's all right. Did you run the vehicle?"

"I did. You clear to copy?"

"Give me a second." I pulled the notebook and pen from the knapsack. "Okay, Tina, go ahead."

"The plate comes back to a 2004 Chevrolet truck registered to a Robert Thayer with an address in Warrenton."

"Well, what do you know, maybe the guy's name actually *was* Bob."

"You sound as if you know him."

"Maybe it's just a coincidence, but someone mentioned that name yesterday at the teddy bear show and it was in conjunction with him having disappeared along with a one-hundred-seventy-thousand-dollar teddy bear."

"You're kidding."

"Nope and if we're talking about the same guy, he's Elizabeth Ewell's nephew. Did you run him through DMV?"

"Yes, and the physical description tallies with that of the victim."

"How about local warrants and NCIC wants?"

"He's got a felony warrant out of Fauquier County for breaking and entering and grand larceny."

"There's a shock."

"So, where are you exactly?"

I looked at Ash. "Honey, where are we exactly?"

"I think somewhere on the Henshaw's land, but it's been over twenty-five years, so I don't even know if the Henshaws are still here."

I told Tina, "She thinks we're on the Henshaw farm."

"That's on Wallace Road off of Route Three-forty."

"I'll take your word for it."

"Okay, I'll be—hang on." In the background I heard a transmission come in over Tina's police radio and then she acknowledged the call. "It's going to be a little while 'til I get there. I've just been dispatched to an injury crash over in Lynwood."

"Not a problem. We'll hang loose here but, before I let you go, one question: Do you have a latent-print kit?"

"Yeah, but I don't have much experience with it."

"Don't worry, I do. We'll see you when you get here."

The moment I disconnected from the call, Ash asked, "What does this have to do with the Mourning Bear?"

"Yesterday, the auctioneer's gofer told me that Liz Ewell's nephew was supposed to be bringing the bear to the show. His name is Robert Thayer—"

"And this is his truck?"

"Well, the registration says he lives in Warrenton, but that isn't really very far from here. And the real kicker is that he's got—had, I suppose, in light of his present condition—an arrest warrant for burglary."

"Oh my God, do you think someone killed him to get the Mourning Bear?"

"Well, the bear is missing and, believe me, one-hundred-seventy-thousand bucks is plenty of motive for murder. And if it is the motive, that puts Poole right back at the top of our suspect list."

"Why?"

"Because he's the nexus. He was Thayer's partner-in-crime and apparently knew Lorraine Cleland."

"What does Lorraine have to do with all this?"

"Maybe nothing, but she wanted the Mourning Bear—remember, she told us that the main reason she'd come to the teddy bear show was for the auction—and I saw her leaving Poole's house."

"And you think Pastor Marc robbed and killed Thayer so he could give the Mourning Bear to Lorraine?" Ash sounded incredulous.

"I don't know what the hell to think, Ash. Too many pieces just don't fit and I guess it's pointless to speculate until we know more." I looked from the truck toward the cornfield. "Tina's been sent to a traffic collision, so she won't be here for awhile yet. You up for a little walk?"

"Sure, but how about you?"

"I'm fine."

"Your leg hurts, doesn't it?"

I lifted my left leg a little and rotated it as far as I could outwards. "Yeah, but it's going to hurt no matter what we're doing out here and I want to take a look at that road leading through the cornfield to see if there's any evidence or tire tracks showing there was a secondary vehicle."

"How about some ibuprofen?"

"Three, please."

Ash slipped the knapsack from her shoulders and, a moment later, handed me the pills and a bottle of water. "This is the girl-cootie-free water, although I think it's a little late for you to be worrying about that now."

"Tell me." I popped the painkillers into my mouth and took several big gulps from the bottle. "You want to know how bad my girl-cootie infection is? I dream up cute costumes for teddy bears, I have an intelligent opinion on textured plush fur with glitter highlights, and I even know the many uses of jacquard ribbon."

"And you're enjoying every bit of it."

"Yeah, I am. It beats the hell out of looking at dead bodies and I get to spend all my time with you." I handed the bottle back to Ash. "How about I carry the knapsack for awhile? Oh, and thanks for being here, honey. I couldn't do this without you."

"I wouldn't miss this for the world because, after all these years, I finally get to see how you investigate a murder."

"*We're* investigating a murder."

We followed the Chevy's tire tracks to where they ended at the lane, and I quickly concluded that even if there had been a second vehicle involved in the body dump, we'd never find physical proof of its presence. There was too much compacted gravel in the roadbed to leave any tire impressions. It would have been easy to call it quits and not follow the road any farther. A lot of investigators might have done so in good faith, believing they'd truly and thoroughly examined the "scene of the crime." However, I have an unorthodox view of that mis-understood expression. The scene of a crime isn't merely a place; it's a continuum that extends across both time and space. It springs into existence when the idea is first formed to commit a crime and the scene conceivably has no terminus point.

Yeah, I know that sounds like sappy New Age psy-chobabble, but consider: The scene of this crime began when someone decided to kill Thayer. Maybe that was also where Thayer died, but there was no way of telling yet. However, the one thing I did know for a certainty was that after the contact between killer and victim, the crime scene began to expand like the Federal budget. The route to the body dumpsite, the abandoned truck, the three miles or so of the Shenandoah that carried the corpse north-ward, and the site where Thayer's body was gaffed from the river—all were part of a contiguous "scene of the crime." And if the killer stole the Mourning Bear, his sub-sequent path was also part of that still-growing scene. Ul-timately, you really have no idea of how large a crime scene is until you begin to really look, and that was why we followed the road farther into the dead cornfield.

I'd never been in a cornfield before and I didn't like it. I couldn't see anything, yet my peripheral vision kept registering movement because the desiccated stalks and leaves were trembling in the soft wind. Despite the breeze, the air was unpleasantly heavy and tasted faintly of dust, mold, and hidden corruption. Then there was the bleak, parched, and almost spectral rustling of the corn shocks, a despairing sound easy to imagine as polite ap-plause from an invisible audience of skeletons.

I wasn't the only one oppressed by the atmosphere. Ash was silent, and wore an expression that was both alert and pensive. I leaned closer and rasped, "If you build it, he will come."

She jumped and pretended to swat my arm. "Don't do that."

We came to a slight rise and about fifty yards ahead we saw a ramshackle two-storied barn that looked as forlorn as the cornfield. The building's white paint had faded to a muddy gray and the tin roof was badly rusted and visibly sagging on the side closest to us. There were a couple of huge black walnut trees just beyond the barn, and even at this distance you could see the green nut pods in the branches.

Ash said, "Okay, this was the Henshaws' farm. That was their old barn. I've just never seen it from this angle."

"Picturesque."

"And dangerous. When I was in high school I used to babysit on Saturdays for the Henshaws while they went into Harrisonburg. Their number-one rule was that the kids were not allowed anywhere near the old barn."

Another minute of walking brought us to the barn, and as we approached the large livestock door, I thought I caught a faint whiff of smoke.

Ash took an experimental sniff. "Something's burning. It smells like a campfire."

The inside of the barn was as black as an electric company's profit sheet during a phony energy crisis. We heard something move inside and froze. Then a large tabby cat emerged. It gave us a long and insolent stare and slowly sauntered away from the barn and into the corn, brown tail flicking back and forth.

Ash's nose wrinkled. "The smoke is coming from that direction."

We walked around the side of the barn and stopped to stare. A five-foot-tall shining copper device that looked like a hybrid between an overgrown samovar and a tactical nuclear missile nose cone sat upon a small brick stove. In stark contrast to the deteriorated barn, the metal was meticulously maintained and gleamed like a newly minted penny. There was a pressure gauge attached to the top of the bubbling contraption and a copper reflux tube, bent in the shape of a curlicue, that led to a three- or four-gallon copper pot. A neat stack of firewood, precisely cut to fit the small oven, was piled beside the giant percolator.

"And now I know why the Henshaws never wanted their kids to come back here," said Ash.

"Well, there's something you don't see every day: a still for making corn liquor. I had no idea that people still made white lightning, but I guess I shouldn't be surprised."

"No, folks have been making moonshine for a couple of hundred years here in the Valley. It's part of the culture."

I bent over to sniff the contents of the copper pot and began to cough. When I recovered my breath, I gasped, "My God, this stuff would remove varnish from a table. Where can I buy some?"

Ash was about to answer when we were interrupted by a sound that's absolutely guaranteed to command your undivided attention: the metallic *rick-rack* of a cartridge being chambered into a twelve-gauge pump-action shotgun.

Chapter 10

"Get your hands up!" shouted a woman from somewhere in the corn.

My cane fell to the ground as Ash and I instantly obeyed. Turning my head slightly, I yelled, "I'm sorry about—"

"Shut up!"

I've found it's always the wisest course not to argue with someone employing a shotgun as a rhetorical tool, so instead, I whispered from the side of my mouth, "Honey, on the count of three, I'm going to fall down and I want you to bail."

Ash squinted at me and her jaw dropped. The truth is, she looked so affronted that you'd have thought I'd asked her to leave so that I could flirt with the woman in the cornfield. At last she said, "Brad, if you believe I'm going to run away while you stay here, you need your head examined."

"I said, shut up!" came the voice from the corn.

"Sorry!" I replied.

"Well, you *should* be for even thinking that." Ash glowered at me.

"Actually, I was apologizing to the lady with the riot gun."

"So you aren't sorry?"

"I'm very sorry for getting you caught in an ambush. I'm not sorry for trying to get you out of it."

"And what would you do if the situation was reversed? Would *you* run?"

"That's different."

"How?"

"Because I couldn't conceive of life without you."

Her eyes softened. "I love you, Brad."

"WILL YOU TWO SHUT UP?"

"Sorry!" I waved in what I hoped was a placating manner in the direction of the voice. "I think we have everything settled here."

There was a second or two of tense waiting, and then two women stepped from behind the screen of cornstalks. Like veteran soldiers on a reconnaissance patrol, they approached slowly and cautiously. Both were armed and both wore belligerent expressions, which is never a good combination.

The younger of the two was pointing the shotgun at us, and the comfortable way she held the weapon snug against her right shoulder told me she was experienced in its use. I estimated her age as being about twenty-eight years and under ordinary circumstances, I'd have considered her pretty. She had curly neck-length brunette hair, rosy skin, and a pleasantly sculpted face faintly dotted with freckles across high cheekbones. Her clothing was guerilla-war chic—a lilac-colored ribbed tee-shirt with a picot collar, baggy desert-camouflaged fatigue pants of taupe, sand,

and bits of chocolate brown, and scuffed black military jump boots. Oh, and if you're a little troubled by the fact that a street-savvy former homicide inspector knows what a picot-trimmed collar is, imagine how I feel.

The young woman's weapon was noteworthy too. With its slate gray matte finish, brutal and utilitarian lines and folding shoulder stock, it looked like something you'd expect Arnold Schwarzenegger to have used in one of the Terminator films—which, in fact, he did. It was a Franchi SPAS-12, the kind of high-tech shotgun used by many police SWAT teams.

I also recognized the gun the older woman held in a professional two-handed combat grip. It was a dated but exquisitely maintained Smith and Wesson .357-magnum revolver with a four-inch barrel and nearly identical to the gun issued to me in the police academy back in 1978. One thing was clear: These women weren't into home DIY projects, but they did take fine care of their firearms.

There wasn't much of a facial resemblance, but the women's physiques were so similar, in that they carried their weight in the belly region—not that I have any room to talk—that I assumed they were mother and daughter. The mother was about sixty years old and looked as tough as beef jerky—but I expect that being both a moonshiner and Liz Ewell's neighbor had a way of aging you. Her skin was leathery from too much sun, there were deep frown lines around her mouth, and her wiry hair was warship gray with a yellowish cast. Mom preferred the retro Hollywood Western look: faded straight-legged blue jeans tucked into mid-calf brown boots, a threadbare blue-and-green-plaid woolen shirt, black leather vest worn unbuttoned, and a tan basket-weave gun belt with a cross-draw holster. I was tempted to ask if she was going to be meeting the Earps at the OK Corral later this afternoon but, for once, I managed to hold my tongue.

"Stand still," the old woman snapped.

I assumed she was talking to me because my left leg was hurting so much I was trying to hop on my right foot without attracting her potentially lethal attention. "I'm having trouble standing. I need my cane."

"Too bad. What are you doing on my property?"

"We came up from the river and just wanted to see where the road went." The answer was technically the truth. I didn't think that mentioning we were investigating a murder was going to improve our situation.

"Yeah, I'll bet. Search 'em, Claire."

Ash's eyes widened. "Claire—"

"Quiet! And don't make me tell you again." Mom pointed the big revolver at Ash's nose to emphasize the point.

Claire slipped up behind me and kept the business end of the shotgun flush against the back of my skull while she frisked me for weapons with her left hand. I discovered she had a melodious voice when she said, "You try anything stupid and they'll be picking up pieces of your skull in Grottoes."

"That's about ten miles from here, isn't it?"

"Yeah."

"There's a visual I didn't need."

As the woman patted me down, I was trying to decide whether I'd been wrong in suspecting Sheriff Holcombe, his son, or Poole of the murder. Maybe these women were the killers—they certainly showed the potential for homicide. Yet I discarded the notion almost immediately and for a couple of reasons. First, why go to the effort of strangling a man when you've got a gun? Manual strangulation requires physical strength and tenacity, even with a garrote. And then there was the truck. It was difficult to believe that if the women had murdered Thayer that they'd leave the truck in plain sight on their property, particularly since the victim was Ewell's nephew. Even if they knew that Holcombe had no intention of investigating the death, the truck would have caused unpleasant questions sooner or later.

When Claire finished the pat down, she yanked the knapsack from my shoulders and tossed it to the ground. Then she reached into my pocket, pulled out the badge case, and flipped it open. The seven-pointed star gleamed in the morning sun and although it was a warm day, I could feel a distinct drop in the conversational temperature. Claire held up the badge so that her mom could see it. "Momma, they're feds. SFPD and it says he's an inspector."

"Likely Special Federal Police . . . for . . . Distilleries."

"Right church; wrong pew. The letters stand for San Francisco Police Department."

Mom's eyes narrowed. "Mister, what kind of fools do you take us for? San Francisco is three thousand miles from here."

"And about a hundred years in the future if you folks still shoot revenuers." I know that challenging her sounds as if I'd suddenly gone suicidal, but there was actually a method to my madness . . . at least, I hoped there was. One of the detectives I used to work with was also a hostage negotiator and he once gave me some advice: If you're ever taken prisoner by a run-of-the-mill crook, talk to your captor and work swiftly to show yourself as another human being—even if that means a little debate, because what's more intrinsically human than arguing? Unlike terrorists, the vast majority of criminals aren't wanton killers and the longer they talk to you, the less likely it is that they'll pull the trigger. I was about to test his theory.

At the same time, I don't want to give the impression that I was calm or thought I had the situation in hand.

Much as I wanted to pretend that the sweat beading up on my forehead was from the heat, it wasn't. I was terrified for Ash and me—the sort of fear that makes your breath shallow, narrows your field of vision, and turns your knees into a mush of overcooked linguine.

"I thought you said you weren't feds," said Mom.

"We're not, but what would you do if we were? Blast us like varmints?"

"Don't you be looking down your nose at us, you Yankee. We just might."

"Will everyone keep quiet for ONE DAMN SECOND?" Ash exploded and then looked a little stunned when we all went silent and stared at her. "Claire! Mrs. Henshaw! Don't you recognize me?"

"How do you know our names?" asked Claire.

"Because I used to babysit you, Claire. I'm Ashleigh Remmelkemp. Don't tell me you don't remember me after all those hours I pushed you on that tire swing in your front yard."

Claire slowly began to lower the street howitzer. "Ashleigh?"

"It's me. Can I put my hands down?"

Mrs. Henshaw peered down the blue-steel barrel of the revolver at Ash for a moment and inhaled sharply. "Lolly's girl? Praise the Lord, it *is* her! When did you get back, girl?"

"A few months ago. We've just been too busy to come by and say hello."

"Ashleigh's come back from California!" Mrs. Henshaw delivered the statement with such a mixture of joyful relief and uncomprehending awe you'd have thought Ash hadn't merely returned from the Golden State, but also from the grave.

Claire leaned the shotgun against the barn and Mrs. Henshaw holstered her gun with a casual spinning flourish that would have made Wild Bill Hickok envious and then all three women began to hug each other. It appeared safe for me to put my hands down, so I did and bent to get my cane. Then, as the tearful homecoming celebration continued, I limped over to the flat stump of a walnut tree cut long ago and sat down to rest my throbbing leg. The women channel surfed through a series of conversational topics: Our marriage, our kids, teddy bears, the death of Mr. Henshaw in a tractor accident back in 1992, Claire's marriage, Claire's nine-year-old son, Claire's divorce, Claire's no-good ex-husband failing to pay child support, and did we ever meet Kevin Costner while we were living in California?

At last, Ash detached herself from the other women and said, "I want you to meet my husband, Bradley. Up until last year, he worked for the San Francisco Police as a homicide inspector. That's why he has the badge."

Claire was the first to approach. She extended her hand and dimpled. "Pleased to meet you and sorry for that part about blowing your head off."

"To Grottoes."

"No offense intended."

"None taken. Besides, it's good for an old guy like me to occasionally get frightened like that. It takes the place of a cardiovascular workout."

"And I'm Abigail Henshaw and I want to apologize too." She handed me back my badge case. "We just wanted to scare you."

"You succeeded. What did we do to merit being terrorized?"

"We thought you were here to wreck the still—that Miss-Holier-Than-Thou Liz Ewell sent you here." Abigail's eyes got icy. "She's tried to do it before."

Ash said, "See, honey? It isn't just the Remmelkemps. Everybody around here hates her."

"What's her problem with the still?"

Abigail sniffed disdainfully. "She don't hold with intoxicating beverages and says that she won't have her land devalued because her neighbors are a bunch of hillbilly moonshiners. So, over the years she's tried to shut our family operation down. First it was the feds, but they didn't find anything."

"Don't tell me. You managed to hide everything because you were warned by the sheriff that the ATF was in town?"

"Of course. I expect *something* for my protection payments to Hokie."

"Sheriff Holcombe? Just to satisfy my curiosity, how much are you paying him?"

Abigail heard the disapproval in my voice. "Three hundred bucks a month. Don't it work that way in San Francisco?"

"I guess it does with some cops. But I never played it that way and not once had a moment's worth of heartache reporting them to Internal Affairs."

"I wouldn't expect anything less from the man Ashleigh married." Abigail patted Ash on the shoulder. "Anyway, after that, Ewell sent two boys over to smash the still—the nerve of that old busybody. Do you know how long Jack Daniel's has been making liquor?"

"No."

"Since eighteen-sixty-three and they act as if that's a long time ago. Well, Ephraim Henshaw began distilling corn liquor on this farm in seventeen-sixty-seven—before there was even a United States—and our family has made it ever since. That's over two-hundred-and-thirty years of family tradition and I'll be darned if that blue-nosed harpy is going to shut us down." Abigail slapped the wooden handle of the revolver for emphasis.

"You mentioned some guys coming over intending to smash the still. When did that happen?"

"Back the end of January."

"Right after the big snowstorm," Claire added with an ominous giggle.

"You work outside in the snow?"

"Come winter we move the rig into the barn. There's another firebox in there."

"So, what happened?"

"These two fellas came creeping through the woods from the direction of Ewell's place. I could tell that from the tracks in the snow. We got nine inches that day."

Claire eagerly cut in, "We were working in the barn, but they didn't know it. They figured we were up in the house."

Abigail gave her daughter a stern look. "Honey, who's telling this story?"

"You are, Momma."

"Then let me tell it."

"Sorry, Momma."

"So, we're working in the barn when these two guys come in. One's got a big sledgehammer and the other has a pry bar—I guess they figured they might have to jimmy the door. Well, Claire gets the drop on them with the twelve-gauge."

"Scared them to death." Claire mimed racking a round into the shotgun, complete with realistic sound effects.

"I can imagine. What did they do?"

"Begged for their lives and I told them, 'Down on your knees, like a rat eating cheese!' Oh, Claire, honey, do you remember the way that one boy almost fainted?" Abigail and her daughter began to howl with laughter. This was obviously a well-beloved family anecdote.

I pretended to join in the gaiety and shot a beseeching look at Ash that silently asked: *Are you* absolutely *sure that when these women finish this story they aren't going to kill us and cook us on a rotisserie for supper?* Her return glance said that everything was all right.

Abigail caught her breath and wiped a tear from her right eye. "So, then I questioned them and found out that Ewell sent them over here. You know what we did then?"

"I'm almost frightened to ask."

"Momma made them—"

"Claire!"

"Sorry."

"I made them take their boots off and strip buck naked and walk back to the Ewell place. Of course, I didn't let Claire watch."

Confident her mother couldn't see her, Claire gave Ash a sly smile that said otherwise and said, "It was twenty-nine degrees and real windy. Can you imagine the things that might have gotten frostbitten?"

A sudden and unpleasant thought—other than what might have been frostbitten—occurred to me. Perhaps I'd been too quick to dismiss the women as suspects in Thayer's murder. Trying to sound casual, I asked, "Was one of the men a small guy in his thirties with a shaved head and a moustache and goatee?"

"You mean Bobby Thayer? Of course not."

"You know him?" I relaxed slightly.

"Sure. In fact, he's the only one from that family we're friends with."

"He's a regular customer," added Claire.

"Why are you interested in Bobby?"

"Because we're investigating his murder."

"What?" The shock in Abigail's voice sounded genuine.

Claire's face went blank for a moment as she tried to process the news. "Bobby's dead? When?"

"We found his body yesterday morning in the river in front of our house."

"Sheriff Holcombe says he drowned, but he was actually strangled," Ash said disgustedly.

"But I saw Bobby's truck two nights ago," said Claire.

"When?"

"I don't know . . . around 1 A.M., I guess."

"You were here at the barn? Why so late?"

"Virginia Tech football," Abigail explained. "We go through our stock pretty quickly this time of year. We started a batch late that day and she volunteered to keep an eye on the still."

"And you saw his truck?"

"He drove down the road to the river."

"Are you sure it was him driving?"

"Well, no. I mean, I saw the truck from the barn and assumed he was driving. I couldn't actually see who all was in the truck."

"Could there have been more than one person in the cab?"

"I don't know."

"Didn't you think it was odd that he came here at that hour?"

"No," said Abigail. "He used to go down to the river sometimes with friends."

"Lady friends?"

"I don't know about them being ladies."

"They were skanks." Claire tried to sound scandalized; however, I could hear a faint but unmistakable trace of jealousy in her voice.

"So, why isn't Hokie investigating this?"

"Oh, Mrs. Henshaw, I think you've already figured that out. Bobby Thayer was involved in things that would make Sheriff Holcombe and some other important people around here look bad—maybe even send them to state prison."

Abigail nodded. She knew exactly what I was talking about. Then her face grew pensive. "So, why are *you* digging into it?"

I shrugged. "Somebody has to do it. A man's been murdered."

"And if we don't do anything we're just as bad as the people trying to cover up the killing," Ash somberly observed.

"Does Hokie know what you're up to?"

"Not so far, I hope. But it's only a matter of time until somebody tells him."

"He won't hear it from us," said Abigail, and Claire nodded in vigorous assent.

"Thanks, Mrs. Henshaw."

"So, what brought you here?"

I jerked my head in the direction of the river. "The truck is still down there. We're pretty sure the killer drove it there and threw Thayer's body into the river. Which reminds me of another question." I looked up at Claire. "Was another vehicle following Thayer's truck?"

"No, that was the only one I saw."

"Then whoever it was walked out—probably right past the barn. Did you see or hear anything out of the ordinary?"

"No."

"Can I ask you guys one more question?"

"Sure."

"Did you hear any gunfire near here that night? On your property or anywhere in the vicinity?"

Abigail shook her head but Claire said, "I think I may have heard a couple shots fired sometime around ten."

"Really? Could you tell whether it sounded like a rifle or a shotgun or—"

"It was a pistol, a nine-millimeter. I know because I've got one—a Ruger. The nine's got a real distinctive sound. You know, *pop*."

I nodded. "And what direction did it come from?"

Claire pointed south. "Over toward the Island Ford Bridge."

"Well, I guess we'd better head up there and take a look just to make sure there isn't any evidence." I pushed myself to my feet and tried to pretend I didn't need the cane. I don't think I convinced anybody. "Can you do me a couple of big favors?"

"What's that?" said Abigail.

"Deputy Barron is helping us and I've already called to tell her about the truck. She's going to be here soon to process it for fingerprints. Would you mind stopping production for awhile and stow the armaments while she's here?"

"I think we can accommodate you on that. What's the other favor?"

"Set aside a quart of that corn-based jet fuel for me. I have a feeling that by the time we're finished, I'm going to need a serious drink."

Chapter 11

We walked back along the dirt road toward the river. Somewhere in the distance a dog barked and far overhead I heard the rumble of a jetliner heading south. It was appreciably warmer and muggy now and my shirt began to stick to my back. Plump black flies the size of blueberries zigzagged lazily through the air while a cloud of gnats danced and hovered around my eyes. The dying cornfield no longer seemed spooky—just forsaken and sad.

I reached out to take Ash's hand. "Hey, you handled yourself like a pro back there. I'm proud of you."

"Thanks for saying that, but I was scared to death."

"Me too."

"You could have fooled me."

"Believe it. I've just had a little more experience camouflaging my terror."

"My mind was just racing and, afterwards, my hands were trembling like I had a bad chill," Ash said musingly.

"Adrenaline palsy. Welcome to the wonderful word of police work." I squeezed her hand and then released it. "Sorry, sweetheart, but I can't hold hands with you and use this damn cane. It's just too awkward."

"No need to apologize, I know."

"I never thought in advance how much it would change everything." I dug my sunglasses out of my shirt pocket and put them on. "When you're young and stupid, you think it's going to be like Tom Selleck in *Magnum P.I.*—you get a 'flesh wound,' wear a white sling for the final minute of the show, and next week you're ready to duke it out with the bad guys again. Sometimes it's hard to believe this is forever and I can't even take a walk and hold hands with my wife without it hurting."

"But I don't know of any other man—handicapped or otherwise—that could have handled that situation so well, and I'm not just saying that."

"Thanks, my love."

"How are we doing for time?" Ash asked, swiping at a fly.

"Fine, I think. It's just a little after ten-thirty now."

"And why are we going up to Island Ford?"

"Maybe it's a fool's errand, but I'd feel better if we took a look. We've got evidence that two pistol rounds were fired at the truck, but it didn't happen here, and then Claire tells us she heard a couple of gunshots from the Island Ford Bridge. It's a long shot but it may be connected."

"And the Island Ford Bridge is where Sheriff Holcombe said that an anonymous witness saw Thayer jump into the river."

"Yeah and I'm beginning to wonder if Holcombe mentioned the bridge because he's concerned about a real witness that saw Thayer's truck on the bridge," I said.

"How do you mean?"

"What if the sequence of events began on the bridge? We know it didn't start here. Thayer was already dead or incapacitated because he arrived here in the back of the truck."

We emerged from the cornfield and I stopped talking to negotiate the descent to the riverbank. From the cautious way I moved, you'd have thought I was descending the narrow trail that leads to the bottom of the Grand Canyon instead of a fifteen-foot-tall and mildly sloped muddy embankment. I got down without falling and limped toward the Chevy. The crime scene was as we'd left it.

Ash said, "So, you think Thayer may have met the killer on the bridge and that some genuine witness may have seen his truck there."

"From what I've seen, Island Ford Road is pretty well traveled, so someone may have driven by. Maybe the driver of the car didn't notice anything—most people don't."

"But Holcombe couldn't depend on that, could he?"

"No, he's too careful." While looking over the truck to see if we'd missed anything during the first inspection, I continued, "He would've wanted an iron-clad excuse for why Thayer's truck was there, just in case someone remembered. So, he invented the convenient anonymous witness that can never be identified or called upon to testify in court."

Ash took a moment to digest the information. "So, are we back to the sheriff and Trent being the probable suspects?"

"Possibly. Or try this one on: Poole, Trent, and Hokie—that nickname is so appropriate and I can't believe I didn't think of it—are in it together."

Ash sighed. "I guess that's possible too."

I took the backpack off and opened it. "You know, before we head upriver, I think we should take some crime-scene photographs of the truck and shoe impressions."

"Whatever you think best, baby doll."

"Let's give Tina a call first." I took the phone out and pressed her number.

Tina picked up after two rings and said, "Sorry, Brad, I'm still here at the crash."

"That's okay. Do you have time to talk?"

"Maybe a minute."

"I want to bring you up to speed on what we've learned. We *are* on the Henshaw farm and we've made contact with Abigail and Claire. I take it you know them?"

"Slightly. I thought they were friends of Sheriff Holcombe, so I never had much to do with them," Tina said stiffly.

"They aren't friends, just clandestine business partners. The Henshaws make moonshine and Holcombe collects three hundred dollars a month from them in protection money. Sweet, huh?"

"Jesus, you're—hang on." The voice grew more remote as she talked to someone at the crash scene. "Yes, he's going to Rockingham Memorial Hospital and she's going to UVA Medical Center by chopper." Then she spoke to me again, "How did you find all this out?"

"It's way too complicated to explain right now but don't worry, the Henshaws have promised that the still and the guns will all be put away by the time you get here."

"And I'm supposed to be reassured by that?"

"Don't worry. They know the score and they're on our side."

"If you say so."

"Item of interest number two: Claire told us that she

saw the truck around zero-one-hundred hours on Saturday morning. It drove past the barn and she assumed that Thayer was entertaining a woman by the river."

"Classy."

"What? Like you've never made out in a car?"

"If I have, it's none of your business!"

Ash sputtered, "Brad!"

"Sorry, Tina. As my wife can tell you, sometimes I'm a smart-ass."

Both women said simultaneously, "Sometimes?"

"Yeah, but I'm only that way with people I like. Now, getting back to business, did I tell you that the truck has a couple of bullet marks in the windshield?"

"No. I guess with you being so focused on my personal life, you kind of forgot to mention that."

"Well, it does. The rounds didn't penetrate and from the position of the truck we're certain the rounds weren't fired down here. Anyway, Claire told us that she heard a couple of gunshots on Friday night, sometime around twenty-two-hundred hours. And, she's almost certain it was a nine-mil being fired."

"And a nine wouldn't go through a windshield."

"Exactly. And just to satisfy my curiosity, does the sheriff's department issue a standard handgun to deputies?"

"Why do you ask?"

"Because I think there's a good possibility the shots were fired by either Holcombe or Trent."

"I was afraid you were going to say that. Yes, we all carry Smith and Wesson nine-millimeters."

"And was Trent working Friday night?"

"His shift started at four."

"Getting back to the guns, do you guys have standardized ammo too?"

"Uh-huh. Winchester one-hundred-and-fifteen grain

semijacketed hollow-points. Could Claire tell where the shots came from?"

"Yeah, and I know you'll be shocked to hear this, but she's certain they came from the direction of the Island Ford Bridge. So, after we get done taking some photos here we're going up there and scout around."

"Want me to meet you there?"

"I don't think it's a good idea for us to be seen together yet. When you clear the crash, head over to the Henshaw farm and hang loose until we get back. We'll process the truck for prints together."

"Sounds good. I'll see you in a little bit," she replied and we disconnected from the call.

"I can't believe you actually said that to her." Ash did her best to sound stern but there was amusement in her voice.

"Of course, you can. I've always been a smart-ass and it's too late in the game to change now. Besides, it's one of the things you love most about me."

"*Uh*-huh."

I put the phone away and got the digital camera out. "Well, let's get started with the photos."

"I downloaded the pictures we took yesterday and deleted them from the camera, so we should have plenty of space on the memory card."

"Thanks, honey." I scanned the scene and walked back over to the base of the embankment. "First we start with the orientation pictures: the truck, the river, the cornfield, and the road leading out. After that, we'll do the close-up shots."

Over the next fifteen minutes I shot twenty-two orientation pictures and drained two AA batteries. Now the hard work would begin of capturing more detailed images of the boot impressions and drag marks in the mud. Barring the recovery of latent and classifiable fingerprints from the Chevy, the shoe prints were the most valuable evidence here because they might eventually be linked to the suspect's boots. However, I needed something to set the scale for the size of the tracks and I hadn't thought to bring a ruler. Reaching into the knapsack, I removed the notebook and placed it on the ground next to one of the patterns in the mud.

Ash leaned closer. "What are you doing?"

"Using the notebook as a scale. It's a standard-sized steno pad—nine-by-six—and we'll keep this one as evidence. It isn't perfect, but the notebook shows approximately how big the boot prints are."

"I'm impressed."

"Don't be, sweetheart. This is about as amateurish as it gets. A defense attorney would begin filing his teeth in anticipation of a deliciously bloody cross-examination if these were offered as the official crime-scene photos."

I took another thirty-seven pictures of the marks in the dirt and used up four more AA batteries. After that, I took some close-up images of the bullet gouges in the windshield, several of the cab's interior through the truck windows, and then a couple of the empty storage bed. I was expending our supply of batteries more quickly than I'd expected. I briefly toyed with the idea of submitting an itemized bill to the Massanutten County Sheriff's Department requesting reimbursement, but knew that the only version of a battery I'd receive from Holcombe would be preceded by and combined with assault. Anyway, by the time I finished, there were only four fresh batteries left and I didn't want to use them in the event we found something worth photographing at the Island Ford Bridge.

"Okay, I think we're finished here. Let's head upriver," I said.

"What time is it, honey?" Ash looked slightly worried.

"Eleven-twenty. We'll be home in time, I promise."

We again churned southward on the Shenandoah. Before, we'd had the river to ourselves, but now we occasionally saw fisherman standing on the bank or in the shallows trying to hook a contaminated trout. Most of the anglers smiled at us and waved, but one guy scowled because our boat motor scared the fish away. This was an uncharitable reaction since we actually did the guy a favor. Nobody with a functioning brain would eat one of those fish. If the folks from the Virginia Department of Environmental Quality are correct, the trout have enough mercury in them to be used as thermometers.

A little while later, we spooked a flock of about a hundred red-winged blackbirds. They rose from the undergrowth on the west bank in a mass of fluttering wings and squeaky discordant cries. I don't know what sort of bird's call Paul McCartney used in his old song "Blackbird" from the Beatles' *White Album*, but it sure wasn't any blackbird from around here. The only sound less lyrical than a flight of startled red-winged blackbirds is that of a food processor chopping raw carrots.

A couple of miles to the west we could see the summit of Massanutten Mountain, while to the east were rolling hills carpeted with emerald green alfalfa. At last, the stark rectangular concrete form of the Island Ford Bridge appeared from around a bend. It was maybe three hundred feet long, supported by twelve tall round concrete pillars, and the roadway was about twenty feet above the river. Envision a two-lane expressway overpass and you have the general idea.

"So, this is where we're supposed to believe that Thayer took his suicide plunge."

Ash measured the distance with her eyes and said,

"You'd run a bigger risk of spraining an ankle in the shallow water than killing yourself."

Ash steered the boat under the bridge and beached it on the other side at a vacant public access lot on the eastern bank. We began our hunt there because the site was lonely, isolated, and at nighttime, probably darker than the prospects I'll be cast in Gene Kelly's old role if they ever remake *Singin' in the Rain*. In short, it was an ideal spot to commit a violent crime without being seen. The half-acre clearing was a mixture of gravel, rutted mud, and tufts of grass, bordered on one side by the river and on the other by a wall of tall sycamores and oaks.

I was also annoyed to discover that big corporations weren't the only ones desecrating the river. The ground was littered with an assortment of beer and soda cans, broken glass, fast-food packaging, candy wrappers, and cigarette butts. I shifted some of the rubbish with my cane, scanning the ground while trying to keep an eye on the traffic that intermittently crossed the bridge. Although neither man was on duty, I was on the lookout for Holcombe or Trent—even though I didn't have the faintest idea of what we'd do if they appeared. Running, at least for me, wasn't an option.

The atmosphere was depressing and I made a feeble attempt to lighten it. "Hey, I didn't know they still made Abba-Zabba bars. But what's with all the Yukon Jack bottles?"

"This is absolutely disgusting and the worst part is that I know this wasn't just caused by tourists," said Ash as she nudged a half-crushed Pepsi can with her foot. "Why do people do this?"

"You can thank Holcombe. Folks don't obey the little laws if they see the big ones routinely violated, especially by the cops."

"Well, the first chance we get, we're coming back here with some work gloves and big trash bags."

That's one of the things I admire about Ash. She's short on noisy outrage and long on action, unlike me. I'm the same as most people. I don't like litter and will noisily complain about it, but it would never occur to me to pick the trash up myself. And, if it did and I actually got up off my butt to do something, I'm honest enough to admit that I'd want everyone to know what a noble fellow I was. Ash isn't like that. She simply does the right thing quietly.

We searched the river access lot for another ten minutes, but there was nothing of obvious evidentiary value, so we walked up the lane to Island Ford Road. There were wide gravel shoulders on both sides of the road just before it transitioned into bridge. Ash crossed the highway to check the north side while I began to search the south. Other than more trash, we came up dry again. That left the bridge itself and its western approach.

The ibuprofen hadn't done much to diminish the pain in my leg, so I wasn't thrilled with the prospect of the hike. Still, I knew we had to go. Remaining on opposite sides of the road we started across the bridge. There weren't any sidewalks, so we carefully walked along the narrow spaces between roadway and guardrail, checking the cement pavement as we went. In fact, I was paying such close attention to the ground that I failed to notice the approach of an eighteen-wheeler as it careened across the bridge on my side of the road. There was the sudden roar of a diesel engine and I clutched the guardrail as I was buffeted by the wind from the passing truck.

We continued our search on the west side of the bridge. I was examining the ground, poking at trash with the tip of my cane, when Ash called to me from the other side of the road, "Brad! You need to come look at this!"

She stood in a grassy lot on the north side of Island Ford Road, just west of the bridge and about twenty feet from the pavement. I crossed the highway to join her and bent over to take a better look. A pair of expended brass cartridges lay on the grass within inches of each other, their positions indicative of two shots fired from the same location.

Ash said, "Is this what we're looking for?"

"Two rounds here and two dings in the windshield. I think so."

I walked a few yards back toward the bridge, my gaze riveted to the earth. "The ground is too hard to show any tire impressions, but I'm pretty certain the truck was parked somewhere near here."

"How can you tell?"

"Auto-pistols eject their brass to the right, usually three or four feet depending on the bounce." I walked back to the cartridges and then took a couple of sidesteps to the left. "Which means the shooter was right about here."

I got the camera out and took a series of photographs of the expended cartridges. Then I bent over and picked up one of the brass cylinders. I used my bare hands and didn't bother with that nonsense you see on television where the brilliant detective uses a ballpoint pen or forceps to carefully pick up a cartridge so as not to obliterate a latent fingerprint. And invariably, the TV sleuth finds an amazingly distinct and complete fingerprint on the expended pistol cartridge; however, it's a little different in real life. In fact, in all the years I'd been a homicide inspector I'd probably picked up a couple of hundred cartridges with a pen and never once did we find a usable latent print.

Anyway, I squinted at the writing that encircled the base of the bullet and said, "It's Winchester nine-millimeter—the same brand of ammo the Sheriff's Department uses."

"So, the truck was coming west on Island Ford Road and stopped here. Why?"

"More than likely pulled over for running an imaginary red light."

"Trent?"

"He'd have been on duty at ten P.M."

Ash looked northward toward Caisson Hill, which was a low green hump in the distance. "And if Thayer was traveling in this direction he might have been coming from his aunt's house with the Mourning Bear."

"Makes sense. He was supposed to have delivered it to the auctioneer on Friday night and this is the road you'd take to go to Harrisonburg." I slowly exhaled and frowned. "However, the problem is that even if Trent is the killer, none of this makes any damn sense. If he robbed and murdered Thayer, why did Trent strangle him instead of shooting him? And here's an even bigger freaking mystery: Why strangle Thayer here and then carpool his body over to the Henshaw Farm to toss it in the river—"

"Three hours later."

"Exactly. What do you do with a dead man for three hours? Stick him in the passenger seat of a car so you have enough passengers to use the HOV lane on the Interstate?"

"That's terrible." Ash tried to suppress a laugh.

"Trent could have just dumped Thayer here from the top of the bridge. He's got the muscles to lift a corpse over the guardrail. So, why run the risk of transporting the body?"

"And who has the Mourning Bear?" Ash stroked my arm. "But I have absolute faith you'll figure it all out.

"Honey, I appreciate the vote of confidence, but there's no getting around the fact that we have more unanswered questions right now than when we began this morning."

Chapter 12

I collected the other cartridge from the ground and put both in my pants pocket. Although they'd never yield any latent fingerprints, the bits of metal nonetheless possessed some potential evidentiary value. The primer cap located on the base of each bullet bore a tiny round depression caused by the impact of the firing pin. This indentation was a unique tool mark that could be matched to a specific pistol by a firearms criminalist. However, unless Trent—and Holcombe for that matter—loaned us their pistols so that we could submit them to the Virginia State Police Crime Lab for examination, that identification wasn't going to happen any time soon.

On the way back to the boat, I took some more orientation photos of the western bridge approach, the span itself, and then finally some of the trash-strewn lot next to the river. I'd put the camera away and was preparing to climb back into the boat when the wireless phone trilled.

"This is Brad."

"Where are you guys?" Tina asked urgently.

"At the Island Ford Bridge—"

"Oh God! Get out of there fast! Sheriff Holcombe just called out over the radio and said he was on his way to the office from home."

"So?"

"So, he lives over at the base of the Blue Ridge and uses the Island Ford Bridge to get to town."

I motioned for Ash to untie the boat. "Do you think he knows what we're up to?"

"I don't know, but he *never* works on Sunday."

"How much time do we have before he gets here?"

"That depends on when he radioed that he was in service. If he was at his house, maybe ten minutes, but if he called along the way—"

"He could be here any minute. I'll call you later, Tina."

I hung up and climbed into the boat. "Let's be shepherds and get the flock out of here."

"Sheriff Holcombe?" Ash held the rope until I was seated and then climbed in.

"Yeah, on his way to the office from home and he uses this bridge."

"I really don't like tucking tail and running," said Ash as she yanked on the starter rope and the engine grumbled to life.

"Me either, but if we stay here we'll lose the evidence and once he finishes looking at the pictures on our camera he'll throw it into the river."

We pulled away from the bank and headed northward at top speed, which probably wasn't much more than fifteen miles-an-hour. I was seated near the prow facing to the rear, watching the bridge intently while Ash kept her eyes on the river. We'd traveled about seventy-five yards and were entering a looping curve that led eastward when

I saw a white and gold police cruiser appear. The car slowly crossed the bridge from east to west and then came to a stop on the side of the road at approximately the same place we'd recovered the expended cartridges. I got the binoculars out of the knapsack and used them to view Sheriff Holcombe climb out of the patrol car. For a second, I was frightened that he'd hear our boat's motor and notice us, but he didn't pay the river any heed. Instead, he began to walk around, hands on his hips and bent over slightly at the waist, examining the ground.

"Has he seen us?" Ash said.

"No, I think we're fine."

"What's happening?"

"Either he's developed a very sudden interest in the litter problem or he's looking for the cartridges. And the only way he could know their precise location was if Trent told him about waylaying Thayer . . ."

"Or he was there when the shots were fired."

"That too. However it happened, he's definitely not a happy boy right this moment."

The distance was too great for me to discern the expression on Holcombe's face, but the rigidity of his posture and the impatient way he occasionally shook his head told me he was annoyed or perhaps anxious over not being able to find the cartridges. Then suddenly my view of the bridge was obliterated as our eastward turn took us behind a stand of trees. I briefly considered asking Ash to turn the boat around so I could watch some more, but instantly dismissed the idea. We'd been lucky to escape and there wasn't anything we might see that was worth the risk of Holcombe spotting us.

I put the binoculars away. "He's very worried."

"About us? Maybe somebody in one of those cars that crossed the bridge recognized us and called him."

"Yeah, but if that's the case, he'd have been looking for us, which he wasn't." I tapped a finger on the aluminum bench. "I think he's nervous about Trent and, hell, I'd be too if I were in his place. Trent has probably never been the brightest bulb in the box and it's hard to focus on cleaning up a murder scene when you're in steroid nirvana. Leaving those expended cartridges there was just plain sloppy."

"But now that Holcombe can't find them . . ."

"Once he learns about our investigation, he'll have to assume we found them."

"What happens then?"

"He'll probably get a search warrant issued on a fraudulent affidavit—I'll bet you didn't know that we're drug dealers—and tear our house apart. And just to be vindictive, he'll cut up all our teddy bears, claiming we had drugs hidden inside them, and believe me, he'll find dope because he'll plant it. Even if he doesn't find the cartridges, we'll be in jail and no longer in a position to hurt the Holcombe family business."

Ash's jaw got tight. "So, what do we do?"

"Find a safe place for the evidence and you go stay with your folks until the case is solved."

"Not happening."

"But—"

"Brad, I am not being driven from our home by filth like them and I'm certainly not going to let you act as some sort of decoy while I hide. Is that clear?"

"You know what I think?"

"What's that?"

"That the monument in town to the Confederate soldiers is a big humbug. If anybody saved that mill from being burned back in eighteen sixty-four, it was the women of the Remmelkemp family."

A few minutes later we approached the Henshaw Farm. I saw Tina's patrol car parked behind the pickup truck and she waved as we motored past. Ash guided the boat to the spot where we'd made landfall earlier and soon we were back at the Chevy.

Tina looked relieved. "Hi, I was beginning to get worried. Did you see him?"

"We just managed to get away," said Ash.

"And you'll find this interesting: He stopped at the bridge to look for these." I pulled the expended cartridges from my pocket. "Fortunately, Ash found them first. Can you do me a favor and let me borrow one of your pistol magazines for a second?"

Tina unsnapped one of her leather ammunition pouches, pulled out a magazine, and handed it to me. "Where did you find them?"

"On the ground on the west side of the Island Ford Bridge. It's probably where that happened." I nodded toward the bullet-scarred windshield. I slipped one of the bullets from Tina's magazine and compared it to the cartridges we'd just recovered. The bottom portions were identical.

Tina was watching intently and sighed. "Oh, Lord."

"Tell me about Trent. How long has he been using the steroids?"

"Probably about a year."

"Have you seen any evidence of 'roid rage'?"

"No, but then again we don't work the same hours—thank God for small favors."

"Has there been any talk about it among the other deputies?"

"If he were going ballistic on people, I'd be the very last person to know. Nobody tells me anything. You think Trent killed him, don't you?"

"I think it's probable, but it doesn't sound as if *you* do."

"Look, I'm not sticking up for him, but we're talking about a murder here. The Holcombes collect graft but . . ."

"So, what you're saying is that they're capable of extortion, but not premeditated murder? No offense intended, Tina, but that's so naive it's endearing. People have been killing to protect their piece of the good life ever since Cain gave Abel the first dirt nap. Besides which, it might have been an accident. Maybe Trent set out to scare Thayer and something went wrong."

"That's possible."

I glanced at my watch. "Look Tina, we'll have to continue this discussion later because we're running out of time, both figuratively and literally. Ash has to be back at our house before three and we have to get this truck processed for prints before somebody tells Holcombe it's here."

"I'll go get the kit."

"You don't keep a toolbox in your unit, do you?"

"No, why?"

"Because I need a big flathead screwdriver and a hammer." I turned to Ash. "Honey, would you do me a big favor? While we dust this thing, would you find one of the Henshaws and see if we can borrow some tools?"

"Sure, but you still haven't told us why."

"Because when we're done printing the truck I'm going to punch the ignition and drive it out of here."

"You're what?" Tina asked.

"I'm going to hide it until we can get it into a crime lab to be processed for trace evidence. As things stand right now, we can't exactly have it towed to the Sheriff's Department parking lot."

"Well, no."

"So, we have to make it disappear until we have enough information for an indictment and then you can have it towed to the state crime lab."

Ash's jaw dropped in disbelief. "Brad, you are not going to steal that truck—"

"I'm not *stealing* it."

"Well, technically, you are," said Tina.

"Okay, but I'm stealing it for a good reason."

"And what happens if you get stopped by Sheriff Holcombe?" Ash demanded.

"I take one of my socks off, turn it into a puppet, and have it talk for me. Holcombe will decide I'm crazy and let me go."

"I don't need to see a sock puppet to know that you're nuts. This is too dangerous."

"Do you have a sock puppet?" Tina eyed me warily.

"Ash collects teddy bears; I collect sock puppets. Why . . . do you think that's weird?"

"Truthfully?"

Ash flung her hands skyward. "He doesn't have any sock puppets! He just says bizarre things like that to divert you from thinking about how bad everything can turn out." She took a deep breath and composed herself. "Brad, let's just say you manage to get out onto the road without the sheriff or Trent seeing you, where are you going to hide the truck?"

"Actually I had an idea about that. Sergei lives up in Thermopylae . . ."

"And you're going to ask him to store a stolen truck for you? Why would he agree to do that?"

"Because he's a bored retired spy and he doesn't like Holcombe. I'll bet he'll be thrilled to help." I took her hand and waited until our eyes met. "Ash honey, we don't have any other options and that piece of evidence has to be protected. It will be all right. I promise."

"Then I'm coming with you."

"You can't. You have to take the boat home because I

don't know how long this is going to take and I don't want you to miss your appointment."

"We can always reschedule."

"There's no need. Tina will follow me up there and bring me home."

Ash folded her arms. "*I'm* the one that's nuts for listening to you, you know that? I'll be back in a few minutes with a screwdriver and a hammer."

"Thanks, my love."

As Ash departed along the road into the cornfield, Tina went to the patrol car. She opened the trunk and returned a moment later with a small and dingy-looking plastic fishing tackle box. I took it from her, opened the lid, and surveyed the contents: a small plastic jar of black powder, a couple of rolls of clear lifting tape, some white latent cards, a Ziploc bag containing a bunch of latex gloves and a wooden-handled camelhair brush stored inside a clear plastic tube. I put the tackle box on the police cruiser's hood, pulled on a pair of the gloves, and took the brush from its case.

"Let's start with the side and rearview mirrors." I began to roll the round brush handle between my palms to separate the long soft camelhairs. "Most people automatically adjust them when they drive a strange vehicle and you'd be surprised how many crooks forget to wipe them down afterwards."

"How can I help?"

"Start filling out the back of the latent card."

"Is Sergei really a retired spy or was that another sock-puppet moment?"

"I don't know for sure, but would you do me a huge favor and forget you ever heard me say that? He's a good man and he doesn't need any grief just because I've got a mouth the size of Wyoming."

You don't need much powder to reveal a fingerprint. I

tipped a tiny amount of the black powder into the jar's cap and dabbed at it lightly with the brush. Then I began to make gentle oval sweeps with the brush in pretty much the same manner Ash applies foundation powder to her cheeks. Ridge patterns, some of them smeared, and at least one big thumbprint appeared on the glass. Several of the fingerprints looked classifiable and I used the clear tape to collect the prints. Then I moved inside the truck where I filled another three of the white cards with fingerprints from the rearview mirror. It had been over a year since I'd lifted any prints and I was a little surprised to learn that I hadn't lost any of my skill.

Next, we went to the rear of the Chevy. The truck-bed interior was covered with a textured plastic liner, so there wasn't any point in dusting there, but I did find some more classifiable prints on the outside of the tailgate. By the time we finished, we'd filled seventeen cards with fingerprints, some of which might have been left by Trent, Holcombe, or Poole, but they weren't going to do us a bit of good until they were submitted to a latent fingerprint examiner for analysis. And in the meantime, I had to find a hiding place for our growing pile of evidence. For now, I'd keep the print cards in our knapsack.

I was putting the print equipment back into the tackle box as Ash reappeared from the corn, carrying a foot-long screwdriver and a claw hammer. Handing the tools to me, she said, "Will these do?"

"Yeah. Thanks, love."

"I can't believe I'm facilitating this. And does this truck have an automatic or manual transmission?"

It was a Homer Simpson moment. "I forgot to look."

We went to the driver's door and I was enormously relieved to see it was an automatic transmission. My bad leg prevents me from operating a clutch pedal and if I couldn't drive the truck, Ash would have to do it. That was an option I dreaded and would noisily but unsuccessfully forbid because Ash could turn right around and point out that I'd assured her the trip wasn't going to be dangerous.

"And have you talked to Sergei yet? What are you going to do if he says no?"

"Consult with my sock puppet." I pulled the phone from my pocket, and tossing my cane in first, sat down inside the truck to give my aching leg a rest.

I emitted the tiniest of groans and Ash asked, "How bad does it hurt?"

"I'll manage. March or die, as they say in the French Foreign Legion."

It was after noon, so I knew Sergei would already be at the restaurant. I pressed the number and he answered, "Pinckney's Brick Pit."

"Good morning, Sergei."

"Brad, where are you? I just left a message on your home phone and I was about to call your cell. Hold on for a moment." The background noise of conversation and the jazz trumpet of Freddie Hubbard receded and I knew he'd gone into the back room. "Sheriff Holcombe went into the Sheriff's Office about ten minutes ago and Trent just arrived. They never come in on Sundays."

"Trent too, huh? We saw Holcombe earlier. He's out trying to tidy things up."

"Did he see you?"

"No, but I think he's beginning to suspect what we're up to."

"Where are you now?"

"On the Henshaw Farm, about four miles upriver from town. We found the truck and identified the dead man. He's Robert Thayer, the nephew of Elizabeth Ewell. I'll explain the rest later, but I have to ask a question: You live up in Thermopylae, right?"

"Yes, and I'm almost afraid to ask why you want to know."

"I need a safe place to temporarily store this truck and the other evidence—someplace the sheriff isn't going to find right away. If we leave it here, Holcombe will discover it and we'll lose any chance at recovering trace evidence."

"Brad, you know I support your goal, but what in the name of merciful God makes you think I'd allow you to conceal a stolen truck and illegally-seized murder evidence on my property, thereby making me an accessory after the fact to homicide?"

"Don't tell me you're frightened? Not an old Borzoi, like you."

"If I knew what that expression meant, I'd be impressed with your knowledge and flattered by your assessment." There was quiet amusement in Sergei's voice. "My home is at six-twenty-two Thermopylae Road. It's on the left side near the end of the paved road. Look for a mailbox painted as a goldfinch and follow the driveway up. There's a small barn behind the house. You can park the truck there."

"Thanks, Sergei, and would you do me one more favor? If you see Holcombe or Trent go mobile in a patrol car, would you give me a call at this number?"

"Brad, this may come as a profound shock to you, but I'm running a restaurant, not a surveillance post." There was a pause and the background noise increased. He'd moved back into the front portion of the restaurant. "Both patrol cars are still at the Sheriff's Office. I'll do my best. You be damned careful."

"Thank you, my friend."

When I disconnected from the call, Ash said, "Honey, why did you call him a Borzoi? Isn't that a Russian wolfhound?"

"Yeah, and it was a title of respect in his former vocation." I reached down and picked up the screwdriver. "Well, I guess we'd better get started."

"Have you ever actually done this before?" Tina watched carefully as I wedged the screwdriver blade in the ignition key slot as far as I could push it.

"No, but since your average seventh-grade dropout can do it, I figure I can manage." I used the hammer to pound the blade farther and farther into the ignition system and the plastic sheathing around the steering column began to crack. Dropping the hammer, I gave the screwdriver a clockwise turn and the engine started. Everyone looked kind of surprised, including me.

"Okay, I'm going to head out to the road and I'll follow you up to Thermopylae," Tina called as she jogged back to her sheriff's cruiser.

I gave her a thumb's up and turned to Ash. "All right, my love, you head home and I'll be back before you know it."

Ash handed the knapsack to me and leaned close to give me a long kiss. "Please be careful."

"Hey, you're the one that needs to be careful. All I have to do is drive a stolen truck across the county and hope the corrupt sheriff and his steroid-addled son don't see me. You, on the other hand, have to negotiate with the Ice Queen of teddy bears."

Chapter 13

Once Ash departed in the boat, I followed Tina's car through the cornfield. We passed the old barn and shortly thereafter I saw what I assumed was the new barn—not that you could have told the difference between the two ramshackle buildings on a moonless night. On the opposite side of the lane was the Henshaw's three-storied Queen Anne Victorian–style house and I slowed down for just a second to look at it. I was stunned.

From the sorry state of the barns, I'd naturally assumed the home would be in similar condition, so I wasn't prepared to drive past a life-size Thomas Kinkade print. The house featured one large turret, a broad wrap-around porch, flowerboxes beneath the ground floor windows, and was painted a sunny yellow with periwinkle trim. A white picket fence circumscribed the grassy front yard, lush and colorful flowerbeds surrounded the house and lined the walkways, and two gnarled old apple trees stood in the front yard. Up on the porch, a tawny tiger-striped cat lay sunning itself on the railing while Claire sat on a white wicker chair and practiced combat loading her shotgun. She waved and I waved back.

The driveway dead-ended at Wallace Road and Tina pulled over to allow me to take the lead. I made a left turn and followed the road for about a mile over the low rolling hills to where it intersects with U.S. Route 340. I had to wait until traffic cleared and then turned north. Route 340 has at least two other names that I'm aware of—the South Eastside Highway and the Stonewall Jackson Highway . . . big shock, that last one. The two-lane highway runs along the base of the Blue Ridge foothills, parallel to the Shenandoah River, bordered mostly by farmland and the occasional home. Overhead and to the east, I could see the black forms of buzzards coasting gracefully on the thermal currents above the hills.

There was a fairly large amount of other vehicle traffic on the road, which was a good thing because it reduced the possibility of the Chevy being spotted. Still, I was apprehensive when I stopped for the red light at the intersection with Coggins Spring Road. If Holcombe or his son somehow learned that we'd found Thayer's truck, or about our other activities, this was the route they'd take to get to the Henshaw Farm. However, the cross traffic passed by without incident and the light turned green.

As I drove, I noticed that the obvious gunshot pockmarks in the windshield didn't draw so much as a curious glance from other motorists. There were two reasons for this: First, hunting is a very popular form of recreation here, and it isn't uncommon for a sportsman to imbibe a little too much Peppermint Schnapps then mistake a motor vehicle for a deer. This isn't a good thing, but it's still much better than mistaking your hunting buddy for a deer, which also happens on a fairly regular basis, courtesy of the German firewater. Second, the local folks have this old-fashioned concept about minding their own business and it's one I find quite refreshing. It wasn't until I'd been away from the city for a few months that I began to appreciate how oppressively Orwellian the atmosphere can be—everybody watching everyone else intently for fear of becoming a victim. But, leaving the Massanutten Sheriff's Office out of the equation, crime is still relatively rare here and that means people don't have to behave like gazelles on the savannah in constant alert mode for lions.

Arriving in the small town of Elkton, I turned east on Highway 33 and headed up the four-lane road toward Swift Run Gap, one of the pathways over the Blue Ridge Mountains. As I drove, I pondered my next move. From their expressions of surprise, Tina and Sergei both thought it was enormously significant that Holcombe and Trent were at work on a Sunday. There were several reasons why they might be breaking the commandment about keeping the Sabbath holy, but the one that made the most sense to me was that they were preparing to implement a damage-control plan, which meant time was of the essence. That, in turn, suggested they at least suspected I was pursuing my own investigation and it was vital they act before I found anything too damning.

It was apparent to me that Holcombe's original plan was to bury Thayer as a John Doe and hope that nobody noticed. But if he believed that plan was no longer feasible, he'd be forced to make an official death notification to Elizabeth Ewell and sell her some fraudulent tale about how Thayer accidentally drowned. However, if I was correct, it also meant that I'd have to interview Miss Ewell and her live-in nurse before Holcombe got there. Unfortunately, that might also cause me to miss the appointment with Cleland—not that I didn't think Ash could handle herself in the encounter with the CEO.

I was still lost in thought when Tina frantically flashed her car's headlights at me, yanking me from my reverie. Looking in the rearview mirror, I saw a police cruiser coming up fast in the passing lane. The patrol car's blue emergency lights weren't on, but the cop was obviously in a hurry. I considered making a run for it, but knew that would be a lethally stupid thing to do. There was no way in the world I could outrun the cop car and police pursuits have a disturbing propensity to end with someone— usually the person being chased—in the intensive care unit or the county morgue. So instead, I got ready to pull over and hoped that if it was Trent, he'd brushed his teeth before going on duty today. I thought I could endure a physical beating, but the prospect of being immersed in his toxic-waste dump quality breath while being transported to jail in the stuffy backseat of a patrol car was just plain terrifying.

Then the car rocketed past and I saw it was a U.S. Park Service unit on the way back up to Shenandoah National Park. The female ranger was gulping down what looked like a Burger King Double Whopper and didn't give the Chevy so much as a second glance. I remembered to breathe and looked in the rearview mirror. Tina mimed mopping her brow.

Just before entering the park, I turned right on Thermopylae Road. For a few moments, I was plunged into cool greenish shadows as the sun disappeared behind a dense canopy of intertwined tree branches. The two-lane highway cut a serpentine course around the west base of a low hill, and when the trees cleared, I could see I'd entered a cleft between the mountains approximately a third of a mile wide. A sign said the road dead-ended in five miles.

I followed the meandering road up the valley, passing through pastureland that was dotted with cattle and cylindrically shaped hay bales sheathed in white plastic. Tidy homes were scattered along the way, some built from brick and others of modular construction. The two-lane asphalt road gave way to a one-lane unmarked road and that in turn became a narrow macadamized lane that began to ascend the south end of the valley. Fields gave way to forest and I began to worry because my odometer indicated I'd gone 5.3 miles and I wasn't seeing any more houses.

I passed a small pond and the road made a hairpin and upward turn to the right. At last I saw the goldfinch mailbox and knew that if Ash ever saw it she'd want one for our house. I turned onto the gravel driveway and saw Sergei's home about seventy-five yards farther up the hill, nearly hidden by the trees. It was a sturdy log cabin resting on a foundation of stacked and cemented flagstones, with a green metal roof and a stone chimney on the far side. There was a little porch and on it a single wooden rocking chair, which accentuated the palpable sense of loneliness exuded by the isolated house.

Evergreens and tall maples surrounded the cabin and the front yard was carpeted with a dense layer of brown pine needles. Suspended from the lower tree branches and hanging from about a dozen black wrought-iron shepherd's crooks was the biggest collection of bird feeders I'd ever seen short of the aviary at the San Francisco Zoo. As I drove past the house, a cloud of sparrows, finches, and chickadees rose from the ground and sought shelter in the nearby trees.

The small wooden barn was behind the house. I pulled inside the building, turned the truck's engine off, and decided to make a quick search of the interior before leaving. Opening the glove box, I found the vehicle registration paperwork, a couple of Lotto South tickets, a yellow receipt from an oil-changing place in Culpeper dated back in August, some Taco Bell hot sauce packets, and a three-quarters-full bottle of toasted hazelnut-scented moisturizing lotion. The last item was as out of place as a furrier at an animal rights convention. I've rummaged through crooks' motor vehicles for a quarter-century and never once found nice-smelling skin care products. You didn't need the investigative acumen of a talking Pomeranian to deduce that the lotion probably belonged to Thayer's girlfriend.

After that, I quickly checked under and behind the seats, but found nothing of evidentiary value. Then I took the expended cartridges and fingerprint cards and put them inside the glove box. It was as safe a place as any for the evidence. Tina sounded her horn for me to hurry and, grabbing my cane and the knapsack, I shut the truck's door and left the barn.

Tina yelled out the car window, "Holcombe just put out a BOL on the truck and Trent went in service a second ago!"

"What sort of BOL?"

"Grand theft auto."

"I wonder why Sergei didn't call."

"He probably tried but you couldn't receive the call up here. Get in and let's get out of here."

I opened the back door. "I think it'd be best if I lay down on the backseat for the ride home."

"You don't mind?"

"Not if it prevents Sergeant Testosterone from seeing me." I shut the door and tried to make myself comfortable on the seat, which smelled almost as bad as Trent's breath. As Tina began to back the cruiser up, another unpleasant thought occurred to me. "What about the park ranger unit we saw on the way up here? Are they on the same radio frequency as the SO?"

Tina turned the car around and began to fly down Thermopylae Road. She glanced into the backseat to answer, which made me wish she were watching the winding road.

"No, but our dispatcher will call them with the BOL information, so there's the chance that Kristine—that's the ranger who passed us—will remember seeing the Chevy and call it in."

"Let's just hope she was more interested in her lunch than the stolen truck she drove by. Tell me about the radio call. Did Holcombe make any mention of the pickup being connected with Thayer?"

"No, only that it was stolen."

"Makes sense. If he linked the missing truck with Thayer too soon, Liz Ewell would probably begin asking uncomfortable questions, and she impresses me as the sort of person with statehouse-level clout and who isn't afraid to use it. The last thing Holcombe wants is the State Police looking into this."

"You've lost me." Tina suddenly inhaled and jerked the steering wheel to the left to bring the car back onto the road.

"You're going to lose us both if you don't pay attention to the road."

"Sorry."

I sat up a little so that Tina wouldn't have to keep glancing into the back seat. "Holcombe knows the truck isn't where he and Trent left it there by the river. Maybe somebody tipped him off or he went looking when he didn't find the expended cartridges. However he found out, they're scared. They don't know if the truck's been actually stolen or if we found it and they can't go to Liz Ewell and ask her if she's seen it because she's never reported her nephew missing."

"Oh. And the only way Holcombe could know Thayer was missing was if he had something to do with it." Tina kept her eyes on the road and I began to relax.

"Exactly, but the ironic thing is that she probably *does* know he's missing. Yesterday—which seems like a hell of a long time ago—I was talking with the auctioneer's gofer. He told me he went over to the Ewell house when Thayer FTA'd with the Mourning Bear."

"FTA'd?"

"Failed To Appear. He told Ewell's live-in nurse what happened, so the Land Baroness of Massanutten County must know by now."

"So, why hasn't he been reported missing?"

"People as powerful as Liz Ewell are seldom stupid. She has to know that Thayer was a crook. Maybe it's part of the family gene pool. Anyway, we can presume she's well enough connected to also know about the felony arrest warrant."

Tina nodded. "And she was hoping to find him and get the Mourning Bear back without involving the law."

"Which brings us to what happened to the bear? Did—"

Trent's voice blurted from the police radio. "Mike Two to Mike Seven, what's your location?"

"God, that's me." Tina picked up the microphone. "Mike Seven to Mike Two, I'm on Thermopylae Road at Powell Gap Road."

"Rendezvous ASAP at that old abandoned gas station on thirty-three just east of Elkton."

"Ten-four, on my way." Tina slipped the microphone back into its holder and glanced back to give me a mildly panicked look. "What do we do now?"

"For starters, don't panic. Isn't that the old stone gas station right there next to the highway?"

"Yes."

"Then it doesn't impress me as the sort of place he'd tell you to meet if he knew I was with you."

"You're right. He'd want to meet someplace where there were no witnesses."

"So go ahead and make the rendezvous."

"But you can't stay there in the backseat."

"I know, so we have two options: You can either drop me off here and come back later to get me or we can pretend I'm a teenager trying to slip into a drive-in movie without paying."

"You mean ride in the trunk?"

"It wouldn't be the first time I've done it in my law enforcement career."

"You're sure? What about the exhaust fumes?" Tina slowed the patrol car and pulled over to the side of the road.

"I won't be exposed to them for long and they can't smell any worse than your backseat. Were *any* of your prisoners potty trained?"

Tina stopped the car and pressed the dashboard button to open the trunk. We both got out of the car and went back to the open trunk. She shoved a cardboard box full of road flares and a first-aid kit in an olive-drab metal ammo box to the side to make room for me. Then she held my cane and the knapsack as I clumsily clambered into the trunk. Once inside, I curled my body into a fetal position. It wasn't going to be very comfortable, but I figured I could tolerate it for a little while—not that I had any real choice in the matter.

Tina handed me my cane and knapsack and looked down at me pityingly. "Boy, I'll bet you wish you'd never gotten involved in this."

"Nope, I'm still having fun, but that could change dramatically if Trent finds me."

"Fun?"

"Fun. If you're lucky, that's what police work is. There were days when I was having such a good time I should have been paying the city to be out there." My voice grew momentarily somber. "Take if from me: Forced early retirement sucks big time. Now, please shut the trunk and let's go before I get *really* maudlin."

Tina pushed the trunk lid closed and I heard her get back into the car. It's a good thing I don't suffer from claustrophobia, because the trunk was absolutely lightless and as cramped as the section of hell reserved for telemarketers. I felt the cruiser pull back onto the road and I rolled over onto my back and tried to relax. After a couple of minutes, the car came to a stop and then turned left. The cruiser sped up and I knew we were on U.S. Route 33 headed downhill.

Maybe a minute or so later, Tina shouted, "We're here!"

The car slowed and made a left turn and I heard the crackle of gravel beneath me. Then came a more terrifying sound: My wireless telephone began to play the Rondo from Mozart's *Eine Kleine Nachtmusik*, signaling that I had a new voice mail message—no doubt the call from Sergei to advise me that Trent had left the Sheriff's Office. I banged my elbow against the wheel well as I rammed my hand into my pocket to get the phone. Fumbling with the device in the darkness, I managed to deactivate it just as Tina shut the engine off.

Tina didn't get out of the car and that meant the cruisers were probably parked with the drivers' windows facing each other so that they could talk without getting out of their units. I lay there quietly and was a little astonished at how easy it was to eavesdrop on the conversation.

Tina said, "Yes, Sergeant?"

"What were you doing up in Thermopylae?" Trent's voice was as hard as a streetwalker's smile.

"I had a 'livestock in the road' call earlier today, but I had to leave to go to a crash before I found the cattle. I went back up there to make sure we still didn't have a problem."

"You heard that BOL?"

"Yes, sir."

"You know whose truck that is?"

"No, sir."

"Have you seen it?"

"No, sir."

"For you and your kids' sake, you'd better be telling the truth. We know you were over at the gimp's house last night." I felt the car jiggle slightly and there was a moment's worth of silence. When Trent resumed speaking, his voice was panicky and stuttering. "Now, now, I didn't mean what you think by that."

It wasn't difficult to figure out what happened. Tina had reacted to Trent menacing her children by pulling her pistol. My attitude on whether she should drop the hammer on the brutal sergeant was almost disturbingly equivocal. It isn't that I countenance murder if committed by a cop, but if she killed him it would be nothing less than an act of self-defense. Furthermore, the world would be a better place without Trent in it. I waited to hear what would happen next. It seemed like a very long time, but it probably wasn't much more than a couple of seconds.

Finally Tina spoke and her voice was as cold as a Martian winter. "You threaten my kids again and they'll be calling you 'Sergeant Golf Course' because that's how many holes you'll have in you. Understand?"

"Yeah."

"Good. Get out of here and stay out of my sight. Run home and tell your daddy you may have frightened that San Francisco cop away from investigating that man's murder, but I don't scare so easy. I'm going to find that truck and when I do you know I'll connect it to that dead man. Now, git."

"You're making a damn big mistake, Barron. My daddy will have your badge."

"Git, before I change my mind, you pathetic excuse for a man."

The engine of Trent's patrol car roared to life and he shot from the parking lot as if hurled from an aircraft carrier fighter jet catapult. Once he was gone, Tina started her car and drove at a more sedate pace down into the Valley. I felt the cruiser turn onto Route 340 and, after a little while, make the right turn onto Coggins Spring Road. Then I heard gravel beneath me and the car stopped. Tina popped the trunk lid and came back to assist me from the compartment. I was home.

Gripping her hand tightly, I said, "Tina, you're a better person than I am. If he'd threatened my kids like that I'd have dropped him like a rabid dog."

"I still can't believe I said it."

"It needed to be said, but let me offer you one piece of advice: Be prepared to back those words up with actions. Whether or not it turns out he's good for the Thayer murder, Trent's a vicious goon and it will drive him freaking nuts that you—a woman—showed him up. Someday he's going to try to get even, and when it comes you'd better be prepared to kill him."

"Or shoot him so he'll be able to sing soprano in the church choir."

"I like the way you think."

I guess Ash saw me climb from the trunk because she came out of the house on the run. "Are you all right?"

"Fine." I hugged Ash. "We got the truck hidden and Tina did something very brave. She offered herself up as a decoy to Holcombe to allow us to continue the investigation."

"How?"

"It's too long a story to tell right now and Tina has to get out of here."

Tina glanced at her watch. "Yeah. I've got just over two hours left on what's undoubtedly my last shift as a sheriff's deputy and I'm going to spend that time leading those dirt-bags on the biggest wild goose chase Massanutten County's ever seen."

Chapter 14

Once Tina was gone, I took Ash's hand and we headed toward the house. She said, "So, do I want to know why you were in the trunk?"

"Tina told me she was developing a serious case of the creeps by me talking to my sock puppet and she finally insisted I ride back there."

"Right." Ash held the door open for me and I was lovingly body-slammed by Kitch.

"Gee, you don't sound as if you believe that. Hi, boy." I scratched Kitch behind his ears as I edged my way past him into the house.

"Picked that up, huh? Did you being in the trunk have anything to do with why Sergei couldn't get through to you on the phone to tell you about Trent leaving the station in his patrol car? He called here a little while ago."

"And you've been worried ever since. Sorry, love. There's no cell service up in Thermopylae, so I didn't get the call. And then, as we were coming down the mountain, Trent called Tina demanding an eighty-seven." I used the California police radio code for a rendezvous. "Getting into the trunk was about our only option to avoid me being treated like a piñata."

"So, does all this mean you're going out again?"

"Unfortunately, yes. Tina bought us a couple of hours of time by convincing Trent that he'd bullied you and me into submission, which means I have to go talk to Liz Ewell and her nurse this afternoon." I looked at my watch and propped my cane in the corner near the door. "The problem is that it's two-thirty now. I won't be back in time for your meeting with Cleland."

"Honey, I'm capable of dealing with Lorraine by myself. Besides, she called and told me she was running late and that she'd be here closer to four."

"I don't doubt for a second that you can handle her." I lowered myself into a kitchen chair and Kitch sat on the floor beside me, resting a drool-drenched chin on my knee. "That's not the point. It's just that we've had such tough times over the past year, I was looking forward to seeing something nice happen to us two whole days in a row."

"Solving this murder is far more important than whether or not I sell the design rights on a teddy bear."

"True."

"And if you do, you'll make something extremely nice happen. Holcombe will be out and Tina will be elected sheriff."

"Good point."

"But before you go, you'd better have some lunch." She pulled the microwave oven door open and took out a Black Forest ham and Muenster cheese sandwich with some potato chips on a plate.

Although I didn't have any time to waste, Ash was right. I'm not exactly hypoglycemic, but I do need to eat on a regular basis or I get a little twitchy and I couldn't afford to be anything but completely mentally focused during the interview. This was the only shot I was going to get to talk to Ewell and her nurse.

Setting the plate before me, Ash asked, "Lemonade?"

"God, that sounds good. Thanks for having this ready."

"My pleasure."

She brought two icy glasses of lemonade to the table and sat down beside me. As I wolfed down lunch, I brought her up to date on everything that had transpired since I'd stolen the Chevy. Meanwhile, Kitch lay sphinx-like on the floor looking as attentive as if he were guarding a flock of sheep—animals he's seen once and that terrify him. He sat in slobbery anticipation of table scraps, a bad habit that I've encouraged, to Ash's mild chagrin. A few months earlier, I'd waited until Ash was drinking something and soberly told her that I wanted to talk to her about how she'd spoiled the dog. The result was a classic Danny Thomas "spit take" with Ash spraying the beverage all over the kitchen counter. It was a funny moment, but also depressing, when I realized I was old enough to remember the *Danny Thomas Show*.

Anyway, when I got to the part of the story about Trent threatening Tina's kids, Ash became thin-lipped with anger and said, "That's despicable. Do you think he actually meant it?"

"Not that I'm trying to scare you, but there's a good chance he did."

"He'd hurt a child?"

"Yeah. Or Tina. Or for that matter, us. Try to look at it from Trent's point of view."

"I can't. I'm not a sociopath."

"But I've dealt with enough of them over the years to pretty much guess exactly what he's thinking. If we solve this case, the very best he can expect to happen is that he'll lose his power, a reasonably well-paying job for this area, the graft, and his macho-man uniform. The worst case scenario is a murder conviction, prison—"

"Which is never a fun place for ex-cops."

"Or maybe he's even looking at the death penalty, depending on whether he's convicted of first degree murder with special circs, or whatever it is they call it here in Virginia." I put the remaining third of the sandwich down, suddenly no longer hungry. I'd scared myself, but Kitch looked very encouraged. "The bottom line is that he has nothing to lose and with those wonderful chemicals percolating in his system there's also the potential he could go postal."

Ash's gaze drifted toward the window that looked out onto the driveway. "And we can't exactly call the sheriff for protection. How about the State Police?"

"Even if anyone believed us—which they wouldn't because we don't have enough evidence—the local office of the State Police wouldn't do anything today." I broke off a tiny portion of sandwich and slipped it to Kitch.

"Why?" Ash watched me feed Kitch and gave me a look that said: *How many times have we talked about you feeding the dog from the table?*

"For starters, it's Sunday and they'd want to consult with State Police headquarters in Richmond before doing anything and nobody would be there and, even if they were, then the office pogues at HQ would need to run the entire thing past the governor." I fed Kitch another piece of sandwich.

"Don't blame me when he drools on your leg at mealtime."

"Who? The governor?"

"Bradley."

"We can't waste table scraps. Dogs in China are starving." I gave Kitch the remainder of the sandwich.

"I give up. Now, explain to me why the governor would have to get involved?"

"Because we're talking about temporarily shutting down an entire county sheriff's department for corruption. The political fallout could be huge. Nobody will do that until the bureaucrats are absolutely sure they've got their asses safely covered and you do that best by kicking the problem upstairs as far as possible."

"What about the FBI?"

"I think the closest office is over in Charlottesville and there's a greater chance of O.J. finding the real killer on the golf course than we have of locating a FBI agent on a Sunday afternoon."

"What about the media?" There was a faint trace of annoyance in Ash's voice. "Couldn't we contact the Harrisonburg newspaper or, better yet, the papers in Richmond and Washington?"

"Again, it's Sunday. Dustin Hoffman and Robert Redford aren't sitting in the *Washington Post* newsroom waiting for our hot tip. We'd get voice mail."

"So, we're on our own."

"Basically. Tina's got to watch out for herself and her kids."

"What are you going to do if Trent stops you on the way to or from the Ewell place?"

"I don't know."

"Your gun is upstairs."

My gun was a Glock .40 caliber semiautomatic pistol. It was in our bedroom inside a zippered leather pouch, tucked away with my black nylon shoulder holster in the bottom of my sock drawer. The pouch also contained three magazines of seventeen bullets each—enough ammunition to ignite a respectable skirmish. During my years at SFPD, I'd shot expert, but it had been over a year since I'd had the pistol in my hand. Besides, the mere possession of a gun didn't mean I was any safer. It'd been in my hand when I was shot and crippled.

"Yeah, I've thought about that, but nothing good can come of it." I swiveled my lemonade glass on the tabletop and studied the wet marks it made. "If he shoots me, he can always claim it was because I pulled my gun on him. If I shoot him, I get arrested for smoking a cop and afterwards very conveniently commit suicide in jail. Better I should go unarmed and hope that if Trent stops me there are witnesses around."

"I can't believe this. This sort of thing isn't supposed to happen here where I grew up. And what are you going to do if you get in to see Liz Ewell and she turns around and calls the sheriff?"

"There's a chance of that, but we've still got to roll the dice, honey. She hasn't called the sheriff yet, which might mean she doesn't trust Holcombe herself." I took her hand. "It's going to be all right. I promise you."

Ash forced a smile. "If you say so."

"I do. Now, it's time I got going. Here's a question: How exactly do I get to the Ewell House?"

"Just cross the river on Coggins Spring Road and turn right on Kilday Road. Believe me, you'll recognize the Ewell place when you see it."

"It's that distinctive?"

"It makes the Winchester House look cheerful."

"Boy, I can hardly wait."

The Winchester House is a huge, gloomy, and very peculiar Victorian mansion operated as a tourist attraction in San Jose. We'd taken the kids there back in the late eighties because they'd seen the famous "haunted" house on some TV show and it was a short trip down the

Junipero Serra Freeway. I don't know if any ghosts actually live there, but I can tell you that the rambling old house was as depressing as a child's wheelchair.

Before heading out again, I used the bathroom and brushed my teeth. I eyed the sock drawer for a moment and then stumped downstairs. Grabbing the knapsack and my cane, I headed for the door where Ash was waiting for me.

She gave me a hug and a kiss. "I love you. Please, be careful."

"I will. I love you too."

It was an old ritualistic exchange and I think we both tried to overlook what had happened the last time we'd spoken those words before I left the house.

I drove to Coggins Spring Road, turned left and crossed the river. Arriving at Kilday Road, I turned right. The lane was fenced on both sides and lined with cedar trees. I saw a driveway up ahead on the right and slowed down in anticipation of turning, but when I got closer I saw the name "Wm. Pouncey" on the black plastic mailbox. There was also a wooden sign affixed to the wooden gate that read, HEADQUARTERS, MASSANUTTEN RANGERS, CSA. Somewhere out there on the farm, Ash's brother and the rest of the Confederate reenactors were camped.

A little later, I came to the edge of the Ewell estate and was immediately reminded of a California landmark: Folsom State Prison. A grimly imposing seven-foot-tall wall of large hand-hewn granite blocks surrounded the property and the only things missing were guard towers. I turned right into the driveway and came to a halt before a tracked steel gate. There was a callbox in a stone pillar by the side of the driveway and I pressed the button.

After a moment, a woman's voice, distorted by static, answered, "Who is it?"

"My name is Bradley Lyon and I need to see Ms. Ewell. She doesn't know me, but it's important we talk."

"Miss Ewell is not seeing visitors."

"I'm pretty sure she'll see me. Tell her I want to talk to her about Robert Thayer and the disappearance of the Mourning Bear."

There was a long interval of silence and then the speaker said, "Drive up to the house."

Chapter 15

After the gate rumbled open, I drove inside the estate. The vast rolling yard reminded me of a memorial park, only much less cheerful. There were severely cut hedges forming a low barricade around the house, clusters of tall bluish-tinted evergreens, a lush lawn with mower tracks so straight it looked as if a surveying team had marked out the paths, and not a single flower in sight.

The house was a three-storied neo-gothic castle constructed from the same bleak stone as the perimeter fortifications and it bore a vague resemblance to the Tower of London. There were turrets at each of the house's four corners, leering gargoyles for rain gutter spouts, and a low crenellated wall running just beneath the roofline. The place was such a grim burlesque of a medieval stronghold that I half-expected to see John Cleese from *Monty Python and the Holy Grail,* dressed in armor up on that topmost battlement, shouting that I was an empty-headed animal-food trough wiper.

I parked the Xterra near the massive oaken front doors and slowly made my way up the broad stone steps. There was a wrought-iron doorknocker fashioned in the shape of a lion's head with a ring in his mouth—another deliciously kitschy touch. I rapped on the door with the ring and waited for perhaps a minute, suspecting the delay in answering was deliberate. That didn't bother me, because I'm an expert at mind games myself and now I could employ some of my own with a clean conscience.

At last, the door swung inward and a woman appeared in the opening, blocking entry into the house. She was nearly my height, with a lithe form, a tiny waist, nicely shaped calves, and a small bust—sorry, but being a guy and, by definition, shallow, I notice those things first. I'd have guessed her as being in her mid-twenties, but the dowdy beige-colored knee-length skirt, matching jacket, and the stark white cotton blouse she wore made her look much older. Her hair was dark brunette, long and straight, and framed a reasonably attractive face distinguished by eyes the same color and luster of smoky quartz and marred by a thin-lipped expression of either anger or worry or both.

"Hi, like I said back at the road, I'm Bradley Lyon and I'm here to see Ms. Ewell."

"Where did you find Robert?" Her voice was resigned. "At that casino down in Charles Town, I'll bet. What does he owe this time?"

"I'm not connected with any casino. I live right here in town."

"Then what do you know about Robert?"

I took my sunglasses off. "That's information I'd prefer to tell Ms. Ewell in person. It's very important I talk to her right now."

"Is he all right?"

"No, he's not. Can I please come inside?"

"Oh, God." She seemed to wilt slightly and stepped away from the door.

Entering the foyer, my footfalls and cane tip echoed hollowly on the pale-gray marble tile floor. I wasn't surprised that the interior of the house was even more funereal than the yard. The foyer walls were papered in murky plum, there were two tiny and uncomfortable looking chairs upholstered in dull eggplant-colored jacquard, and the stairway and second-floor landing woodwork were varnished in a dark muddy color that should have been called "black hole" because it absorbed all light and reflected none. Overhead, six faux candlelight bulbs flickered inside a large cagelike black metal light fixture decorated with protruding spikes that looked as if it had been modeled after a gibbet: I wondered if whoever had done the interior design for the house had been on suicide watch at the time.

Noticing the wheelchair lift on the stairway, I asked, "Are you Ms. Ewell's nurse?"

"Not her nurse—her live-in physical therapist. She had a minor stroke about eighteen months ago and, well . . . I guess I shouldn't be telling you any of this."

"I can keep a secret. Are you okay? You looked bad there for a second."

"I'm fine. Robert just has a way of wearing you out. Is he in jail?"

"I don't really want to get into details until Ms. Ewell is here, but I'm sorry this has upset you, Ms . . . ?"

"Audett. Miss Meredith Audett and I should warn you: Don't call Miss Ewell, Ms.—she doesn't like it."

I extended my hand. "It's good to meet you and thanks for the guidance."

Her skin was soft and her grip strong. "Let's go into the parlor and you can wait there while I go get Miss Ewell."

She led me through a doorway that led to the left and into a room decorated in various coordinating and depressing shades of blue. The stucco walls were painted the chilly pallid hue of cyanotic skin, the matching wingchairs and sofa were melancholy cobalt, and the area rug covering the polished hardwood floor was dingy sapphire with a perimeter of faded flowers. Another light fixture purchased from Dungeons R Us hung from the ceiling, and the window curtains were made of white damask that reminded me of burial shrouds. Above the marble fireplace mantle was an age-darkened oil portrait of a stern-faced man with muttonchop whiskers and steely gray eyes, attired in what looked to me like a businessman's suit from the late nineteenth century.

"Who's that?" I jerked my head in the direction of the painting.

"Hosea Ewell—Miss Ewell's great-grandfather. He built one of the first modern factories in this part of the Valley."

"Right next to the river, I'll bet," I muttered.

"Pardon me?"

"Nothing. If you don't mind me asking, just what do you do for Miss Ewell?" I motioned with the cane toward my bum leg. "I'm interested because, as you can see, I'm a little handicapped myself."

"Well, I supervise her physical workouts, give massages, make sure she takes her medication, and I oversee her diet."

"And you obviously work out. You look as if you're in great physical shape—and I hope I'm not coming across like a dirty old man because that's certainly not my intention."

That elicited a shy smile from her. "Thank you for the compliment. There's a weight-training room in the back of the house and I work out for a couple of hours every day."

"I admire that sort of dedication."

"I guess I'd better go up and get Miss Ewell now. Why don't you sit down and make yourself comfortable until I get back."

"Thanks."

Meredith left the parlor and I heard her start up the staircase. I lowered myself into one of the wingchairs and stretched my leg out. There was an old clock on the mantle and its mellow tick was hypnotic. The house was so hushed, the day had already been long and taxing, and the atmosphere so soporific that it wasn't long before I was trying to suppress a yawn.

I thought: *Great! All I need now is to fall asleep, have my head slump forward, and begin drooling on my shirt.*

I reached up intending to rub my eyes—something Ash says I should never do because it stretches the skin and I've already got bags the size of Samsonite luggage beneath my eyes—but paused to sniff my fingers when I detected a strange delicate aroma. My right hand smelled faintly of one of the perfumed hand lotions that Ash wore . . . but not the one she'd put on this morning. That had been scented with sweet pea. What I smelled now wasn't floral but vaguely like a baked dessert.

From out in the foyer I heard a small electric motor begin to hum and I presumed it was the wheelchair lift bringing Miss Ewell downstairs. The hum stopped after about thirty seconds and was replaced by the sound of a higher-pitched motor. She rolled through the doorway at bumper car speed in a motorized wheelchair with Meredith a few steps to the rear, half-jogging to keep up with the old woman. I struggled to my feet because I knew that someone like Miss Ewell would expect someone like me to stand when royalty enters the room.

One of the first things a young rookie cop ideally learns after leaving the police academy is that bad people usually don't look bad. For instance, serial killer Ted Bundy could have been considered handsome, personable, and intelligent . . . so long as you weren't one of his many victims. Lifelong successfully bad people are chameleons; masters of improvisational acting for an audience of dupes—that's all the rest of us, by the way. They wear the ultimate disguise: They look just like us. Still, I had to admit I was a little surprised when I finally got a look at Miss Ewell. Based on everything I'd heard about the woman, I was expecting someone dour and hatchet-faced like Carrie Nation; what I got was Mrs. Santa Claus.

She had a round cheerful face, Delft china-blue eyes, plump pink cheeks, and a curly corona of glossy white hair. Other than the fact she was in a wheelchair, the only evidence of the stroke she'd suffered was an opaque plastic support brace that was tucked inside of her sensible left shoe and Velcro-strapped to her left calf. She wore a sweet, matronly pink dress and a tiny gold cross on a matching modest chain around her neck. The only props omitted in this archetypal grandmotherly persona were oven mitts and a metal baking sheet loaded down with oatmeal cookies.

"Good afternoon, Mr. Lyon. I'm so sorry to have kept you waiting. Please, sit back down." Her voice was a strong contralto and although she was a Southerner, the accent struck me as sounding contrived. It was over the top—too musical and way too much Vivian Leigh *Oh-Rhett-whatever-shall-become-of-me?*

"Thank you for seeing me." I sat down.

"Meredith tells me that you may have some bad news about my nephew." Miss Ewell glanced backwards at Meredith, who was standing behind the wheelchair. "Honey, please sit down. You aren't a servant."

"Yes, ma'am." Meredith looked a little surprised and sat down.

Miss Ewell nodded at me to begin. I said, "Before I get started, I have to explain a few things. I used to work for the San Francisco Police Department as a homicide inspector, but my wife and I moved here a few months ago. You may have known my wife when she was young. Her name is Ashleigh and her maiden name was Remmelkemp."

"Of course. Laurence's daughter. I'm certain they've told you just dreadful things about me."

"Actually, Lolly's never said a word to me about you. Ash, on the other hand, loathes you." I thought it wouldn't hurt to find out sooner rather than later how she was going to react to unpleasant truths.

Meredith blinked nervously while Miss Ewell looked a little sad. "I suppose that's understandable. She was very young when that unfortunate dispute over the land occurred and didn't realize that it wasn't personal—just business."

"Children often have a great deal of trouble telling the difference between grand larceny and business." I tried my best to sound reflective and not sarcastic.

Furthermore, I was fascinated with Ewell's behavior. If someone came to my house hinting at possessing bad news about a relative who'd disappeared while in the possession of an item of great value, we wouldn't have sat and chitchatted about what other people thought of me. We'd have gotten to the point immediately. It was possible this was an insight into how Ewell viewed herself and other people. On the other hand, it was also likely she assumed I bore terrible tidings and might have been trying to delay delivery of the news—I'd encountered that too. I didn't know quite what to make of her yet, but I hoped to have a better idea in a moment.

I continued, "But, to get back to the reason for my visit. Yesterday morning I found a dead man in the river near our house."

"We heard something about that after church today, Miss Ewell."

"Hush, dear. Let the inspector talk."

"Well, there's no good way to say this, but I'm almost one-hundred-percent certain it's your nephew."

I've always hated making death notifications to next-of-kin. It's almost always the same: You break the terrible news and there's a second or two of tense silence not unlike the reaction of a stunned victim to an ugly practical joke. Both women's faces revealed shock and then the customary swift denial.

Ewell said, "That can't be. Are you sure?"

"I watched the body being pulled from the river. I'm as sure as I can be . . . under the circumstances."

"Under *what* circumstances?"

"Before we get to that, I'd like to describe the man, just to make sure that we're talking about the same person. He was about five-five, maybe thirty-five years old, thin build, had a shaved head, with a moustache and goatee. He was wearing jeans, an orange tee-shirt, a leather jacket, and tennis shoes."

"Oh my God," moaned Miss Ewell and she reached out for Meredith's hand.

"I'm genuinely sorry for your loss and that you had to learn about it this way."

"How? What was he doing in the river?" Ewell began to cry.

"Forgive me, but some of the things I have to say now are going to be graphic and probably very upsetting. Your nephew was in the river because someone threw his body in there. But he wasn't drowned, he was strangled."

"Oh my God, oh my God!" Ewell wailed.

Meredith wore a look of sick shock. "But the people at church told me that the sheriff said the man had drowned."

"The sheriff was lying and we'll get into his reasons for that in a little bit. But right now, I'd like to ask some other questions first, if you're up to it." Ewell seemed to gather herself up and nodded in assent. I continued, "On Saturday morning you knew he was missing. If you don't mind me asking, why didn't you call the sheriff when Robert disappeared with the Mourning Bear?"

"Robert's been in his share of trouble over the years and I was just hoping . . ." Her voice trailed off and her body was wracked with a fresh spasm of pathetic sobs. After a few moments, she caught her breath and said, "Meredith, will you please get me a box of tissues?"

"Yes, ma'am." Meredith slipped from the room.

I completed Ewell's unfinished statement. "You were hoping that he hadn't come to the point where he was going to begin victimizing you and that he'd come back."

"That's true."

"Did Robert own a red Chevrolet pickup truck?"

"I bought it for him."

Meredith returned with a box of tissue. I waited until Miss Ewell dabbed her eyes and blew her nose before I broke more bad news. "I found that truck abandoned up-river a little way. The windshield has two gouges from gunfire and there was no sign of the Mourning Bear."

"Shot at?" squeaked Meredith.

"How do you know about the bear?" asked Ewell.

The cold incongruity of the old woman's question caught me flatfooted. I'd just informed her that Thayer's truck had been used for target practice and that the odds were good that the same person who'd done the shooting had also murdered her nephew. Yet for all her tears, she wasn't as curious about that as she was the extent of my knowledge about the Mourning Bear.

I said, "My wife and I were at the teddy bear show yesterday. I happened to be talking to one of the auctioneers and he told me that Robert was supposed to have delivered the Mourning Bear on Friday night."

"You said that *you* found Robert's truck. Why isn't the sheriff investigating?"

"Now we come to the interesting and very confusing part of the story. I hope you'll bear with me. When we found the body we called the rescue squad. The fireman that pulled Robert from the river was Pastor Marc Poole."

"Pastor Marc knew he was dead? But . . . this happened yesterday morning?" Miss Ewell looked at Meredith and back at me, her moist and reddened eyes sick with betrayal. "This morning he met us at the door, when services were finished, shook my hand, and wished us a good day and he *knew*."

"Pastor Poole didn't give us any indication either that he knew Robert. However, I've since learned that they were very well acquainted." I didn't think it was the right time to define Poole and Thayer's relationship as co-conspirators in what was likely a statewide burglary ring. Things were bewildering enough already.

Miss Ewell frowned and her eyes became hard. "I should say they knew each other well. What's more, they were supposed to meet Friday night! They were going into Harrisonburg together to deliver the Mourning Bear to the auctioneer."

"Why would they have gone together?" I kept my voice nonchalant, as if the question was of minor interest.

"Because Pastor Marc was on the board of directors for the regional charity group that set up the auction."

"So, I guess you would have called Pastor Poole when you learned that Robert had disappeared?"

"Meredith did. When she woke me up to tell me that the young man from the auction house had come by to tell us that Robert had disappeared with the bear, I was too angry and embarrassed to talk to anyone."

It was another major *Twilight Zone* moment—so much so that I half expected to see Rod Serling standing in the doorway, puffing on a coffin nail and delivering an ironic prologue to this episode into which I'd wandered. If everything I'd heard about the autocratic Miss Ewell was even partially accurate, the idea of her being embarrassed to talk to anyone was far stranger than the bizarre concept that Madonna can act. I added this anomaly to the growing list of things that didn't make any sense and asked, "Why was that?"

"Because the biggest charity event in the Shenandoah Valley was ruined by my nephew, the thief. It was the last straw." The flare of anger was replaced by mortification and she began to cry again. "Oh God, I've been thinking nothing but bad things about him ever since and all this time he's been dead."

I looked at Meredith. "When did you talk to Pastor Poole?"

"Yesterday around noon—right after I learned that nobody from the auction house knew where Robert was."

"What did he say?"

"Actually, I don't know if I should say this . . . but, he was kind of evasive."

"He was what? Why didn't you tell me that?" Miss Ewell peered at the younger woman accusingly over a wad of crumpled tissue.

"It was just a feeling, ma'am, and you were already so upset I couldn't see any point in telling you."

"What did the pastor say?" I asked.

Meredith's gaze shifted upward and became momentarily unfocused. "Well, I told him that Robert hadn't shown up at the teddy bear show and asked him if he'd seen Robert on Friday night, like they planned. Pastor Marc told me that Robert had called to say he was going into Harrisonburg by himself to make the delivery."

"But that didn't make any sense to you, did it?"

"No, especially since when Robert left he mentioned that he didn't know which motel to go to." She looked at me and I saw her eyes were now rimmed with red. She continued in an acidic voice, "The last thing Pastor Marc told me was that I shouldn't worry, Robert was fine. But if what you say is true, he must have already known Robert was dead."

"Yeah."

"Why would a minister of the gospel lie like that?"

"For the same reason everyone else lies. He was afraid of being caught for doing something wrong."

"Did Pastor Marc kill my nephew?" The old woman wore an expression that was as hard and cold as the rock face of Half Dome at Yosemite in January. I realized that I'd just caught a glimpse of the real Miss Elizabeth Ewell.

"I think he's up to no good about something—he may even know who killed Robert—but at this moment I don't believe Poole did it."

"Why?"

"This is going to answer your earlier question about why I'm investigating this murder and not the Sheriff's Department. A deputy came to our house right about the same time the rescue squad was pulling Robert's body from the river. I saw evidence that told me Robert had been strangled and I showed it to the deputy."

"What sort of evidence?" Meredith asked.

"How descriptive do you want me to get?" I directed the question at Ewell.

"It's enough that you're certain he was strangled and you are, correct?"

"There's no doubt in my mind whatsoever."

"Please continue."

"The deputy was ready to initiate a homicide inquiry, but was immediately stopped by Sheriff Holcombe.

Without even looking at the body, he determined that Robert had drowned accidentally. Then he tried to feed me an unconvincing story that someone had seen your nephew jump or fall from the Island Ford Bridge."

"That's patently ridiculous."

"That's what I thought too, but when I told the sheriff that, he promised to toss me into jail if I did anything to undercut his authority."

"Yet you proceeded with your own inquiry. Why?"

"I'll admit part of it was ego. I don't like being bullied and I *really* don't like anyone threatening my wife. Mostly, though, it was because it was just the right thing to do. Call me old-fashioned, but cops aren't supposed to cover up murders."

"Do you know why he was trying to conceal the true cause of Robert's death?"

"I have a hypothesis, but before I share it, I need to ask some questions and some of them are going to be disturbing."

Chapter 16

Miss Ewell peered out the window. "I think it's late enough in the day for a drink, and even if it wasn't, I need one. Inspector Lyon, you look like a Scotch-drinking man."

I knew Ewell wasn't scatterbrained, so this was the second time she'd deliberately tried to butter me up by using my old SFPD title. That, along with the unexpected offer of booze from a supposed belligerent teetotaler made me wonder why she was so interested in securing my goodwill. My guess was that—like a shark smelling blood in the water—she detected the opportunity to file a multi-million-dollar lawsuit against the Sheriff's Department and realized she'd need my assistance.

Deciding to match flattery for flattery, I replied, "You're an excellent judge of a man's drinking habits."

"Can I interest you in a wee dram of Lagavulin?"

"That would be wonderful."

A teetotaler with excellent taste in booze, I thought. Lagavulin was a premier single-malt Scotch whiskey and a bottle of the stuff was priced at over eighty bucks, which placed it well beyond our budget.

"Meredith, go into the library and bring the decanter and two glasses. Oh, and get yourself a soda."

"Yes, ma'am, and I don't need anything to drink. I'm not thirsty." Meredith slipped from the room like a wraith.

"Suit yourself, dear. I'm not thirsty either, I just want a drink."

I did my best to chuckle appreciatively at the feeble wisecrack. Also, I noticed that, for the moment at least, Miss Ewell seemed to have fully recovered from the shock and anguish caused by the loss of her nephew. Then, as if she'd read my mind, she clouded up like an approaching summer thunderstorm, plucked several more tissues from the box, and moaned, "Oh, Lord, poor Robert. You said you have questions. Go ahead."

"I take it from your earlier allusion to Robert's—let's call it *checkered*—history, that you knew he was a professional burglar."

"Of course. I blame my youngest sister for that. She never provided him with any rules. I did what I could to straighten him out."

And took advantage of his connections in the local criminal community when you wanted to hire some muscle to destroy the Henshaws' still, I wanted to add, but resisted the impulse. Instead, I nodded empathetically and asked, "And did you have any idea that Pastor Poole was Robert's fence?"

"Fence?"

"A dealer in stolen property. The good reverend was probably paying your nephew a dime on the dollar for the hot merchandise being funneled through the church's monthly flea market."

Ewell's eyes narrowed. "And do you know what the topic of that hypocrite's sermon was this morning?"

"No, what?"

"The whited sepulcher from the Book of Matthew."

"Full of dead men's bones and of all uncleanness," I quoted what I could remember of the biblical text I'd learned as a child. "It kind of makes you wonder whether that's evidence of a guilty conscience on Poole's part or a sick sense of humor."

Meredith came back into the parlor carrying a cut-glass decanter half-full of Scotch and two small glasses on a silver tray. She put it on the coffee table and looked expectantly at Ewell for further orders.

The old woman said, "Inspector, will you do the honors?"

I poured two fingers' worth into both glasses and handed her one. We chinked glasses and I said, "Cheers."

We both took sips and I savored the smooth peaty taste. Then Ewell glanced at Meredith, who was still standing by the coffee table and said, "Sit down, dear."

Meredith sat and I wondered what she'd do if the old lady told her to heel or rollover.

"So, back to my original question: Did you have any idea that Pastor Poole was selling Robert's stolen property?"

"Of course not."

"So, it would follow that you also don't know that Poole is paying the sheriff protection money. He has to if he wants to stay in business."

"Can you prove that?"

"I can prove Holcombe collects protection money from local folks. As far as Poole is concerned specifically, I haven't talked to him yet to determine the extent of his rendering unto the local third-rate Caesar."

"My God, that's awful," she said, but it wasn't her most convincing moment. Maybe I was imagining things, but I detected the faintest element of predatory glee in her voice and I wondered why. "You said you found Robert's truck. Is that important?"

"Yes, but it's also confusing. This morning my wife and I took a ride upriver in a boat to look for clues. We found the pickup abandoned by the river a few miles south of here." I deliberately blurred the location because there was nothing to be gained by pulling the Henshaws into the story.

"But how did you know it was Robert's truck?"

"We had some preexisting information about the vehicle, and once we learned it was registered to Robert Thayer, we connected the name to the auction."

"You said there were bullet holes in the windshield," said Meredith.

"Yeah. Somebody took two shots at the windshield but the rounds didn't go through and it was obvious they weren't fired where the truck was abandoned. That didn't make any sense until we cruised up to the Island Ford Bridge where we found some more evidence." I paused to take a sip of Scotch.

"And how does it make sense?" Ewell studied me over the rim of her glass.

"While we were there we—actually Ash—found two expended nine-millimeter pistol cartridges. It's the same ammunition used by the Massanutten Sheriff's Department. Not long after we left, we saw Sheriff Holcombe stop at that precise spot and look for the cartridges."

"Speak plainly. What are you suggesting?"

"I believe that on Friday evening, shortly after he left your house, Robert was stopped at the Island Ford Bridge by a member of the Sheriff's Department. More than likely it was Sergeant Trent Holcombe, because he was on duty that night and has much greater 'loose cannon' potential than his dad."

"Why?"

"Because he's stupid, addicted to steroids, and a bully by nature . . . other than that, he's a wonderful fellow. But to continue, shots were fired, Robert was strangled—in what order, I can't say—and then his body was thrown into the river in the hope of concealing the murder."

"And the Mourning Bear was stolen."

"True. Which could make this a murder in the commission of a robbery. I'm not completely plugged into Virginia law, but I believe that makes this a potential capital murder case."

"And that means?"

"Potentially the death penalty for whoever committed the murder."

"And by that you mean Trent."

"He's our best suspect right now and it would explain why his dad tried to cover the murder up as a suicide. However, there isn't anything close to what cops call 'probable cause' to make an arrest. That's why I'm here. Maybe if you can tell me a little more about Robert, I'll know which direction to go next."

"I'll help in any way I can."

I was growing to admire the old lady's superb ability to parse words. One of the most important things a homicide detective learns is to take note of what people say, how they say it, and what they don't say, which is often the most important of the three. In this instance, Miss Ewell didn't agree to tell me all she knew; only what she could.

I stretched my leg out and said, "So, even though he was a thief, you allowed him to take the Mourning Bear to Harrisonburg. I don't mean to be rude, but talk about assigning the fox to guard the henhouse."

"Robert had never stolen from me."

"And I'll bet that was because he was scared of crossing you."

"That's probably true." She gave me a tight smile as if modestly acknowledging a compliment. "But regarding the bear—had Robert stolen it, he wouldn't have known where to sell it."

"I see what you mean. The average person wouldn't pay one-hundred-and-seventy grand for a teddy bear, so Robert would have needed to know a collector with the financial wherewithal to buy."

Miss Ewell gave me a reassessing gaze. "Quite correct. I wouldn't have guessed you to be an aficionado of collectible teddy bears. How do you know so much about the Mourning Bear?"

"My wife makes bears and I've gotten very interested in them myself. The fact is, I enjoy them."

"That's very sweet." Ewell made no effort to conceal the contempt in her voice. Her underlying message was clear: There was something intrinsically flawed about a grown man interested in stuffed animals as anything other than valuable and rare collectibles.

Like the cleaning of an old oil portrait, the interview was slowly but surely revealing large patches of the real Ewell, and it wasn't a pretty picture. Furthermore, I knew that we'd reached a crucial point in our conversation. There comes a moment in every investigative interview with a hostile witness that decides who will be the dominant party afterwards. Ewell had just thrown a gauntlet down. I could submissively ignore the jibe—which is probably what she expected I'd do—or drop the hammer on her. The trick was in asserting myself without enraging her to the point where she'd terminate the interview. Anger wouldn't play well since it connotes a certain loss of control and Ewell was an archetypal control freak. Instead, I opted for pity mingled with ironic humor.

I leaned back in the chair and grinned. "You know, there is something so utterly pathetic about *you* sneering at me over my interest in teddy bears that it's almost heartbreaking. Here you sit in Castle Dracula, hated by everyone for fifty square miles, you've spent a lifetime as a brigand and a tyrant, and you're so screwed up in the head that you're looking down your nose at *me*. If it weren't so sad, I'd laugh."

Meredith gasped and Ewell glared at me. "Nobody speaks to me that way."

"And yet you'll notice the earth still spins on its axis. Miss Ewell, I'm not stupid. I realize the only reason you're talking to me is because you think you might be able to use my investigation later on to sue Massanutten County in a wrongful death action. And you know what? You have a good case. But that means you need me a lot more than I need you, so what are you going to do? Throw me out for being rude?"

Ewell took a noisy sip of Scotch and turned to Meredith. "His glass is empty. Pour him some more."

I held out the glass as Meredith poured the liquor. Her hand was shaking and the bottle tinkled against the rim of the glass. I thanked Meredith and looked back at Ewell. "So, back to business. Why did you decide to donate the Mourning Bear to charity?"

"Don't I impress you as a charitable person?" Ewell's tone was wry.

"Truthfully? No."

"My accountant suggested it as a tax deduction. I've made too much money."

I wanted to add: *Yeah, I always hate it when that happens,* but kept quiet. There was no point in unnecessarily goading her. I said, "Getting back to the Mourning Bear, how was it packaged when Robert left here on Friday night?"

"It was inside a hinged wooden box."

"And what time did he leave the house?"

Ewell looked at Meredith, who said, "Sometime around nine-forty."

"And who, other than you, Meredith, and Robert would have known that he was making the delivery that night?"

"The auctioneers, my lawyer over in Charlottesville, and Pastor Marc," said Ewell.

"Who couldn't identify Robert's body the following morning. What a remarkable coincidence."

"Do you think Pastor Marc told Trent about the delivery?" Meredith asked.

"If he did, that makes him just as culpable for the murder as the person that strangled your nephew, but right now there's no proof of that." I said to Miss Ewell, "Can you tell me a little more about Robert? Did he live here with you?"

"Mostly during the week. On weekends he stayed at his apartment in Warrenton."

"Was he employed?"

"He worked for me." She held out an empty whisky glass and Meredith poured her some more.

"Doing what?"

"Whatever I needed him for." Ewell gave me a chilly smile.

It was obvious I wasn't going to receive any specific information on Robert's undoubtedly unlawful duties, so I tried another tack. "Did you ever have any conversations with the sheriff about how Robert would be dealt with by local law enforcement?"

"Why do you ask?"

"Knowing Robert's relationship with the local law might help."

Ewell was silent for a moment and then nodded. "I told Sheriff Holcombe that I wanted Robert treated properly and that my nephew would be on his best behavior."

"Which is a sanitized way of saying Robert wasn't to be stopped or arrested for that felony warrant in NCIC and, in return, he wouldn't embarrass the sheriff by committing burglaries in Massanutten County."

"I never used those words."

"No, I understand that," I said in a placating tone. "Did Sheriff Holcombe receive anything in return for this agreement on how Robert would be treated? A reelection campaign contribution? A donation to the sheriff's widow and orphan's fund? Not that I actually think there are any widows or orphans."

"Are you suggesting I bribed the sheriff?" Ewell sounded immensely amused.

"I'd have a hard time believing he agreed to what you asked out of the goodness of his heart."

"I don't *ask* for things from people like Sheriff Holcombe."

"I see." In her own way, this woman was more frightening than Trent. I shifted the axis of questioning again, "Did Robert have any girlfriends?"

"None currently."

"I assume he had a room here in the house?"

"He stayed in the guesthouse. It's behind the main house."

"When we finish here, could I take a quick look in there?"

"Would it help find Robert's killer?"

"It might. I can't promise anything."

"Meredith will show you out there when we're done. Inspector, may I ask *you* a question?"

"By all means." I sat back and took a sip of Scotch.

"You said that you believe Trent Holcombe murdered my nephew. Do you have *any* proof?"

"Nothing that would result in an indictment. We've got some circumstantial evidence to show that his dad covered up a murder and was trying to clean up the crime scene, but I'll admit that we still don't have a firm nexus between Robert and Trent. We can't even really show that they knew each other."

"But they did," blurted Meredith.

We both turned to stare at the young woman.

"Explain," said Ewell.

"A couple of weeks ago, Robert was in the kitchen and he mentioned having a run-in with Trent over near Power Dam Road. He said Trent pulled him over and waved his gun around and threatened to . . ."

"To what?" Ewell demanded.

"To shoot his," her voice descended to a whisper, "*private parts* off unless he was paid some money."

"Sounds like Trent—except he wouldn't have used the expression 'private parts,' " I said.

"Nor would Robert. What else did he say about what happened, Meredith?"

"Only that he wasn't scared, but I could tell he was."

"Why didn't you say something about this earlier?"

Meredith studied her hands. "It was two weeks ago and I didn't think it was connected. I just kept hoping that he'd gone to Charles Town again."

Remembering Meredith's initial comments at the front door, I said, "That's over in West Virginia, right? I take it Robert had a gambling problem."

Ewell gave Meredith a smoldering glare. "He thought he had a talent for picking horses. He bounced a check at the off-track racing facility. I took care of it."

"Did he have any other vices?"

"What a pleasantly old-fashioned expression. I didn't think there were any vices in the world today—just lifestyle choices."

"Drugs?"

"Definitely no," said Ewell and Meredith shot a quick glance at the ceiling.

"Alcohol?"

"The occasional beer."

"Tobacco?"

"I've never allowed smoking in this house." Miss Ewell handed her glass to Meredith. "Inspector, as you said a few minutes ago, you aren't stupid, so I won't play word games. I'd like to make you an offer."

"What sort of offer?"

"Whether or not you can prove Trent killed my nephew, I'm going to sue the Sheriff's Department for their conspiracy to cover up the murder of my nephew."

"And your damages are?"

"The grave emotional distress caused by Robert's death and their unlawful actions." Ewell said piously and we both struggled not to chuckle.

"Yeah, I can see you're devastated. And, of course, you'll ask for punitive damages too. What are you thinking, an initial demand for fifteen million with the expectation the county will settle out of court for something in the high six-figure range? Say nine-hundred grand?"

"As I said, you aren't stupid at all."

"So, your offer to me is?"

"How would you like to be my private investigator?"

"And that would entail?"

"Continuing your inquiries and solidifying an iron-clad civil case against Sheriff Holcombe."

"And what about recovering the Mourning Bear?"

"If in doing so it further implicates Holcombe, but my focus isn't on getting the bear back. That's why I have insurance. So, are you interested?"

"Not really and, even if I were, there's the issue of me lacking a state PI license."

"That's a paperwork problem and easily resolved. I'm offering an initial non-refundable retainer fee of five thousand dollars, and once that's used up, I'll pay you four hundred dollars a day, plus expenses."

"Still not interested."

"Why not? That's a lot of money."

"Not enough to sell my soul to you."

"What if I included a finder's fee? You and your wife like teddy bears. I'll give you the Mourning Bear if you find it."

"Again, not interested. That teddy bear's value rests solely on the fact that it commemorates the deaths of over fifteen hundred people and that's a notion so ghoulish that I wouldn't have it in my home if you paid me." I put the Scotch glass on the coffee table. "Besides, you don't need to buy me off. I don't expect you to understand this concept, but when the time comes for your lawsuit, I'll testify honestly—even though the thought of you stinging the innocent taxpayers of Massanutten County for a large chunk of blood money frankly sickens me."

Ewell wasn't even slightly upset. In fact, she seemed quietly pleased that she'd gotten what she wanted without an additional outlay of money. She said, "Then I believe we're finished here. Meredith, please take the inspector to the guest cottage and allow him to look around. I'm going to go upstairs."

"And call your lawyer," I said.

"Of course."

Chapter 17

Meredith and I stood in the hallway and watched as Miss Ewell rode the wheelchair lift to the second floor. Once the old woman vanished upstairs, Meredith led me down the corridor toward the rear of the house. We paused at the doorway leading into what I assumed was the library. There were shelves packed with leather-bound books, a large globe that was probably so old it showed places such as French Indo-China and the Belgian Congo, and a dark wooden desk the size of one of the stone support plinths at Stonehenge.

Meredith said, "Hang on a second and I'll get the key."

She went to the desk, opened the top drawer, and took out the key. We resumed our journey, passing the dining room and a closed door to our right that Meredith told me led to the kitchen. After that, we came to the exercise room. It was the only place in the house that didn't look as if the Spanish Inquisition had designed the lighting fixtures and I paused in the doorway.

I was impressed. The room was equipped with everything you'd possibly need for a fitness program. There was a treadmill, a name-brand elliptical cross-trainer, a top-quality weight machine, a recumbent stationary bicycle, two weight-lifting benches, elastic workout bands, a large inflatable ball, and a wooden rack containing dumbbells ranging in weight from five to thirty-five pounds. Attached to the wall, just below the ceiling, was an enormous plasma television. For the first time I was slightly envious of Ewell.

"This is very nice. Did you pick out the equipment?" I asked.

"Thanks. Yes, Miss Ewell basically gave me a blank check."

"Do you like working for her?"

Her voice lowered. "She isn't the nicest person I've ever met, but she pays well. I was lucky to get this position." There was a long pause and then she continued, "I don't mean to pry, but what happened to your leg?"

"I don't mind talking about it. A murder suspect shot me in the leg back in April of last year. The doctors did what they could to repair the damage, but there was just too much bone destroyed."

"Did you shoot him back?"

"No. I was too busy bleeding on the pavement. My partner got him though." I saw her wince and added, "Sorry."

"That's all right. Have you ever killed anyone?"

"Why do you ask?"

"Sometimes I've thought about becoming a police officer. I've got all the physical tools, but I don't know if I could shoot anyone."

"Most cops never fire a shot in their career."

"Was that the case with you?"

"No. About twenty years ago, I ran into a guy that wanted to commit 'suicide by cop.' He wanted to die and didn't have the courage to do the job himself, so he grabbed a butcher knife and went looking for a blue-suit. He found me and got his wish."

"How did that make you feel?"

"Pretty bad. For awhile I considered leaving the job altogether."

"So, how do you ever forget something that awful?"

"You don't. You learn to live with it."

"Ready to go outside?"

"Yeah, let's go see the cottage."

She opened the backdoor and I slowly followed her down the steps. There was a cement-paved courtyard behind the house. On the right was a detached three-car garage that looked as if it had once been the carriage house. To the left was the guesthouse. It was an ivy-covered Tudor Revival cottage constructed from half-timbering set against beige plaster. The narrow arched windows were decorated with inset iron latticework in a repeating diamond pattern, the roof was a brown mosaic of wooden shingles, and the chimney was composed of red brick in an intricate hounds-tooth pattern. It wasn't even a contest—the guesthouse was easily the most attractive building on the estate.

As we walked, I said, "I couldn't help but observe your skeptical reaction when Miss Ewell told me that Robert didn't use drugs."

"Was it that obvious?"

"Don't worry, she didn't notice. However, when I search his room is there any chance I'm going to accidentally stick myself on a syringe?"

Meredith was flabbergasted. "You're kidding."

"I've seen it happen."

"No, he didn't use anything like that. He smoked marijuana."

"Forgive me for asking, but . . . how do you know that?"

"Sometimes he'd just reek of it."

"And Miss Ewell never noticed?"

"Of course she noticed. She lied to you about that."

A tall wall of shrubbery bordered the tiny half-circle of brick steps that served as a front porch. While she unlocked the door, I asked, "Did he own any weapons?"

"Like a gun?"

"Guns or knives."

"Not to my knowledge."

"Did you like him?"

"Not particularly. He was a con artist."

She pushed the door open and I went inside. When she didn't follow, I looked back and said, "Aren't you coming in?"

"I wouldn't really feel comfortable."

"I know this can be kind of creepy—going into a dead person's room. But it would be a big help to me, just in case I find something and later we need a witness to testify to what happened."

"If you think I should, all right."

I turned on the light as Meredith came inside. The guesthouse was composed of a bedroom, connecting kitchenette, and a bathroom. Although the queen-size and quilt-covered bed was unmade, the quarters were clean, nicely decorated in warm pastel colors, and the air smelled pleasantly of lemon from an unlit scented candle on the dresser. If this was Thayer's room, I'd just wandered into a bizarre alternate reality. Early in my police career, I learned an almost immutable law of the universe: Male crooks live in places that are invariably filthy and that possess a miasmic atmosphere of dirty clothing, decaying food, tobacco and marijuana smoke, and other stuff that smells so bloody awful you *really* don't want to know the cause. And in such a place you'll find piles of pornographic magazines, drug paraphernalia, and possibly even Jimmy Hoffa's body— but definitely not a quilted bedspread and a lemon-scented candle.

I stood there gaping. "*This* was his room? Has anyone tidied up in here since he left?"

"Why do you ask?"

"Because this doesn't look like any burglar's place I've ever seen. It's way too sanitary and—look, oh my God—clean curtains! My old partner back in San Francisco wouldn't believe this. Does Miss Ewell have a domestic staff?"

"Yes, a cook and a woman that comes to clean three times a week, but I don't think she was here yesterday."

"Well, is this the way it normally looks?"

"I really don't know." Meredith's voice was chilly.

"Hey, I apologize if you took that wrong. I didn't mean anything by it. I just assumed that at some point you might have seen inside the guesthouse."

"And I'm sorry for overreacting, but I really didn't like him. And if I didn't know what the inside of his place looked like, it wasn't for lack of trying on his part."

"Really?"

"It's true. I wasn't interested, but he wouldn't take no for an answer, which just showed how vain he was. Do you want to know what he thought?"

"What's that?"

"That he looked like Vin Diesel." Meredith snorted with bitter humor.

"Did Miss Ewell know about the situation?"

"No, and how could I go to her and accuse Robert of all but stalking me?"

"Oh, I don't know. It didn't look to me as if she had too many illusions about Robert."

"Maybe you're right. But I guess it's a moot point now."

"And as long as we're talking about their relationship, do you have any idea of how Robert viewed his aunt?"

"He never said anything directly to me, but I always got the impression he didn't really like her, but put on this big act of being affectionate because he didn't want to be written out of her will."

"It sounds as if everything about him was a con."

"From what I could see, yeah." She shifted her weight onto one leg and sighed impatiently. "So, what exactly are you looking for in here?"

"I don't know yet. This should only take a couple of minutes."

I began with the nightstand and opened the top drawer. There wasn't much inside: a tube of cherry-flavored Chap Stick, a small baggie of inferior-grade marijuana, a package of rolling papers, a couple of matchbooks, and a box of condoms. The last item meant that, regardless of Miss Ewell's belief that Robert didn't have a girlfriend, he'd had some female company here in the room. There was another small bit of evidence to support that belief because there were three or four long brown hairs on one of the bed pillows.

Those definitely hadn't come from Thayer and I couldn't help but notice that Meredith's dark brunette hair was about the same color and length as those on the bed—not that that necessarily meant anything. No doubt, there were thousands of brunettes in the Shenandoah Valley. Yet, I also realized that it was Meredith who'd spontaneously raised the topic of her rebuffing Thayer's romantic advances. I didn't know quite what to make of it, but even if the hairs belonged to her, what difference did it make? The most it likely meant was that she'd had a sexual relationship with a lowlife and wasn't eager to advertise the fact.

The bottom drawer revealed a little bit more of the real Thayer. There was a key ring with all sorts of shaved and filed-down keys—ideal for stealing cars—and a baggie containing tiny broken pieces of ceramic from automobile spark plugs. Although they looked innocent enough, the chips were also burglary tools because, when thrown, they could break a car's passenger window. These items rested atop Thayer's respectably large collection of well-thumbed smut magazines. The discovery of the burg tools and the hardcore porn restored my faith in reality.

"Why do men look at that stuff?" Meredith asked scornfully.

"For the same reason bodice-ripping romance novels are so popular among women. I think it comes down to how both sexes have been culturally conditioned for thousands of years."

"Humph."

"But I suspect you believe the reason is because men are pigs . . . and in all fairness, it was my experience as a cop that the guys with big porn collections *were* pigs."

Next, I made a quick search of the cedar dresser and we were back in a strange realm. There weren't a lot of clothes, but they were clean, neatly folded, and sorted into drawers by items of apparel. Perhaps that doesn't sound peculiar to you, but that's only because you haven't had my wealth of experience in looking inside men's dressers. As a general rule, guys, including myself, don't invest a lot of worry over maintaining our clothing in assigned drawers. Indeed our attitude can be summed up in a Johnny Cochran-esque rhyme: *If it can fit in the drawer, then I'm out the door.* Therefore, the presence of order, attention to detail, and aesthetic arrangement of folded clothing told me that the odds were very high a woman had put the stuff in the drawers—a woman that was something more than a casual girlfriend or just a one-time sex partner.

After peeking into the fireplace to make sure there was no evidence of anything having been recently burned, I limped into the bathroom. The medicine cabinet contained a small assortment of men's cosmetics, and the shower contained nothing but a tiny fragment of bar soap and a serpentine arrangement of soap-scum-coated brown hairs on the drain cover. The only remarkable element was that the towels were clean.

After that, I checked the kitchenette. Opening the refrigerator, I caught another glimpse of the genuine Thayer. There was a grease-stained cardboard pizza box tipped sideways so it would fit, a couple of cans of beer, and a package of lunchmeat colored the same shade of verdigris as the tarnished copper roof of the Rockingham County courthouse over in Harrisonburg. There were only a few dishes and glasses in the cupboard, and the contents of the pantry consisted of a bag of potato chips and a box of Count Chocula cereal.

"Well, I guess that's about it," I said.

"It doesn't look as if you found anything."

"Nope."

"What do you want me to do with the marijuana and the other . . . stuff?" Meredith was already heading for the door.

"Nothing. Leave it exactly where it is for now. Hopefully, we'll get the State Police involved soon and they'll probably send over a photographer to take pictures of everything."

I followed her outside and she locked the door. We stood for a moment in the bright afternoon sunshine and I savored the fresh air, the sound of the trees rustling in the gentle breeze, and an almost iridescent blue sky dotted with puffy white clouds. It was a tranquil moment in a long and frantic day, and I was enjoying it right up until the moment a volley of gunfire erupted from over the ridge and just to the north. I flinched and turned, then saw a thin wispy cloud of white smoke rise from behind the hill and begin dissipating as it drifted westward on the wind.

"What the hell was that?"

Meredith glared at the hillside. "It's those idiot reenactors over at Bill Pouncey's farm. They're out there almost every weekend playing soldiers like a bunch of kids. Sometimes I think they camp as close as they can to the property line just to bother Miss Ewell."

"Considering how popular she is with her neighbors, you may be right."

My tone was jocular, but that was intended to conceal my sudden and stomach-flipping realization that I might be wrong about almost everything. Remembering the conversation I'd overheard yesterday morning near the church, I realized that I had to get over to Pouncey's farm and talk to the reenactors before they broke camp and there wasn't a moment to waste. Yet there was also a chance to resolve this mystery here and now.

I fixed her with a sad, knowing smile and said, "You know, Meredith, I've been completely focused on Trent Holcombe as the suspect, but it occurs to me that it's also possible Bobby's death had nothing whatsoever to do with the theft of the Mourning Bear. Can you think of anything else you'd like to tell me?"

Meredith looked very thoughtful and shook her head. "No, I've told you everything I can."

But not everything you know, I wanted to add. Instead, I offered her my hand. "Please tell Miss Ewell good-bye for me and thank you for all your help. I'll just go around the side of the house to get to my truck."

I followed the driveway to the front of the castle and saw a sheriff's patrol car come to a stop behind the Xterra. Sheriff Holcombe was behind the wheel. It looked as if he'd aged perceptibly over the past thirty-six or so hours and he definitely wasn't happy to see me. He got out of the cruiser, slammed the door, and approached me with his hand resting on the butt of his pistol. Up close, I could see that Holcombe looked fatigued beyond measure and his eyes were feverish.

"What are you doing here?" He did his best to sound menacing, but the demand came across as merely querulous.

"What you should have been doing—investigating a robbery and a murder."

"It was an accidental drowning."

"Right. And you're late making the death notification because you didn't recognize the victim as the man you'd been ordered to treat with kid gloves by Czarina Ewell. Great story."

"You don't know what you're talking about."

"Funny, Miss E seems to think I do. And a word to the wise, if you've come to tell her that Thayer accidentally drowned, I wouldn't waste my breath. She already knows the truth, and I think at this very moment she's talking to her lawyer about suing you personally and the Sheriff's Department for fifteen million bucks."

"There is no murder."

"Tell me something, Hokie. The local folks say there was a time when you were an honest cop. Naturally, I don't believe that, but if it's true, how does it feel to have so thoroughly pimped yourself for a freaking teddy bear?"

"Shut your filthy mouth. I told you yesterday what would happen if you began interfering in official sheriff's business." His hand tightened on the pistol.

"What are you going to do? Shoot me? Put me in jail? Take me over to the Island Ford Bridge and have Trent shoot up my truck and rob me? I guess I should warn you that I've only got a couple of dollars in my wallet." Holcombe winced at the mention of the bridge and I continued, "Oh yeah, I know all about the Island Ford Bridge. In fact, I even have the evidence you were looking for earlier today—not on me of course."

"You don't know anything. You're bluffing."

"Dude, get this through your head. This is over and killing me or putting me in jail isn't going to solve your problems." Knowing that now it *was* time to bluff, I continued, "And the reason for that is because my old partner back in San Francisco is sitting by the phone and if I don't call at the prearranged time and say the proper code phrase, he's going to call his old friend at FBI headquarters. After that, how much time do you think it'll take before the State Police and all the Washington TV reporters are here? Do you really want to add another murder to the charges you're going to be facing?"

As I spoke, Holcombe seemed to sag and his hand fell away from his gun. "What do you want?"

"Stay out of my way while I finish this investigation and I'll let you leave with some dignity. Go back to your office and keep that lunatic son of yours there until I arrive." I paused and assumed a more gentle tone. "And I know you're crazy with worry because you think Trent killed Thayer, right?"

"Yes." The sheriff's voice was a sick whisper.

"Well, he may not have, but believe me, he will take the fall for a capital murder unless I get to the bottom of this mess. Oh, and one other thing: If you've got any brains you won't call Poole and tell him what's happened."

"Why?"

"Because if he learns that this thing is going south he's going to shovel every bit of the blame onto you and Trent. There's no honor among thieves . . . or corrupt pillars of the community for that matter."

Chapter 18

Okay, I know what you're thinking. Why was I suddenly on a crusade to clear Trent's name? Well, I wasn't. My goal was still to identify Thayer's killer. That required viewing the fresh facts dispassionately and not trying to twist them to fit my old—and as I now suspected— obsolete theory of how and why the killing occurred. As much as I despised the Holcombes, I wasn't going to try to pin a murder on Trent if he hadn't committed it . . . even if Massanutten County would be a better place if he were locked up for life.

Besides, I had nearly enough proof to send Trent and his dad to prison for robbery and attempted malicious wounding, which is what they call assault with a deadly weapon here in Virginia. The evidence seemed pretty clear that Trent had robbed Thayer of the Mourning Bear on the Island Ford Bridge and taken a couple of shots at the truck. Then, afterwards, the elder Holcombe attempted to conceal the crimes, making him an accessory after the fact.

However, I was now almost sure that neither of the rogue cops had killed Thayer. I'd know for certain in a few minutes when I interviewed the faux rebel soldiers camped on Pouncey's farm. Everything depended on whether they could remember what time and from what direction they'd heard the violent argument on Friday night.

I followed the patrol car down the driveway and stopped while Holcombe continued on through the gate and turned north onto Kilday Road. Getting out of my truck, I limped over to the two-foot-tall metal box housing the gate motor. As I expected, there was an external power toggle switch on the box and I flicked it to the "off" setting, locking the gate in the open position. The Ewell house was invisible behind a wall of trees, so with any luck, no one would notice the gate was open and I could come back into the estate without announcing myself.

Getting back in the truck, I drove down the driveway and out the gate, but stopped again before turning back onto Kilday Road. I pulled the phone from the knapsack and pressed the auto dial for our home number. Ash answered on the first ring.

"I was beginning to get worried. Are you all right?"

"I'm fine. Is Cleland still there."

"Her highness has come and gone." Ash was clearly fuming.

"What happened?"

"She got here, looked at Susannah, and said that she'd changed her mind. I asked her why and she said," and now Ash's voice slipped into a wickedly accurate caricature of Cleland's Boston Brahmin accent, "that, upon further reflection, Susannah just wasn't right for her company."

"That's all she said?"

"That was it and then she bailed out of here so fast, I'm surprised you didn't hear the sonic boom.

"That doesn't make any sense, especially when she seemed so enthusiastic yesterday. Unless . . ."

"Unless what?"

"Unless the reason I saw her Saturday morning at the church was because she was going to cut a private deal with Poole to buy the Mourning Bear. Maybe she knows that we're investigating the murder."

"But how would Pastor Marc have known to contact Cleland and how would he have gotten the bear?"

"Because he's on the charity committee that organized the auction and he and Thayer were supposed to deliver the bear to the auctioneers on Friday night."

"Oh my God."

"Look, sweetheart, this thing has gotten even more bewildering and I don't have a lot of time to talk. Please call Tina and tell her that she's no longer being hunted and she should come to our house immediately."

"Sorry, but I have to ask—how do you know that?"

"I ran into Holcombe and he's run up the white flag—at least for now. He's a complete basket case because he thinks Trent murdered Thayer."

"Well, didn't he?"

"Probably not, and please don't ask me to explain because it would take way too long. I'll be home in a little bit. Oh, and tell Tina to be prepared to take over as interim sheriff sometime tonight, okay?"

"I'll call her the moment I hang up from you. Good job, honey."

"Thanks, but let's hold off on the congratulations for now, sweetheart. This case has had more twists in it than Lombard Street and we aren't finished yet. I love you and I'll see you in a little bit."

I disconnected from the call and turned left onto Kilday Road. A minute later, I turned left again onto the asphalt lane leading to the Pouncey home and farm buildings, which were about a quarter mile from the road. Arriving at the two-storied white clapboard house, I came to an intersection of four gravel lanes and I selected the one that led in the general direction of the Ewell estate. The rutted track took me over a grassy hill and down into a meadow where I saw an encampment of about twenty tents in two perfect rows facing each other. Beyond the tents, twenty or so Massanutten Rangers were engaged in close-order drill on a grassy field. The stone wall separating the Ewell and Pouncey farms was less than thirty-five yards from the tents and, in fact, the tops of two of the castle towers were visible just above the trees.

There was a makeshift parking lot about a hundred yards from the camp but I drove past it because my leg was hurting like hell and I didn't have the time to plod across the field and back again. Instead, I guided the Xterra off-road, slipped the transmission into four-wheel drive, and slowly proceeded toward the encampment, hoping the pastureland wasn't too soggy from the recent heavy rains. I didn't get stuck and parked the truck near the tents.

Climbing from the Xterra, I wandered into the camp, astonished at how authentic everything looked. The tents were small and low to the ground and made from sun-bleached canvas. There weren't any sleeping bags or other modern conveniences inside the tents—just replica Civil War–era knapsacks constructed out of tar-coated canvas with uncomfortable-looking leather shoulder straps. I also noted that the soldiers had slept on the wet ground, protected only by rubber ground cloths and bundled up in threadbare woolen blankets. It was a commitment to recreating history that I admired, but not so much that I wanted to enlist.

However, as long as I'm on the topic, why is it that the entertainment industry sneeringly portrays reenactors as ignorant and crazed trailer-park-trash losers? The fact of the matter was that most of the guys out there drilling on the grassy field knew as much about the American Civil War as a university professor. Furthermore, I defy anyone to explain to me how reenacting is intrinsically any more stupid than a mainstream pastime such as golf, where you're obligated to pay two hundred bucks or more to hit a little ball into a hole with an assortment of expensive crooked sticks. Oh yeah, *that's* a much more sensible form of amusement than discovering something about the realities of American history.

I looked toward the drilling green and saw Josh Remmelkemp jogging across the field toward me, his bayonet-tipped rifle slung over his right shoulder. Meanwhile, the men continued to march back and forth to the tinny beat of a drum. As he got closer, I saw that Josh looked anxious.

"Hey, Brad. Is everything all right? Is Ash okay?"

"As of five minutes ago, everything was fine. I take it you've heard that we're investigating the murder?"

"My folks told me at church this morning. They also told me about what that SOB Trent did last night. Nobody threatens my sister like that and gets away with it." Josh shifted the rifle to port arms and ran his thumb over the large firing hammer. Although the musket was a replica, it was still a lethal firearm capable of shooting a Minie ball and I hoped he wasn't considering an extreme makeover of Trent's head to make him look like an oversize Life Saver.

"Nobody does that to my wife either, so I'm afraid you're going to have to wait your turn until I'm done with him."

"If you say so." He didn't sound convinced.

"Josh, he isn't worth it. Think about your wife and kids—you'll break their hearts and your parents' and Ash's too. Besides, Trent is going to prison and for an ex-cop that's a lot worse, for a lot longer than anything you've got planned."

Josh nodded, slowly exhaled, and lowered the rifle. "What brings you out here?"

"The murder investigation. While we were in town yesterday morning I overheard a couple of your men talking about hearing a violent argument on Friday night. You didn't happen to notice anything like that, did you?"

"No, I was already asleep but some of the fellas mentioned it. Apparently it was a doozey."

"What time did you go to bed?"

"Around nine, I think. Is this argument important?"

"It might be very important and that's why I need to talk to your men to find out what time it happened and from what direction they heard the voices."

"Well, the fellas said it came from the Ewell place, but I'll call them in and you can ask them yourself." Josh turned toward the men and shouted, "Captain Pouncey! With your permission, sir, would you please bring the company here?"

A lanky man waved his sword in acknowledgment and the soldiers turned and began to march toward the camp.

"Thanks, Josh."

"No, thank you, Brad . . . for the advice. So, have you identified the dead man yet?"

"Yeah, his name is Robert Thayer, Liz Ewell's nephew. Did you know him?"

"Not really. I've heard his name and seen him around town a couple of times. As you probably heard from Ash, our family doesn't associate with the Ewells."

"And with good reason."

"So, do you know who killed him?"

"I've got a pretty good idea, but I know you'll understand that I can't talk about it right now."

"If there's anything I can do to help, just let me know."

"Thanks and when this thing is wrapped up I'll tell you the whole story."

The column of Rebel troops entered the camp and halted. Captain Pouncey gave them a couple of brisk commands and the men stood at ease. The reenactors looked happy for the break. Most were sweating profusely, a couple of them began gulping water from button-shaped canteens, and one poor guy was breathing harder than an obscene phone caller. I scanned the ranks and was relieved to see the two soldiers I'd seen yesterday at the church.

Pouncey was strikingly handsome and looked as if he'd stepped right out of an antique daguerreotype. He had an aquiline nose, a strong jaw, shaggy drooping moustache, and an athletic physique. His weather-beaten uniform coat was butternut-colored, with a double row of brass buttons on the chest and gold embroidery on the sleeves in a pattern that vaguely reminded me of a Celtic cross. He wore a black leather belt with a scabbard hanging from it, and an old-fashioned revolver in a leather holster. His broad-brimmed, black felt hat was faded and battered.

Josh saluted. "Sir, I'd like you to meet my brother-in-law, Brad Lyon."

"William Pouncey. Pleased to make your acquaintance, sir. Your brother has told me all about you and your former career in San Francisco." Pouncey extended a gloved hand.

"Thanks for allowing me to interrupt, but it's very important that I ask your men a few questions. It won't take long, I promise."

"Is this about the man they found in the river yesterday? Sergeant Remmelkemp told me that you are conducting an investigation because the sheriff refused."

"That's true, but I also need to stress that I'm not a cop, this isn't an official investigation, and your men are under no legal obligation to talk to me."

"I understand that, but I believe there is a moral obligation, and I'm certain we'll do everything we can to help." Pouncey turned toward the troops and spoke in a stentorian voice. "Men, I want your attention. This is Mister Bradley Lyon and he wants to ask you some questions that may pertain to a murder. I wish you to understand that you're under no compulsion to answer, but be warned . . . if I learn that any man deliberately withheld information, his name will be immediately stricken from the company roll. I will not serve with a scoundrel. Am I clear?"

"Questions about what?" one of the soldiers asked.

Pouncey glanced at me and I said, "The questions pertain to an argument that some of you may have heard on Friday night."

Several of the men began to chuckle and I knew I'd struck pay dirt. Now, back in San Francisco, I'd isolate the witnesses and question each one separately to ensure that they told me what they actually knew, rather than what they might have heard someone else say. But I didn't have the time for that.

"With a tongue that sharp, I'm surprised that gal didn't cut her mouth," a reenactor called from the rear rank.

The man beside him added, "My daddy used to say that you can *always* tell a lady by how she uses the word mother-f—"

"Actually, I think that's two words hyphenated. Okay, so how many of you actually heard the argument?" I saw six men raise their hands. Pulling out my notepad and pen, I pointed to a tall soldier in the front rank. "Let's start with you, and guys, please don't interrupt, even if you disagree with what's being said. Name?"

"Walter Welford."

Josh said, "I can get you their phone numbers and addresses later on."

"Thanks, I'll need them. So, Walter, what direction was the sound coming from?"

Walter hooked a thumb toward the Ewell estate. "Over there."

"What were you doing at the time?"

"Sitting around the campfire having some drinks with my pards."

"Would you describe yourself as being intoxicated?"

"Who said we were drinking alcohol? Mister, I'll have you know that I don't drink anything stronger than pop."

"Sorry, I didn't mean anything by that." As I apologized I noticed Captain Pouncey's head shaking slightly and his eyes turning heavenward. I suddenly suspected I was interviewing the company comedian and was about to be the straight man for some of his really old material.

Bubbling with suppressed laughter, Walter couldn't wait to deliver the punch line. "And my Pop drank two pints of rye whiskey a day!" There were a few groans from the men and Josh gave Walt a glare. The reenactor sighed heavily, as if profoundly perplexed and saddened that his brilliant comedic talent wasn't appreciated and added, "Okay, okay, I'd had a few but I wasn't drunk."

"And what did you hear?" I asked.

"A man and a woman arguing. Well, it wasn't so much arguing as her calling him all sorts of filthy names."

"Disregarding the obscenities, can you recall anything specifically that was said?"

Walter pulled on his earlobe and thought for a moment. "The only thing I can definitely remember is that she told him he wasn't going to get away with it."

"Did you recognize either of the voices?"

"No."

"How long did they argue?"

"Maybe a minute or two."

"And how did it end?"

"It just quit. It suddenly got quiet. She was yelling and I think he said something and then it was over."

If I'm right, it was over in more ways than one, I thought. I asked, "Any idea of when this happened?"

"Oh, it had to have been some time around eleven— but that'd just be a guess."

"Uh, sir?" A young bearded soldier in the rear rank raised his hand.

"Yes?"

"Uh, I think I can tell you exactly what time it happened." The man sounded a little worried.

"Really? What's your name?"

"Randall Bell."

"And what was the exact time?"

"I'd just called my wife on my cell phone when the argument started. If we check the call history, it'll tell us the time I made the call."

Josh leaned close to my ear and whispered, "Uh-oh. Captain Pouncey doesn't allow *anything* modern in our camp. Even the booze the boys drink has to be poured from the bottles into historically accurate ceramic jugs."

Bell noticed Pouncey glaring at him and said to his commander, "I'm very sorry, sir. I realize that cell phones are forbidden out here, but you know I just got married last week and I wanted to call and tell Monica good night and . . . and that I loved her."

I gaped at Bell in disbelief, the investigation momentarily forgotten. "Let me get this straight, you got married last weekend and you've been out here *this* weekend sleeping on the wet ground in tents with a bunch of guys in stinky woolen uniforms when you could have been in bed with your newlywed wife?"

"Uh, yes, sir."

"You look young. Is this your first marriage?"

"Yes, sir."

"Did you live with her before you got married?"

Bell got red-faced. "Of course not! We both vowed to wait until we got married before we, well, you know . . ."

"Yeah, I do know and, Mr. Bell, I truly don't mean any offense but, no matter how much you like reenacting, you need your head examined."

"That's what Monica says," Bell said quietly.

"Listen to her. She's a smart woman. Now, getting back to the time, where is your phone?"

"In my knapsack in my tent." Bell looked at Pouncey. "Permission to fall out and get my phone, sir?"

"At the double-quick!" Pouncey barked.

Bell jogged to his tent and returned a moment later with a wireless phone. I signaled him to come to me instead of returning to the ranks. He turned the phone on and began pushing buttons while squinting at the tiny screen. At last, he handed me the phone and said, "Here. Look."

The screen showed a column of phone numbers with corresponding columns of dates and times. There was only one listing for September 30 and that was for a telephone call made to a local number at 11:09 P.M. That was almost an hour-and-a-half after the time Thayer had purportedly left the Ewell estate, never to be seen again.

"Thank you, Mr. Bell, and I expect at some point the State Police are going to want to take a look at your wireless phone bill, so you might want to keep it handy."

"This is important?" Bell swallowed nervously.

"Very important. You heard what Walt had to say about the argument. Is that basically what you heard?"

"I didn't even notice that much. All I heard was shouting, mostly by a woman. I was on the phone, so I wasn't really paying attention to anything that was said."

"Okay, thanks."

"Fall in, Private Bell," said Captain Pouncey.

As Bell returned to the troop formation, I resumed questioning the other four witnesses. All their statements were essentially the same. They'd heard an unidentified couple involved in a savage argument that had ended as quickly as it started. One of the soldiers thought the woman might have been crying, but he couldn't swear to it, and another concurred with Walter. The woman had shouted out something to the man about not getting away with it.

And the fact that Robert Thayer was found strangled and floating in the Shenandoah River less than eight hours after that threat was delivered, clearly demonstrated that the woman—undoubtedly Meredith Audett— had been absolutely correct. He hadn't gotten away with it. But now I had to find out precisely what "it" was.

Chapter 19

Thanking the reenactors for their time and cooperation, I limped back toward the truck. Pouncey dismissed the troops and as they broke ranks, Josh caught up with me. He said, "I'll stop by your house later tonight and drop off a list of those six guys and their phone numbers."

"Thanks. If we're not home, just go in through the back door and put the sheet on the table."

"Why wouldn't you be home?"

"I've still got several people to interview today."

"Including Holcombe and his son?" He gave me a sidelong and suspicious look. "Is Ash going with you?"

"You know your sister. If she wants to come, do you think I could actually prevent her?"

"Well, you could tell her 'no.'"

We looked at each other for a moment and then both of us exploded into laughter. Catching my breath, I said,

"I can't believe you said that with a straight face. But, I really don't want you to worry. I'm not going to do anything to endanger her."

"If you say so, Brad. Still, please be careful," he said as we shook hands.

I climbed into the truck and drove back across the farm to Kilday Road. Less than ten minutes later, I turned onto our driveway and as the house came into view I saw an unoccupied sheriff's patrol car parked near the house. I felt a tiny prick of fear and tried to reassure myself that it was Tina's cruiser, because the only other option was that Holcombe hadn't been able to rein in his son and that Trent had come to eliminate us as a problem. Then I relaxed as the front door opened and Ash, Tina, and Kitch came out of the house.

Ash gave me a hug. "Hi honey, I'm glad you're home."

"Me too, even if it is only for a few minutes." I gave her a kiss on the forehead and then glanced at Tina. "So, how did the wild-goose chase go?"

"Fine. In fact, it was kind of fun. First, I drove up to the ski area on Massanutten Mountain and then over to the Island Ford Bridge where I stopped and pretended to look for evidence."

"Was Trent following you?"

"Not at first, but he picked me up when I came down from the mountain. He kept his distance though. I think I scared him."

"I guess he's not as stupid as he looks."

"Then, about twenty-five minutes ago he just took off, so that must have been when you ran into Holcombe at the Ewell estate."

"Fortunately, Trent's still lucid enough to follow his daddy's instructions, although we can't continue to count on that."

Ash knew how much my leg was hurting and she guided me toward the picnic table. "So, where did you go after you finished with Ewell?"

"Over to interview Josh and the other Massanutten Rangers." I settled onto the bench and sighed with relief. Kitch sat down and rested his damp chin on my knee. Scratching his head, I continued, "Yesterday I overheard a couple of reenactors talking about an argument between a man and a woman they'd heard on Friday night. I didn't mention it because it didn't seem significant at the time."

"And the reenactors have their camp at Pouncey's farm, which is next to the Ewell estate." Ash sat down beside me.

"Right. It turns out that six—count 'em, six—witnesses heard this donnybrook at eleven-oh-nine P.M., which contradicts the story I'd just gotten from Ewell's live-in physical therapist."

Tina made a capital T with her hands. "Time out. You're saying that Trent isn't the murder suspect?"

"Unfortunately not, and Thayer's death probably had nothing to do with the theft of the Mourning Bear—which, by the way, Trent probably took."

"Then who killed him?"

"I strongly suspect it was Meredith Audett—the physical therapist I just mentioned."

"Why?" both women demanded simultaneously.

"I don't have time to tell you the entire story, so briefly, there's evidence of a sexual relationship between Thayer and Meredith, although she claims to have despised him. Also, from a purely physical standpoint, she's big and muscular enough to have committed the crime."

"You said that she lied," said Ash.

"They were lies of omission. She and Liz Ewell—who's a real gem of a human being, by the way—said that Thayer left the house with the bear at about nine-forty P.M. en route to Poole's place. However, Meredith neglected to mention that she became involved in a loud argument with a man ninety minutes or so later."

"But how do you know it was Thayer?" asked Tina.

"It had to be. For starters, unless you have a key to the gate, you have to call the house on an intercom to get into the estate. Neither Ewell nor Meredith said anything about any visitors coming to the house later that evening, so that means the man in the argument was someone who had access to the property."

"So, what else did Meredith lie about?" said Ash.

"Ewell told me that Thayer didn't have a current girl-friend. Meredith didn't disagree. That was another lie by omission, although I didn't realize it at the time. Yet when I searched the guesthouse where he lived, I saw long brown hairs on the bed pillow and in the shower."

"And he was bald," Tina said.

"Correct, and Meredith's hair is the same color and about the same length. And, the place was clean, so the hairs had been left recently."

Tina rubbed her chin. "So maybe they were in a ro-mantic relationship. It still doesn't prove she killed him. What's the motive?"

"Rage. Early on, Meredith told me that Thayer was a con artist and she wasn't lying when she said that. I think he probably tricked her into his bed and she, like so many nice women, thought she was going to rehabilitate the bad boy. Maybe when Trent robbed Thayer, he told him to get out of town."

"And he went back to the estate and told her that what-ever they had was over," Tina finished the scenario for me and I thought I heard a distant echo of pain in her voice, as if I'd just provoked some ugly memories.

"Do you think Liz Ewell knows?" Ash asked.

"There's no way of telling. She didn't give any indica-tion that she was aware of the relationship or the argument, but that doesn't mean anything. That old woman's got more dark layers than a freaking chocolate torte."

Tina finally emerged from her brief reverie. "So, what do we do?"

"Leave Meredith alone for now. She isn't going anywhere and we need to know the entire story before we re-interview her. And we're going to need an arrest warrant and a search warrant when we go back."

"I've written a few search warrants for burglary and dope cases, but never one for a homicide."

"The affidavit format isn't really much different. You've got nothing to worry about."

"Really?"

"Yeah, you'll just be including a larger list of items that you hope to find during the search. I'll be happy to help you with that, but you've got some much bigger issues to consider right now. For instance, are you prepared for what's going to happen when you arrest Holcombe and Trent?"

"I think so."

"You know as well as I do that this level of corruption is never really a secret. You can take it to the bank that your Commonwealth's Attorney knew what was going on, as did the county board of supervisors. Some of them may have even directly profited from it and they're going to be terrified that the Holcombes are going to roll—"

"And cut a deal to tell everything they know. I realize that I'm going to be under a lot of pressure to cover everything up."

I locked eyes with her. "Exactly. The bottom line is that you are going to be the ranking law enforcement officer in the county that's on duty and not under arrest—you are going to be the interim sheriff for at least a couple of hours. Are you ready for that?"

Tina didn't look away. "Absolutely."

"Good. Then you can count on Ash and me to stand by you and do everything we can."

Ash nodded vigorously and reached over to squeeze Tina's hand. "I'm so proud of you. You'll do fine."

"And not that I'm trying to run the show, but have you given any thought to calling in some backup? I'm assuming there are at least a few honest cops in the county."

"Most of the deputies are honest," Tina said in a slightly brittle tone, and I instantly realized that I'd touched a nerve by insulting the entire Sheriff's Department rather than just the Holcombes. "I've already thought of two or three guys to call in, but I'm not going to do that until Holcombe and Trent are in custody. That way we'll avoid an argument over whether I'm issuing legal orders."

"Good idea and I'm sorry if you took that last comment as a slam."

Tina looked down at the tabletop. "No, it's me that should be apologizing. You have every right to be suspicious of the department, but I'm going to do my best to change that."

"We know you will," said Ash.

"I agree. So, let's decide on our plan of action. I strongly believe our next move should be to go and interview Pastor Poole."

"Why Poole? I mean, I understand he lied about knowing Thayer, but how is he connected with everything else?" Tina asked.

"Ewell told me that Poole was on the organizing committee for the charity auction and that he and Thayer were going to transport the Mourning Bear into Harrisonburg on Friday night. Based on the facts that Poole didn't raise the alarm when Thayer was a no-show and Lorraine Cleland was at his church the following morning, we know that something was up."

Ash was the first to comprehend what I was suggesting

and she blanched a little. "Then, Pastor Marc had contacted Lorraine before the auction and she was there at the church to pick up the bear. Oh my God . . . he never planned to take the bear to Harrisonburg. He and Thayer were going to sell it directly to her."

"Or something like that. I'm not going to pretend I understand all the details, but there was some very important reason he didn't want Ewell to know what happened to Thayer. The thing that threw the monkey wrench into the works was Trent's deciding to play Jesse James."

"And the only reason Trent would steal the bear was if someone told him it was valuable," Tina added. "And the only way he could know *that* is if Thayer told him at the time of the robbery—"

"Exactly, and if Thayer didn't know who the buyer was, then the Holcombes would have had to contact Poole to let him know they had the bear now and that the deal was still on—but with a few minor revisions."

"Such as Poole's cut going from fifty percent down to a three-way split."

"If it was even that generous," I said with a bitter laugh.

"So, what you're saying is that the Holcombes and Poole got together and sold the Mourning Bear to Lorraine Cleland." Ash's eyes were brilliant with anger. "And you know what? It probably happened earlier today. That would explain why she was late and then so distant with me when she got here. She must have been told that we were investigating."

"That scenario fits the facts best, honey."

"What a bunch of scheming monsters. When are you going to talk to Pastor Marc?"

"Just as soon as we have a game plan. Why?"

"Because I'm coming with you. I want to give that creep a piece of my mind."

"Absolutely you're coming with me, but you'll have to

wait until the end of our chat with the good reverend to blast him."

"Why is that?"

"Because, with your permission of course, I'm going to use you as a twist. Your presence will motivate him to talk and tell me all sorts of wonderful lies that I can later use to ram down his throat and eventually get to the truth."

"How will me being there do that?"

"Honey, I know you don't believe me, but Poole's got a serious case of the hots for you and he won't be able to help himself. He'll be compelled to show you that he's a super genius and in order to do that, he has to show off as he outwits me."

Ash looked doubtful. "Brad darling, I've told you this before: I'm certain Pastor Poole just thinks of me as an old friend."

"You're kidding, right?" Tina laughed in disbelief. "Everybody in town knows that Poole has done nothing but talk since you came back. And he was probably the one that started the rumor . . ."

"What rumor?" Ash demanded.

"That . . . well, maybe this isn't the time."

"*What* rumor?"

"Okay, but I want you to understand I never believed it. The story is that, once when Brad was at a doctor's appointment over in Harrisonburg, you invited Poole over to visit, but that he told you no because it wouldn't be right."

"Oh, *really*?" Ash's eyes enlarged to the size of Ping-Pong balls and her hands curled into fists. Then she turned to me. "Brad, I'm so sorry I didn't believe you and I promise I'll maintain my composure in the interview with that rotten dirt-bag as long as you think it's necessary. But after that . . ."

I took her hand. "After that, he's yours to abuse. Now,

let's get back to our action plan. Once we finish interviewing Elmer Gantry we'll go over and interrogate the
Holcombes and that brings us to a problem."

"What's that?" asked Tina.

"We need to lock Holcombe and Trent into statements
that they can't deny later, which means secretly recording
the conversation."

"Can we do that?"

"I can't as a private citizen. However, you as a peace
officer can and you can also authorize me to do so as your
official agent."

"Okay, you're authorized, but that still doesn't solve
our problem."

"I know. Do you have a micro-cassette recorder?"

"No."

"Probably just as well. I'd have to put it in my pocket
and even then it would be almost impossible to conceal."

"How about a cell phone?" Ash said. "We could call
Tina at a number with a recorder attached to the line."

"That's not a bad idea," I said.

"But you'd have the same problem as with the cassette
recorder. The Holcombes might see the phone was on.
Besides, the cell phone reception is lousy in there." Tina
shook her head. "So what do we do?"

"We call our local expert in espionage." I pulled the
telephone from my pocket and pressed the number for
Sergei's restaurant.

Sergei picked up on the fourth ring. "Pinckney's Brick
Pit, how may I help you?"

"Hello, I'm looking for the Red Menace."

"Speaking. Hello, Bradley, and I want to congratulate
you on whatever campaign of terror you're running. The
sheriff and Trent both came back to the station about a
half-hour ago and then they stood out in front of the building arguing before going inside."

"Are they still there?"

"So far."

"Good. Hey, I've got an Aquarium pop-quiz question," I said, and Ash and Tina exchanged puzzled looks.

Sergei made an amused sound in the back of this throat. "It's a shame I don't know anything about tropical fish, but go on."

"I want to secretly record a conversation inside the sheriff's office. A micro-recorder isn't an option and neither is using a wireless phone as an impromptu bug. Obviously I don't have a body-mike, so how would I go about doing this?"

"You need to get a body-microphone."

"*There's* some expert advice! Oh, yeah, I'll just run over to Garber's and pick up a wire transmitter and base-receiving unit. I think he keeps them behind the cans of bug spray."

"No, you borrow mine."

"Some company equipment you forgot to turn in when you quit your last job?"

"I'm stung at the suggestion, old boy. It actually does belong to me. I bought it because we could never depend on the Soviet-made garbage they issued us. Come by and I'll give you my house keys and directions where to find the equipment."

"Can I send Deputy Barron? We're about to pay a visit to Pastor Poole. Ash just heard the racy rumor that's been circulating through town and she's really looking forward to discussing it with him in brutal detail."

"I'd pay to watch that."

"You could if you had one of those little TV cameras."

"Sorry, you're out of luck."

"Too bad. I guess you'll have to hear the bloody details over cigars and whiskey. Thanks, Sergei."

"You're welcome, but a word of advice. Watch yourself

when you meet with Holcombe and Trent. The son is a murder-suicide looking for a place to happen. You might want to consider having a gun."

"I've given that some thought, but I think me having a gun would just increase the chances of him going postal. I'll just have to rely on my empathetic conversational skills to maintain the peace."

"Can I cater your wake?"

I chuckled. "Go to hell, you Bolshevik spook. I'll talk to you later tonight."

Once I disconnected from the call, Ash said, "Okay, you've officially lost us. What does an aquarium have to do with anything?"

"It's the nickname of the building where he used to work and someday when we have more time—and with his permission—I'll tell you more."

"You have something for me to do?" asked Tina.

"Yeah, you need to go over to the restaurant and pick up Sergei's keys and make a speed run up to his house. He's loaning us a body wire. Meanwhile, we're going to go receive some spiritual guidance from the esteemed Reverend Poole."

Chapter 20

As Tina departed, we led Kitch into the house and put him inside his crate. I took some more ibuprofen, power-chugged a can of Diet Coke for the caffeine boost, and hit the bathroom. Five minutes later, we were on the road to town.

Ash tapped out an arrhythmic beat on the center console with her finger. "Okay, so how do you want me to act when we get to Poole's?"

"Surprised, a little disappointed, and secretly wanting to be convinced that we've misjudged the poor man." I couldn't help but notice that Ash was no longer calling him Pastor Marc.

"So, when do I get to throttle him?"

"Not until we get done. Think of it as dessert."

"Yeah, a nice fiery dessert, like cherries jubilee or crepes suzette—something that will cause third-degree burns."

"And here's something else to be prepared for: He's undoubtedly going to tell us lies, so at first you can't react with any disbelief. We want lies so we can use them later as leverage. If Poole tells us that he's the grand high emperor of Alpha Centauri, you nod in agreement," I said, turning west onto Coggins Spring Road.

"Does he really think we're that stupid?"

"Yes, as a matter of fact he does. Look at it from his point of view. He's already fooled us once by pretending not to know Thayer. Keep in mind that some of the aspects of his type of personality are above-average intelligence, an ability to manipulate others, and extreme arrogance."

"And what sort of personality type is that?"

"Borderline sociopath. If we can be patient and engage his craving for adulation, Poole will eventually tell us the truth."

We drove into town and I saw two patrol cars parked in front of the Sheriff's Department, which hopefully meant that Holcombe and Trent were still there. It being a Sunday afternoon, there weren't many people on the sidewalks, but those few I saw seemed to stop and watch us go by with an inordinate amount of interest. Apparently word of our investigation had begun to circulate among the townsfolk. As we passed Pinckney's, Ash waved at Tina who'd just emerged from the restaurant and was returning to her cruiser. A moment later, I turned into the driveway of the Apostolic Assembly.

Poole's home was behind the church. It was an unprepossessing single-story brick rancher with white trim and black vinyl shutters. The yard was depressing: a lawn that seemed mostly composed of yellowing crabgrass and a three-foot tall yew tree cut in the shape of a coffee canister that stood forlornly in a small planter surrounded by dying day lilies. Off to the side was a cement birdbath and the basin was drier than a life insurance agent's dissertation on actuarial tables.

Parking the truck, I looked at Ash and noticed she'd undone her topmost blouse button, exposing a tiny bit of cleavage. I took her hand and said admiringly, "That almost isn't fair. He won't be able to concentrate at all."

"Oh, you think he'll like it?"

"It'll drive him to distraction and you want to know the best part? Poole will be just like Moses . . . he'll be allowed a glimpse of the Promised Land from afar but never get there."

Ash gave me a sassy grin. "Let's go. I can't wait to watch you take that fraud apart like a two-dollar watch."

We got out of the truck and went to the front door. Giving Ash a nod of encouragement, I rang the doorbell. I heard the approach of footsteps on a hardwood floor and the door opened. Poole stood in the doorway and his eyes flicked from my face, to Ash's chest, and then to Ash's face. I couldn't blame him. If I'd been in his shoes, I'd have been admiring that view—and wouldn't have been anywhere near as subtle.

"Why, Brother Brad and Sister Ashleigh, I am *so* glad to see you. I was just about to call you."

"Really? Why?"

"I've heard about the brave thing you're trying to do and I want to help." Poole's head fell and he looked downward and away. "Yesterday morning, I did something quite shameful by lying to you. I was frightened, but that's no excuse."

I wasn't particularly surprised by Poole's spontaneous and ostensibly heartfelt prelude to a confession. Sometimes crooks offer their version of a story before any questions are asked, hoping it will be accepted as the truth because it is seemingly unsolicited. More often than not, such a "confession" is a blend of disinformation and harmless facts. In short, this was a fairly clever interrogation defensive tactic I'd encountered in the past. My task was to allow Poole to believe I could be manipulated into believing his tale without making myself appear a total moron. He knew me better than that.

I heaved a mighty sigh of relief and said, "I can't tell you how glad I am to hear that. Can we come in? This might take a little while."

"Of course. Please, come in."

He held the door open for us and we went inside. He led us through the characterless living room, down a shadowy corridor and into his office—a converted bedroom with a couple of windows overlooking the pasture behind the house. The room's only decorations were Poole's Doctor of Divinity diploma hanging in a cheap burnished steel frame on the wall and an artificial ficus tree in a straw basket in a corner. Both badly needed dusting. A pair of thirty-year-old Danish-modern chairs, upholstered in high-grade burlap and dyed the same shade of orange as a road crew worker's safety vest, faced an old wooden desk. Behind the desk were sagging shelves loaded with Bibles, theological volumes, and dozens of religious-themed books about marriage counseling, premarital sex, domestic violence, alcoholism, drug addiction, and child abuse. The remedy for almost every form of social malady was represented, with the exception of preachers who'd strayed from the ethical reservation.

"Please, sit down." Poole gestured toward the chairs as he moved behind the desk.

The decision to conduct our conversation in the office and his assigning of seats were also techniques calculated to place Poole in a position of unspoken control. Rather than sit in the living room and talk as equals, Poole had placed himself behind a powerful authority prop—the desk—while we were instructed to sit in the chairs customarily occupied by people seeking guidance.

We all sat down and I took out my notebook and pen. "I'm ready whenever you are, Pastor."

Poole leaned forward to rest his chin wearily on his hands. "When I pulled that man from the river, I recognized him but didn't say anything. I've felt awful ever since because I lied to you and Deputy Tina."

"So, who is he?"

"His name is Robert Thayer and he lived with Elizabeth Ewell."

I wrote the name down. There was no point in advertising how much I actually knew this early in the interview. I turned to Ash. "Liz Ewell? Isn't that the lady you told—"

"Yeah, that's her and she's no lady," said Ash, flawlessly supporting the ruse that this was all new information to us.

I looked back at Poole. "I've got to tell you, Pastor Marc, I'm a little surprised at your behavior."

"You're being charitable. Actually you're disgusted. That's all right, I am too." He looked broodingly out the window.

"Why didn't you tell us you knew him?"

"As I said at the door, I was very afraid. I suppose I need to back up a little to explain." He turned back to us and I pretended not to notice his eyes lingering for a second on Ash's bust as she leaned forward attentively to listen to the explanation. Poole cleared his throat and continued, "When Robert came here, Miss Ewell told me that he was what you'd call a career criminal—a burglar. Miss Ewell asked me to intercede and try to bring him back to the Lord."

"Did you make any headway?"

"Not enough. I think Robert wanted to follow the path of our Redeemer, but the old habits were too strong."

"Does that mean he continued to steal things?"

"I believe so."

"What caused you to think he was committing burglaries?" *Other than the fact he was delivering truckloads of swag to your house every freaking week,* I wanted to add, but suppressed the urge and waited with my pen poised.

"I don't have any direct proof. It was just a feeling. As a minister, you learn to trust your instincts about people."

"So, what made you afraid?"

Poole looked as if he were struggling mightily to control his temper and then shouted, "That pair of robbers across the road! Sheriff Holcombe and his son Trent are out of control and have been for some time. They told Robert they'd kill him if he didn't pay them protection money."

"How do you know that?"

"Robert told me on Friday afternoon. He came by the church just terrified and said he'd been stopped by Trent and threatened with death unless he was paid that night. And, God forgive me, I told him not to worry because I didn't think the Holcombes would be so stupid as to harm Liz Ewell's nephew. I was so very wrong." Poole looked upset and his voice was full of self-reproach, yet I noticed his eyes again drifting toward Ash's blouse.

I let his gaze rest there for a moment and then said, "But you still haven't explained why you were frightened enough to help conceal the identity of a man you knew had been murdered—a man who'd come to you in search of salvation."

Poole had the disheartened sigh down to an art form. "I know. The fact is, when I saw Robert's body I immediately suspected he'd been killed by Trent and I knew that if I said anything . . ."

"You'd have been the next victim. It's a perfectly natural reaction. You shouldn't be so hard on yourself."

"Thank you for saying that, but we both know I acted about as cravenly as possible. I'm ashamed of what I've done. But thanks to you, I can try to atone for my failure."

"Does that mean you'd be willing to testify to what you just told me in court proceedings against the Holcombes?"

"I'm still scared, but I'll use your bravery as an example."

Now I wanted to retch, but his unctuous Eddie Haskell impression told me that he'd come to the conclusion that I'd buy any bill of goods he had to sell, including brazen flattery. Fortunately, I didn't need to collect any more lies and it was time to have some fun. I said, "There are just a couple of things I don't understand and I'd like to clarify them before I write my report."

"I'll answer all your questions."

"Great, then I'd like to go back to your 'feeling' that Robert hadn't stopped engaging in his nasty habit of pillaging homes. Would you say that 'feeling' was based on the fact that you routinely bought stolen property from him and then sold it at the church flea market?"

"I don't know what you're talking about." Poole looked to Ash for moral support.

"Just answer the question and stop leering at my boobs, you hypocrite." She buttoned the blouse.

"Let's try an easier one. While you were baring your soul a moment ago and begging for forgiveness, why didn't you tell us about how Robert was supposed to meet you on Friday night so that you guys could deliver the Mourning Bear to the auctioneer in Harrisonburg?"

Poole's mouth hung open.

Ash said chidingly, "I'll bet it was because he was *so* afraid of Trent."

"Don't know the answer to that one either, huh? Okay, how about this question: What did Lorraine Cleland pay you for the bear, and how much of that do you have to give to the Holcombes?"

"How can you accuse me of such things?"

"Oh, man, listen to yourself," I said with a humorless laugh. "Think carefully about the words you just used. You aren't denying a single thing I've said. You just want to know how much information I have and who my sources are. Take it from me, they're impeccable sources and I know enough to ruin your day—the rest of your life in fact. So, how much did she give you for the bear?"

"I really think you should leave." Poole began to stand up and I noticed that his face had grown hard.

"By all means. The Holcombes are waiting for us over at the Sheriff's Office and I'm certain they're eager to tell us all about how you led them into temptation—not that I don't think they're perfectly capable of finding it themselves."

"I don't believe you."

"That's a shame because we're at that delightful point in a multi-suspect criminal investigation when the crooks begin pointing fingers at each other in the hope of being the penitent offender who gets the light sentence. I enjoy it because I get to play Monty Hall and decide who gets to make the deal."

"What deal?"

"To betray your partners in crime. It's obvious that you're by far the smartest of the bunch, so I was going to give you first shot." I made to push myself up from the chair. "However, if you're not interested I'll take my offer across the street, where I'm certain it will be accepted."

Poole slowly sat back in his chair. "What do I get out of it?"

"No reduction in charges, if that's what you're thinking. However, you will have the opportunity to cover yourself in advance from the Holcombes, who are going to accuse *you* of murdering Thayer."

"I didn't kill him!"

"I know that, but it will be the word of two witnesses against one, and they can point to your theft of the Mourning Bear as the motive."

"So, how can you help me?"

"Cooperate and we can show it was the Holcombes that contacted you after Thayer's death. You might even be able to argue that, believing that Trent had murdered Robert, you went forward with the deal to sell the bear under duress. Perhaps even because the Holcombes threatened to kill you unless you assisted."

Poole nodded thoughtfully. "That's true."

"And it also eliminates the possibility of being charged as an accessory after the fact to homicide."

"What about full immunity from prosecution?"

"I'm not in any position to make you that offer and I wouldn't offer it even if I had the authority."

"Why not?"

"Because you can't tell me anything specific about the murder."

"Oh, yes I can. What if I were willing to testify that Trent confessed to killing Robert Thayer?"

"Forgive my disbelief, but why would Trent tell you he'd killed Thayer?"

"So that I would understand that he and his dad meant business. He told me that he stopped Robert on the Island Ford Bridge and strangled him. Then he said that if I didn't wise up and get in contact with the buyer for the teddy bear, the same thing could happen to me." Poole sounded as if he were telling the truth.

Ash's eyebrows arched slightly and I shot her a warning glance. "Really? When did that happen?"

"He called here late on Friday night."

"All the previous BS you told us aside, I bet that did scare you."

"Yeah, and the most frightening part was, he didn't sound troubled by the murder at all."

"Well, I'm certain the Commonwealth's Attorney will find that information very interesting, but you'd have to prove Trent actually called here."

Poole allowed himself a slight smug smile. There was a phone with a built-in answering machine on the desk and he turned it toward me. The number "1" showed on the LCD screen, indicating one recorded message. Poole said, "I started recording shortly after the lummox called. Press the play button."

I did and we heard an excellent recording of Trent's voice say, ". . . you need to shut up and listen."

Poole's voice replied, "All right."

"I guess by now you know what happened to your friend, and in case you're wondering, I've got the teddy bear. Now unless you want to end up like your burglar buddy you'll do exactly what I say. Thayer told me about the deal."

"I understand."

"It's still on but Thayer's out and I'm in. Call me when you've contacted the buyer."

"Is it going to be the same split?

Trent guffawed. "Seventy percent for me, thirty for you, and you're damn lucky I'm being that generous. Oh, and Mr. Preacher?"

"Yes, Sergeant Holcombe?"

"You crap backwards on me and you'll end up in the river trying to swim to Front Royal just like Thayer. Do I make myself clear?"

"Yes, sir."

"Good. Get to work. I'll be waiting for your call."

There was a double-click as the call was terminated, followed by an artificial woman's voice that intoned, "Friday, October first, one-ten A.M."

Poole wore a look of serene satisfaction. "I even got him to acknowledge his name."

"I wouldn't be too proud over tricking Trent. His IQ is about the same as his belt size."

"But it proves my point. Trent killed Thayer." Poole sat back in his chair, placing his hands behind his head.

"So it would seem. Of course, you realize what would happen if Trent knew you had that recording, don't you?"

"Who'd tell him about it?"

"I will if you don't answer all my questions to my liking."

His hands came down and Poole leaned forward. "I don't like to be threatened."

"I don't like being crippled, but we both have to deal with reality. Now . . . are you ready to chat in detail?"

Poole looked as if he'd just tasted something awful. "Yes, damn you."

Chapter 21

"Let's start at the beginning. How long had you been Thayer's fence?" I asked.

"About seven months. Shortly after he moved here, I learned he could obtain merchandise and I offered to buy it from him."

"At the usual dime on the dollar?"

"Yes."

"And by 'obtained' you mean that Thayer was committing residential burglaries in Northern Virginia and bringing you the stolen goods, correct?"

"I didn't know all the details."

"C'mon Poole, let's not play semantic games. Were you aware the merchandise was stolen? And remember what will happen if I decide you're yanking my chain."

"Yes, I knew," Poole said, through clenched teeth.

Ash couldn't help herself. She glared at Poole and said, "People had their homes violated and their things taken. How could you do such a thing?"

"Because it was necessary and I'd even argue that it was the moral thing to do." Poole's stern demeanor softened a little as he looked at Ash. "This is the richest country in the history of the human race and we give next to nothing to help others. Those things the people lost can be replaced, but a starving or diseased child's life can't."

"You're rationalizing, Marc. It's burglary. Think of how frightened those people were when they came home and found their houses had been broken into."

"Think of the people who are starving or haven't heard the word of our Lord. Every penny I raised from the sale of those stolen goods either went to charity or missionary work—and without the customary 'administration' fee taken out so that the charity CEO can buy a condo on Maui." Poole's tone was acidic.

"Sorry, I'm not buying the Robin Hood act."

"I'm sorry you feel that way." Poole waved a hand at the stark office. "Look around this house. I certainly didn't benefit from the thefts."

"Oh, yes you did," Ash pointed an accusing finger at him. "You got to feel good and holy about yourself because you gave so much. But I'll bet you didn't tell those charities and missionaries how you came by your donations, did you?"

Poole was silent.

"I thought as much."

I decided to interrupt before she could continue flaying Poole. There were other important questions to be asked and, as much as I enjoyed watching him squirm under Ash's inquisition, we were short on time. I said, "Getting back to your relationship with Thayer, who came up with the idea of circumventing the auction and selling the Mourning Bear to a private buyer?"

Poole paused before answering and I knew he was weighing his options. By acknowledging that he'd originated the idea to steal the bear, he'd incriminate himself and probably earn another flaming from Ash. On the other hand, I didn't think he could quite bear the idea of giving Thayer credit for such a clever scheme, and he was also probably worried that if he did, I'd know it was a lie and terminate the interview. At last, he said, "It was my idea."

"Thanks for being honest. What was your deal with Thayer? I'm assuming he wasn't going to be satisfied with just ten percent."

"He wasn't. We were going to split the proceeds fifty-fifty." Poole wiped something from his right eye with his fingers. This symbolic blocking of vision suggested to me that whatever the pair had agreed upon, Poole never had any intention of honoring the deal.

"Did either of you have any second thoughts about stealing from Liz Ewell? After all, she was Thayer's aunt and you were her spiritual shepherd."

"I've agreed to answer your questions, so there's no need to be sarcastic."

"You're absolutely right, Poole. It's a bad habit of mine."

"Thank you. Do you know Liz Ewell?"

"Only by evil reputation."

"Everything you've heard is true. If anyone on this planet deserves to be stolen from, it's Liz Ewell."

I looked at Ash and saw her nodding slightly in agreement. "We have a consensus here. How did you select Lorraine Cleland as the buyer?"

"How did you find out about her?"

"That isn't important right now. So?"

"Actually, Lorraine was the one to contact me. Apparently she saw my name on some of the auction house literature and somehow found out that Ewell attended my church."

"Did Cleland know she was making a deal to purchase stolen goods?"

Poole snorted. "Of course."

"What was the purchase price?"

"One-hundred-and-seventy-thousand dollars."

"I'm impressed. Your run-of-the-mill grifter doesn't make one-tenth of that in a lifetime. How was the money going to be paid?"

"A cashier's check to the church. It's a charity donation."

I began to laugh and Poole watched me with a bemused smile. I said, "Oh, this just keeps getting better and better. Let me get this straight: Cleland gets a charity tax deduction for buying stolen property?"

"Essentially."

"Your idea?"

"Yes."

"Love it. I'll give you this, man, you're smart and you've got some real guts."

"Thank you."

"So, what was the original plan on Friday night? Were you actually going to take the Mourning Bear to the auctioneers?"

"Yes. We were going to go into Harrisonburg and I was going to take the bear to the motel room."

Suddenly suspecting the rest of the plot, I nodded in reluctant admiration. "And once you'd identified the room where the auctioneer was staying, Thayer was going to break in sometime during the middle of the night and take the bear, right?"

"He *was* a skillful burglar." Poole couldn't resist smiling.

"One problem though: The kid working for the auction-eer told me that Robert was supposed to make the delivery. Had they ever seen him?"

"No, and the plan was that I'd tell them I was making the delivery for Robert."

"And if you planned to steal the bear, the very last thing you'd do is deliver it to the auctioneer and Robert isn't suspected because he was never seen."

"Exactly."

"Once more, I'm impressed. So, you had this great plan, but then ten o'clock came and went on Friday night and Robert was a no-show. What were you thinking?"

"That he'd double-crossed me or said something to make that old witch suspicious." Poole frowned with the memory.

"What did you do?"

"Waited. Then I called his cell phone, but didn't get an answer."

"Probably because the circuitry was shorted out from being immersed in water. How did you find out about Robert being killed?"

"When Trent called."

"And when were you supposed to have originally made the sale to Cleland?"

"Saturday morning. She was supposed to come here. That's why I was in such a hurry to leave your house." Poole turned to meet Ash's gaze and answered her unspo-ken question. "And yes, I genuinely feel ashamed over how I behaved when I recovered Robert's body."

"But not ashamed enough to do the right thing."

I said, "Gee, it must have been fun telling Cleland you didn't have the bear and that your partner had been mur-dered."

Poole shook his head as if to dispel an unpleasant mental image. "At first, she was very apprehensive . . . and angry. But I managed to calm her down when I assured her that I could still get the bear for her, but it might take a little more time. I called Trent while she was there, but all I got was his voice mail. I left a message, but didn't hear anything from him."

Ash was outraged. "Hold on a second! She was aware that Thayer had been murdered and she *still* wanted to buy the bear?"

"Sure, so long as she could be guaranteed that her name would be kept out of any death investigation."

"And with Trent and his dad in possession of the bear, you naturally assumed there *wasn't* going to be an investigation," I added.

"Right."

"Which reminds me—not that this has anything specifically to do with Thayer's death—but just to satisfy my curiosity, how much in protection money were you paying the Holcombes in order to operate the flea market?"

"It had just gone up to four hundred dollars a month."

"Yow. He was in danger of killing the goose that laid the golden egg."

"Tell me."

"Okay, getting back to Saturday morning with Cleland, when Trent didn't call, what happened?"

"She left for the teddy bear show."

"In a hurry, I might add." Poole looked puzzled, and I continued, "I saw her take off out of here like she had the pole position at the Indy 500. Why did she go to the teddy bear show?"

"She thought that the deal had fallen apart and that the bear might actually go up for auction."

"So what did you do while she was gone?"

"I must have called Trent ten times, leaving messages

and telling him I was ready to deal. He finally called back and told me that there'd been a temporary delay and to stop bugging him."

"That doesn't make any sense," I said, not adding: *unless there'd been some sort of dispute between Trent and Holcombe over the sale of the teddy bear.*

"But at some point you finally did hear from Trent."

"It was Gene Holcombe that called . . . earlier today. He told me he was going to be handling the negotiations from now on and that he was ready to sell the bear."

"Did he change any of the terms?"

"No, it was still seventy-thirty and he told me that if I talked to you, the very best I could expect out of the rest of my life was becoming an inmate's girlfriend and making license plates at the state penitentiary."

"At least he didn't threaten to toss you into the river. What happened next?"

"We met this afternoon right here around three-thirty." Poole gestured listlessly at our chairs.

Ash looked stunned. "That means the Mourning Bear was out in her car while she was at our house . . . which explains why she was in such a hurry to leave."

"I wonder why she even bothered to come by. She could have just called you and cancelled." Turning to Poole, I said, "Did she know we were investigating?"

"Holcombe mentioned it. He wasn't happy."

"There's your answer, sweetheart. She was concerned that if she cancelled and we later learned she was in town, we might have connected her to this carnival of crime. Okay, back to the meeting. What happened?"

Poole grimaced. "There isn't much to tell. Holcombe brought the Mourning Bear and Lorraine had the cashier's check. I have no idea of where Trent was. Anyway, it took all of five minutes, but there was one kind of funny moment."

"Really? What happened?"

"Holcombe got all puffed up and started to threaten Lorraine about what would happen if she talked about the deal. Well, she turned right around and told him to 'shove it' and said that she had investors up in Boston who were experts in making troublesome people have fatal accidents."

"Mob connections?"

"That's how I took it."

"That's how I'd take it too. What happened next?"

"Lorraine left with the bear and Holcombe took the check."

"I take it he didn't trust you'd be here tomorrow morning so that you could go to the bank together?"

"I don't know what he thought. You'll have to ask him." Poole suddenly sounded very tired and petulant. "So, what's going to happen to me?"

"You'll probably be booked into jail sometime tonight, but you're going to have to wait your turn because you're relatively low on the list. I expect that the interim sheriff, Barron, is going to be very busy for the next few hours arresting Holcombe, Trent, Cleland, *and* the murderer."

Poole blanched. "But I thought Trent was the murderer."

"Nah. Trent robbed Thayer, shot his truck up, and probably threw him in the river to scare the bejeezus out of him, but he didn't kill him. Somebody else did that later."

"But the recording—the message."

"The message hurts you almost as much as it does Trent because it shows your participation in a preexisting criminal conspiracy to steal and sell the Mourning Bear."

"But he admitted to killing Thayer."

"No, he didn't. You need to listen to that recording

more carefully. Trent just said that he'd thrown Thayer into the river—which he did. And do you want to hear the most deliciously ironic part about all of this? Trent didn't know that Thayer was dead when he made that call. In short, you've got no leverage, and the Commonwealth's Attorney is going to try and crucify you in order to show the voters that he's lily white and *shocked* at your criminal behavior. And even if you avoid a prison term, once people around here understand the depths of your misconduct, you'll be a pariah."

"You deliberately misled me."

"But it was for a good cause." I kept the mockery from my voice and it seemed to sting Poole that much more. "I wanted the truth and that seemed more of an effective tool than appealing to your conscience. Would you have told me anything otherwise?"

He looked out the window. "Then I guess that's it."

"Oh no, that isn't 'it.'" Ash stood up and placed her hands on the desk so that her face was only a few inches from Poole's. "The last time I looked, lusting after another man's wife was a sin. All those hugs and—stupid me—I thought it was innocent. After all, you're an old childhood friend and a clergyman. But then I learned about that rumor you started—I guess I was one of the very last ones in town to hear it—and now I know the truth."

Poole looked down at the desktop and remained silent.

"Oh, spare me the I'm-so-ashamed act. You aren't capable of understanding how dirty and idiotic you've made me feel in front of my husband, family, and neighbors."

Looking up, he began to say something.

"So help me God, if you say you're sorry, I'll slap you."

Poole shut his mouth.

"One other thing: You've got to have several screws loose to be able to rationalize all the evil things you've done. But you have to be a raving lunatic to think I'd leave this man for anyone on earth, let alone for a selfish and cowardly little nothing like you."

Chapter 22

As we drove down the driveway toward the road, I asked, "Feeling better?"

"A little."

"I really enjoyed that last part when you threw Poole's framed Bible College diploma against the wall and then kicked it to pieces." I quietly chuckled.

"I *warned* him not to say he was sorry. He's lucky I didn't break it over his head." Ash took a deep breath and then smiled slightly. "Actually, I'm beginning to feel pretty good. Can I smash something in Holcombe's office?"

"Probably not."

"But if you decide you need something smashed, I'm your girl."

"You've always been my girl, Ash. Always and forever."

"Thank you, sweetheart." She leaned over to kiss my cheek. "So, how are you going to handle the interview with Holcombe and Trent?"

"That we're the only people in the world who can keep Trent from taking the lethal-injection elevator to hell and we don't want our time wasted. I'm not going to be anywhere near as circumspect at getting to the point," I said, turning the truck into Pinckney's lot and parking beside Tina's patrol car.

The front window of the restaurant had a CLOSED sign on it, but Tina opened the door. "Come on in. Sergei decided to close for the afternoon and help us."

We went inside and I saw Sergei bent over some electronic equipment on a table. He grunted, "Business was slow, so I thought it would be a good idea to make sure this was done properly."

I went to the table and took a closer look. The base radio receiver was the size of a large toolbox with a four-foot-tall antenna jutting from the top and contained a built-in cassette tape recorder. Beside the receiver was a transmitter power pack of roughly the same dimensions as a small wireless phone and attached to the bottom was a flexible two-foot-long beige-colored wire microphone. The equipment had to be at least fifteen years old, yet it was lightyears ahead of anything I'd ever used while working for SFPD.

"So, who's going to wear the wire?" Sergei asked.

"I think it has to be Ash. You okay with that, honey?"

"Sure. What do I have to do?"

"I thought you'd never ask. We both go into the backroom and you undo your pants."

"Brad!"

Sergei laughed, as did Tina, who also blushed.

"I'm not kidding. We have to put this in the small of your back below your waistband." I held up the transmitter. "We'll tape it in place to make sure it doesn't move. Then, we take this wire antenna and bring it around front and up under your blouse. We'll secure it in such a manner that our radio surveillance team can keep abreast of the situation."

She gave me a mischievous grin. "And I suppose you'll help me with that too."

"I live to serve. Got some bandage tape, Sergei?"

"There's a roll of it in the medicine cabinet in the bathroom."

"If we're not back in ten minutes . . . give us another ten minutes."

It took considerably less than ten minutes to tape the transmitter to the small of her back and to slip the microphone wire into the right cup of her bra. Ash buttoned everything back up and I closely scrutinized her chest to make sure the wire wasn't visible through the fabric.

"Are you enjoying yourself?" she asked.

"This is purely professional."

"Right. Are you making all these jokes because you're scared?"

"Petrified. This could turn very bad and it'll be my fault if it does. Add the fact that I can't envision life without you and it's a wonder I can even function."

"You'll bring us through this just fine." She took my face in her hands and gave me a long, slow kiss.

"Okay you two, you can come on out! We're receiving you just fine! In fact, right down to the smacking lips!" Sergei called from the dining room.

Emerging from the back of the restaurant, I said, "You're just jealous, Sergei."

"That's true," he said gravely.

I turned to Tina. "All right, here's how we'll do this. You wait here until we've finished the interview. You'll be able to tell if it's gone well and can be standing by to take them into custody. However, if this goes to hell and one of them begins cranking off rounds, under no circumstances are you to John Wayne–it and try to make a

rescue, pilgrim. There'll be no point in charging in because it will be too late to do anything for us. Secure the
scene and get some reinforcements. Understand?"

Tina nodded, shook hands with me, and gave Ash a
hug.

I started to give Sergei a handshake but—Russians being some of the most sentimental people on earth—he
yanked me close and gave me a bear hug. He said quietly,
"From one Borzoi to another, you must assume an attitude of icy and total moral ascendancy when you enter
that office. I know their type and they will submit if they
unquestionably believe they've met their master."

"Thanks, that's damn good advice. Let's just hope I
can fool them into thinking I'm moral."

"Just be yourself . . . except not quite such an insuffer-
able smart-mouth." He gave me a wry grin.

"Much as I'd love to, I can't argue with that advice.
Ready, honey?" I held out my hand.

Ash took it and we left the restaurant. As I've mentioned before, it's very difficult for me to hold hands and
walk while using my cane, but this time I gritted my teeth
and ignored the pain. I wasn't going to let go. As we
walked, I thought about the first time we'd ever held hands.
It was on our second date as we were exploring the Tor-
pedo Factory Art Center in Old Town Alexandria and her
hand slipped into mine as if it had always belonged there.

We crossed the road, passed the courthouse, and arrived in front of the Sheriff's Department. I considered
pausing before the glass door to tell Ash I loved her one
more—and perhaps last—time, but there wasn't the opportunity. Trent was waiting just inside and he shoved the
door open.

"Get in here! Where have you been?" His voice was
menacing yet there was a barely suppressed look of panic
in his eyes.

I straightened my back and fixed him with a chilly stare. "Young man, in light of the fact that we are the only ones capable of keeping you from finishing the remainder of your life on death row, let's establish the ground rules right now. You will lower your voice, you will speak courteously to my wife and me, and you will behave as an adult. Do I make myself abundantly clear?"

Trent was the first to blink. "Yes . . . sir."

"Good. Take me to your father. We don't have all day."

Ash squeezed my hand as Trent led us past the reception desk, down a corridor, and into an office at the back of the building. The office wasn't quite how I imagined it would be. Holcombe had impressed me as being austere, yet his workspace was anything but. Hanging on one wall was a hand-made quilt composed of gold, brown, ivory, and russet fabric in a striking design that incorporated the six-pointed star of the Sheriff's Office. On the opposite side were framed color pictures of the Blue Ridge Mountains and lovely shots of the river. The only overt bit of evidence that the office belonged to a lawman was the black-and-white photograph of a younger and smiling Eugene Holcombe having a badge pinned to his uniform shirt by a pretty woman with a Farrah Fawcett hairdo and wearing a dark dress with tiny white polka dots. And now the older and spent version of that man sat behind an oak desk.

I pointed to one of the chairs and said to Trent, "Sit down. Now before we get started, take off your badges."

"Why?" Trent slouched into the chair.

"Because criminals aren't supposed to wear badges." I kept my voice dispassionate. "You've both betrayed your oaths of office and have no right to wear any symbols of law enforcement authority."

Holcombe didn't argue. Indeed, he almost looked as if he were in a trance. He took his badge off and set it on the desktop. Trent sighed, gritted his teeth, and finally removed his badge.

"Good. The next order of business is to establish the ground rules for this interrogation. We have neither the time nor the inclination to play word games, or Trent-has-selective-amnesia, or 'twenty questions.' You will answer my questions truthfully and not hold back any information."

Trent sat back in the chair and folded his arms. "If you know I didn't kill Thayer, why should I sit here and be interrogated?"

"Because it's in your best interest. Even though I know who actually killed Thayer, the best evidence points directly at you. Without my help, you'll be charged with first-degree murder and a local jury will convict you—even if they have doubts—just for the sheer joy of getting rid of you."

Holcombe finally seemed to pay attention and said in an old man's querulous voice, "Trent, just shut up and answer the man's questions."

"All right."

I leaned a little on my cane and tried not to fidget too much. My leg was beginning to ache, and as much as I wanted to sit down, I remained standing since it placed me at a psychological advantage because the Holcombes had to look up at me. I asked, "Okay, so what happened on the Island Ford Bridge on Friday night?"

"I decided to stop Bobby Thayer," said Trent.

"Why? Hadn't you and your dad been told by Liz Ewell to leave him alone?"

"Yeah, but . . ."

"But what?"

"I was . . . Hell, I just didn't like the fact that Ewell told us to leave him alone. This is our county."

"Thanks for being honest. Were you staked out and waiting for him or did you just see the truck?"

"I just saw it going by."

"Where did you pull him over?"

"On the west side of the bridge."

"What happened?"

"Well, I walked up to the truck and the first thing he does is begin yammering at me about how I've made this *big* mistake because his auntie would have me fired. So, I got a little mad and . . ."

"And what?"

"I walked to the front of his truck and fired off a couple of rounds at the windshield. Not near him, mind you! I just wanted to scare him."

"And did you?"

"Yeah. He started screaming at me not to kill him."

"Then what happened?"

"I got him out of the truck and told him that I knew he was a burglar and that he was going to have to start paying up like everyone else. He didn't have much in his wallet, and then he started yelling about telling his aunt again, and I kind of got real angry, and that's when he showed me the teddy bear."

"You glided past becoming real angry and how this caused Thayer to tell you about the bear. Did you do something to make him show you the teddy bear?"

Trent looked at the floor. "I stuck the barrel of my gun in his mouth and told him I was going to kill him and throw his body into the river."

I resisted the urge to sarcastically say: *Yeah, that would certainly cause me to think you were 'real angry'—or freaking nuts.* Instead, I said, "What did he tell you about the Mourning Bear?"

"Only that it was worth a lot of money and that he and Poole had already found a buyer. He said I could keep the bear."

"Believing that if he didn't surrender the bear, you'd shoot him, correct?"

"Yeah."

"So, he didn't actually give you the bear. Wouldn't it be more accurate to say that you robbed him at gunpoint?"

"I suppose."

"What happened after you robbed him?"

"I, uh—I threw him off the bridge and into the river."

"Why?"

"To show him I meant business."

"Is that another way of saying you meant to terrorize him?"

"Well, yeah."

"What happened when he hit the water? Was he hurt?"

"No! He was fine! I was watching him with my flashlight. He was swimming like a damn fish!"

"What happened after that?"

Trent shrugged. "I drove over to my folk's house with the bear to show it to my dad. Then I gave Poole a call."

"That wasn't smart, by the way. He recorded the call and if it weren't for what we know, your comments could well convict you of murder. Why did you take so long to contact Poole about making the sale?"

"You'll have to ask my dad that. It was his decision."

"Did your dad tell you to threaten the lives of Deputy Barron's children?"

Holcombe sat up straight and looked at his son, his eyes showing surprise and loathing.

There was a long pause before Trent answered and I knew he was thinking, which is always a suicidal pastime for thugs because they're never as clever as they imagine themselves to be. The worst part about waiting for him to speak was that I strongly suspected what he was pondering

and hoped there was still a milligram of decency in his
bloated body. This investigation was already too squalid
for my tastes, but Trent sent it plummeting to a new level
of filthiness when he finally said, "Yeah, he told me to
do it. In fact, all along I've just been doing what I was
told. What I said before about it being my idea to stop
Thayer—that was a lie. It was my dad's idea and he told
me to shoot at the truck and throw Thayer in the river."

As the litany of betrayal came spilling out, Holcombe
sagged in his chair and his lips twitched slightly. It was
hard not to feel profoundly sorry for him because I knew
Trent was lying to save his own wretched skin. I looked at
Holcombe and said, "Is any of that true?"

"It *is* my fault, but not in the way he's saying it."

"Would you like to explain?"

Holcombe's gaze drifted to Ash and then back to me.
"It's obvious you truly love your wife. What would you
do if she got sick? I mean, *really* sick. Would you do anything to make her better?"

"Absolutely."

"Anything? Even violate the oath you swore to uphold
the law and . . . do what needed to be done to ensure she
received the necessary medical treatment?"

"Your wife has cancer."

"Pauline has non-Hodgkin's lymphoma." He pointed
at the photograph of the woman pinning the badge on
his chest. "That's her. We've been married twenty-three
years and I love her more now than the day I married
her."

"When did she become ill?"

"She was diagnosed two years ago. It was shortly before the county changed over to a better HMO system and
we didn't mention her condition on the application forms
because they wouldn't have covered her."

"Due to a preexisting illness."

"Exactly. The treatment for NHL is very expensive: chemotherapy, radioimmunotherapy, MRIs, tests, tests, and more tests . . . most of it very painful. And through it all, my angel has stayed cheerful and brave." Holcombe smiled sadly and swallowed hard.

Ash's hand found mine and she asked, "What happened?"

"About six months after we enrolled in the new HMO, they somehow learned that we'd concealed the information about her illness. I think the doctor's receptionist told them because I'd arrested her brother for drunk driving. Anyway, they cancelled our policy and said that we'd have to repay them for all the bills they'd already paid because we hadn't told the truth on the application documents."

"And don't tell me, they wanted their money back immediately."

"Of course."

"How much do you owe?" I said.

"Counting everything, probably close to six-hundred-thousand dollars, but that doesn't count yesterday's mail." Holcombe flashed a bittersweet smile. "And the bills keep rolling in because Pauline still needs her treatment. I maxed out our credit cards and took out a second-mortgage on our home, but it wasn't nearly enough . . . just a drop in the bucket."

"So you decided to supplement your income by collecting a tariff from the local criminals."

"It wasn't an easy decision, despite what you undoubtedly think about me." He nodded at the badges on the desktop. "I was as proud of what that badge stood for as you are, but if it came down to you having to choose between your wife's life and your pride, which would you pick? Be honest."

"I'm pretty certain I'd have done the same thing."

"That's what I thought."

"Tell me about Friday night. Did you send Trent out to intercept Thayer?"

"No, but I've known since the beginning that my son lacks the ethical and emotional maturity to be a deputy sheriff. I know he's a bully and uses steroids, but I kept him on the job because I needed his help."

"But unfortunately, he didn't view your criminal fundraising efforts as an ugly necessity."

"No, much to my shame I discovered he enjoyed it." Holcombe glanced at Trent, who was glowering at the floor. "So, I have to accept moral responsibility for whatever happened on the Island Ford Bridge."

"When Trent showed up at your house on Friday night, why didn't you contact Poole immediately?"

"I was afraid that we'd gone too far and not just because we'd crossed Liz Ewell. When Trent told me that he'd shot Thayer's truck and thrown him in the river, I realized that we were no longer merely collecting graft. It'd become armed robbery and malicious wounding."

"And then Thayer's body was found in the river the following morning. You thought Trent killed him, didn't you?"

"Of course. He denied it, but he's a congenital liar." He glanced at Trent again and said sarcastically, "Can you *ever* forgive me for not believing you, son?"

Trent muttered something under his breath and his hands balled up into fists. The atmosphere in the room was swiftly changing and becoming charged with tension. It was like the breathless calm before a thunderstorm struck. The problem was that Ash and I were the obvious lightning rods.

I tried to return Holcombe's focus to telling the story. "So, when Deputy Barron radioed the description of the man pulled from the river . . ."

Holcombe looked back at me. "I knew it was Thayer.

That's why I insulted you and told you to mind your own business. It's a day late and a dollar short, but I *am* sorry for that."

"And you did that because you figured concealing the murder as an accidental drowning was your only option, right?"

"Yes, because I was certain that if Trent were arrested he'd immediately implicate me." He shot a brief spiteful look at his son. "And if that happened, who'd be left to take care of Pauline?"

"What you did was wrong, but I can sure understand your dilemma."

"It was my fault. I'd created the situation."

"At some point on Sunday you finally decided to sell the bear. Can you tell me about that?"

"Yes, I thought about it all day Saturday and decided to go ahead with the deal. Our portion of the proceeds would have been over one-hundred-and-twenty-thousand dollars. It was simply too much money to turn my back on."

"And so you met here in town a little while ago with Cleland and Poole."

"She gave me the cashier's check and I gave her the bear."

"I'm assuming the check is here. Can I have it?"

"It's in the drawer."

I should have been prepared for what happened next, but even if I'd known, there was nothing I could have done about it. There was a desk between us and it all happened far too fast. Holcombe turned in his swivel chair and bent slightly as if to open the top desk drawer, but at the last second his hand shifted to his pistol. The gun was out of his holster in a nanosecond and pointed directly at Trent's head. Trent's mouth flew open in shock and he sat back rigidly in the chair.

"Son, I'm going to kill you in a second, but I want the

pleasure of telling you why before we both die. I raised you right and your momma and I loved you, yet you turned out to be the biggest piece of gutter trash in the county. You're a hoodlum, a drug addict, a liar, and a coward. But I do have some good news," said Holcombe, mimicking an old car-insurance television commercial. "Your life is insured for two-hundred-and-fifty-thousand dollars."

"Daddy, don't do this. I'm sorry. I promise I'll do better."

Holcombe continued as if he hadn't heard, "Now, there won't be a payout for me since it'll be a suicide, but they'll have to pay off on your policy because you'll have been murdered. At least your momma won't be left penniless."

"Sheriff, don't kill him," I said, trying to move crabwise in front of Ash. "If you do this, Pauline will never understand and she'll be left alone. She needs you alive."

"Even if I am alive, I won't be there to help her. I'll be in prison."

"Maybe." My mind was racing, trying to think of some way to minimize the gravity of the charges against him. I continued, "But maybe the charges you're facing aren't that serious."

Holcombe looked at me, but kept the pistol pointed at Trent. "You mind if I call you Brad?"

"Not at all."

"Well Brad, don't piss down my back and tell me it's rain."

"I'm not. Just think for a second before you do this. Okay, so you collected graft from a bunch of crooks. How many of them do you think are actually going to come forward and sign a criminal complaint against you?

They'd have to get up on the stand and incriminate themselves. That isn't going to happen."

"Maybe, but I'm also an accessory after the fact to murder."

"No, you're not. Pay close attention, Sheriff. If Trent didn't kill Thayer, you can't be an accessory after the fact. At worst, you covered up an armed robbery and a misdemeanor assault, because Thayer wasn't injured by his fall into the river."

"And I engaged in a criminal conspiracy to sell stolen property." Holcombe turned his attention back to Trent. "Son, if I were you, I'd keep that hand right where it is or I will open your head up like a ripe melon."

"Sheriff, listen. Those are first-time offenses, you've got mitigating circumstances, and you've cooperated fully. Once the story of why you did all this comes out—that it was done because you love your wife and some soulless HMO screwed you guys—the Commonwealth's Attorney will recommend probation," I said and paused to take a deep breath. "But most of all, don't do it because it's wrong. Pauline would expect better of you."

Holcombe was silent for a moment and I could see his eyes were moist. Finally, he said, "I'll keep him covered. Get his gun because he told me before you came in that he wasn't going to jail and he'd kill anyone that tried to arrest him. Be careful."

"Thanks, Sheriff. I will be."

I edged up to Trent and leaned over to take his pistol from the holster. There was a feral look in his eyes and at the last moment he made a grab for the gun. I struck Trent with my cane right between his running lights, but it was like hitting that hundred-year-old oak in our yard. It bounced off, opened a bloody gash on his brow, but otherwise had no effect. Trent and I wrestled for possession of the gun, but he was bigger, stronger, and younger and I was quickly losing the struggle. I saw Ash jump on Trent's back and try to choke him, meanwhile Holcombe tried to get a clear shot at his son without hitting one of us. I shouted at Ash to run for it, but she ignored me.

Trent finally wrenched the pistol from my grasp and I tried to grab his hand. As I fought, my mind flashed back to that first moment when Ash had slipped her hand into mine and I felt a terrible sadness that this was how our lives were going to end. I hoped that if there were an afterlife, we'd be there together. I heard the sound of a shot and was surprised to find us both still alive.

Then I saw Tina and Sergei in the office. Tina had her pistol in hand while Sergei was armed with an AR-15 assault rifle. Both weapons were pointed at Trent and I saw a hole in the wall behind him where one of them had fired a warning shot.

Tina said, "Drop the gun, Trent. You're under arrest."

Trent gave a sideways glance in Ash's direction and I knew he was weighing the odds of taking her hostage. I began to wish I hadn't been so hasty in preventing Holcombe from offing his son. The guy was like a shark—almost no brains and an excess of killer instinct.

Sergei looked down the barrel of the rifle and said, "If you so much as look at that lady again, it will be my pleasure to shoot you in such a way that you'll wish I'd killed you. Be a good boy and put the gun down."

A couple of seconds passed—but believe me, it seemed like a lot longer—and then Trent sighed and slowly placed the gun on the desk. After that, Tina ordered him to lay face down on the floor. The fight seemed to have gone out of him. He meekly complied and was immediately hand-cuffed.

A moment later, Ash and I were hugging each other tightly, and after I made sure that she was all right, I demanded, "Why didn't you run when I told you to?"

"And leave you here alone fighting that psycho? Brad honey, I could no more do that than stop breathing."

"Hey, you're the best partner I've ever had . . . and the only one I've ever wanted to kiss." I leaned over to give her a peck on the cheek.

"Well, I certainly hope so," said Ash.

Another deputy appeared in the doorway and Tina pointed at Trent, "Get him out of here and into the jail. Oh, and leave his uniform on for now. The other inmates will enjoy that."

The cop pulled Trent to his feet and hustled him out the door. Meanwhile, I noticed that Holcombe had also put his pistol on the desk and was now taking his leather gun belt off.

Holcombe looked at Tina and said, "I'm assuming you're the interim sheriff. Good. You'll do a fine job. I can find my way back to the detention facility."

"Mr. Holcombe, I can't see any point in booking you into jail right now. Your wife needs you at home, and considering everything you've done to help us this afternoon, I'm very confident you won't flee this jurisdiction." Tina reached out to gently touch his arm. "Go take care of Pauline."

"Thank you, Sheriff."

Once Holcombe was gone, I said, "That was really classy, Tina."

"Thank you. It just seemed like the right thing to do."

"Yeah, and as long as you've brought up the subject of

doing the right thing, I thought I told you not to charge in here if things went to hell in a handbasket."

"You did, but Sergei and I decided that it would be way too boring around here if you went and got yourself killed."

Chapter 23

Going to Holcombe's desk, I opened the top drawer and found an unsealed business-size envelope that bore the logo of the Massanutten Crest Lodge where Cleland was staying. I looked inside the envelope and saw a cashier's check in her name for 170,000 dollars and made out to the Remmelkemp Mill Apostolic Assembly.

"The check?" Tina asked.

"Yeah, and although we've got confessions from nearly all the principals, you still might want to consider having the crime lab process it with ninhydrin for latent fingerprints." I handed her the envelope.

"Just in case somebody wants to change their story later?"

"It's been known to happen. So, you don't need an unofficial investigative team anymore, Tina—sorry, I mean, Sheriff Barron."

"Stop that."

"So, would you like Ash and me to go home, and can we resume our lives as mild-mannered artisan teddy bear makers?"

"You fraud. What would you do if I actually said, 'Yes, go home'?"

"Have a temper-tantrum and hold my breath until I turned blue. I want to finish this case."

"I know and I need you to finish it. You guys are the only ones that can. I'm going to be stuck here for a while because I have to call the State Police, get the Commonwealth's Attorney in here, *and* go over and arrest Poole." Tina shook her head in frustration. "Where are you going next?"

"Back to Chez Ewell to reinterview Meredith Audett and see if we can get her to cop to murdering Thayer. But whether she does or not, you're going to need an arrest warrant to take her out of the house and a search warrant for the evidence in the guesthouse."

"See? Two more things to add to the list," said Tina.

"So, if we're going to talk to Meredith, should I keep this body mike on?" Ash asked.

"I don't think that'll be necessary."

"Good, because this is uncomfortable." Ash reached behind her and I heard the sound of tape being pulled from flesh. After that, she slipped her hand under her blouse and pulled the wire antenna lose.

"I'd have done that for you," I said earnestly.

"Brad, you have a one-track mind." She handed the transmitter to Sergei, gave him a hug and a kiss on the cheek, and said, "Thank you for everything, Sergei."

"You're welcome, and please," he shot me an impish look, "try to keep him out of trouble."

Ten minutes later we'd arrived at the Ewell estate, and I was relieved to see that the gate was still open. I drove up the driveway and parked in front of the castle. I used that absurd-looking knocker and Meredith opened the door after a brief delay. She wore a baggy pair of black sweatpants, an oversized white tee-shirt with an athletic shoe's company logo on the left breast, black workout gloves, and her hair was gathered up and banded in a lime green scrunchy. It was obvious that we'd interrupted her in the midst of an exercise session in the home gymnasium.

"Oh, Mr. Lyon, this is a surprise." She had a small white towel in her left hand and she wiped at her brow, concealing her eyes.

"No, it isn't, Meredith. I think you know exactly why we've come."

"Is this your wife?"

"Yes, this is Ashleigh and she's been investigating Robert's murder too. Can we come in?"

"I don't know if that's such a good idea." She slung the towel around the back of her neck and glanced nervously back toward the stairway.

"Fine, we can talk out here then."

"Talk about what?"

"Meredith, we know what happened to Robert. We even think we know why it happened, but we'd like to hear it from you."

"I haven't done anything and I think you'd better go." She began to push the door shut.

There often comes a point in an investigation when it's necessary for a ruse and a truly skilled homicide inspector can bluff like a Mississippi riverboat gambler. I said, "We're not guessing—we *know*. Your fingerprints were on Thayer's truck's rearview mirror."

The door stopped moving.

Ash said gently, "Meredith, please listen. Sometimes a good person is so hurt and betrayed that she just snaps and does something awful. What did Robert do to you?"

Meredith tried to keep her face emotionless, but her lower lip began to quiver. A glistening tear appeared beneath her left eye and she swiped at it savagely with one of the towel ends. "He said he loved me."

"And he lied. Some men do that to get what they want."

"I'm not the sort of woman that just jumps into bed with a man. I loved him. For four months I believed all his promises about how we'd get married and not have to sneak around anymore." More tears were running down her cheeks and she leaned her head against the doorjamb.

Realizing that Ash had attained an empathetic connection with Meredith, I kept my mouth shut and paid attention.

Ash reached out to take Meredith's hand. "And you were devastated when you found out that you didn't mean anything to him."

"Oh, God . . . I felt so hurt and dirty and humiliated and . . . used."

"And finally, so enraged you were out of control."

Meredith sniffled and nodded.

"And this happened on Friday night, didn't it?"

"Yes." She took a deep ragged breath and seemed to recover some of her composure. "When Robert left with the Mourning Bear, he told me he probably wasn't going to get back until very late and suggested I sneak into his room early the next morning before Miss Ewell woke up. No 'I love you,' no 'I'm gonna miss you,' just a suggestion that I come to his place and service him when he decided to come home."

"That must have made you feel cheap."

"It did. I got angry, so I decided to work the energy off in the exercise room."

"When did Robert get back?"

"Sometime around eleven—maybe a little after. I was

working on some stretching and flexibility exercises when I heard his truck pull up to the guesthouse."

"What happened then?"

"I couldn't figure out why he was home so early, so I went outside. I thought . . ."

"Maybe he'd come back to see you?"

"Yes. Stupid, huh? Anyway, I'd been working with one of those elastic tension bands with the plastic handles on both ends and I had it when I went out there. Robert was sopping wet and had just put something in his truck. I asked him where he was going and he told me he was leaving."

"Did he say why?"

"Yes. He told me that Trent had pulled him over near the Island Ford Bridge and fired his gun at the truck and stolen the teddy bear. I asked him how he'd gotten wet and he said that Trent had thrown him into the river."

"What happened when you realized that he was leaving without you?" Ash's tone was sympathetic.

"I asked him what was going to happen to us. He got this annoyed and surprised look and shouted that it was time I got a f-ing clue—there never was an 'us.' I'd been a convenient lay and nothing more. I started to cry and begged him to stay." Meredith's eyes began welling up with fresh tears.

"But he refused."

"I tried to hug him and he knocked my arms away and when I tried to grab him again, he slapped me. Right here." Meredith touched a spot on her left temple. "Robert didn't hit me hard enough to leave a mark, but that didn't make any difference. I was suddenly so furious, so angry over being used and then thrown away like a gum wrapper or something, that I just exploded."

Ash waited for a second before saying, "I know this is hard for you, but what happened next?"

"I looked down and realized I had that elastic tension cord in my hand. Robert had just turned his back on me to go into the guesthouse and I . . ." She faltered for a moment, and when she resumed speaking, her voice was flat with detachment. "I looped the band over his head and around his neck and began tightening it just as hard as I could. He jerked and struggled and tried to scream but couldn't. He just sort of gurgled. One part of me knew I was killing him, but I was so crazy with anger that—God forgive me—I didn't want to stop."

Ash's eyes were moist and I realized that listening to Meredith's tale of humiliation and the graphic description of the murder had taken a huge emotional toll. I caught her eye and glanced in Meredith's direction, silently asking if she wanted me to take over. She nodded.

I said, "Meredith, would you mind if I asked a few questions?"

She nodded and continued to hold Ash's hand.

"What did you do after Robert was dead?"

"I, uh—that part is actually a little hazy. I just sat on the cement next to his body for a long time. I couldn't believe what I'd done."

"But at some point you came up with the idea of putting him in the bed of his truck and driving him over to the river, right?"

"Yes. I couldn't let anyone find him here."

"Why did you go to the Henshaw farm?"

"I didn't know who owned the property. I just knew the place because Robert and I had been there a couple of times."

"And did you throw him into the river because you were hoping to shift suspicion onto Trent?"

"I don't know. Maybe. All I can remember was thinking that I had to get rid of him because if I didn't he'd go right on hurting me." Meredith gazed at me with fatigued eyes. "Does that make any sense?"

"Yes, it does."

"So, what happens to me now?"

"You've got a choice, Meredith. You can either wait here for the sheriff to arrive with an arrest warrant charging you with murder or go in voluntarily and surrender yourself. I won't kid you, neither option is pleasant, but cooperating will work out better for you in the long run." I jerked my head in the direction of the Xterra. "We'd be happy to drive you to the Sheriff's Office and you can sit down with her and—"

"Her?"

"That's right, Holcombe is no longer sheriff and Trent's in jail for the robbery and trying to kill us. Tina Barron's the sheriff, at least for now."

Meredith looked at Ash. "What do you think I should do?"

"I think you should come with us. It's time to be brave and face what you've done."

"I know. Thank you, Mrs. Lyon."

I heard the wheelchair lift's electric motor start and realized that Ewell was coming downstairs to investigate. I said, "Meredith, I think you should go to the truck with Ash. Miss Ewell isn't going to want you to come with us."

"Why?"

"Because you'll ruin the big payday she's got planned."

Ash and Meredith got into the Xterra as I waited for the old woman. I pushed the door open a little and saw Ewell arrive on the ground floor. As the wheelchair approached, it made a sound that reminded me of agitated bees in a hive.

Ewell gave me an imperious glare. "Who gave you permission to enter my property? Where is Meredith going?"

"We've come to give her a ride into town. She wants to confess to Robert's murder and don't bother trying to look surprised because you knew all along."

"You can't prove that."

"I realize that, but you *did* know. I'll bet your bedroom window on the second floor overlooks the guesthouse, because you're such a tyrant you'd want to keep an eye on Robert whenever he was here. You knew Robert and Meredith were lovers."

"The slut seduced my nephew."

"Oh yeah, everybody knows how virtuous Robert was—a regular Sir Galahad. There's no way you couldn't have heard their argument on Friday night when she begged him to stay and—gallant guy that he was—he slapped her for the crime of imagining a Ewell was capable of behaving decently."

"I'm not interested in your little sermon."

"Too bad. You sat up there like a fat spider in a web and watched as Meredith murdered him in an uncontrollable rage. And what did you do?"

"Leave my property now." Ewell turned the wheelchair and grabbed the door.

I placed my hand against the door to prevent her from closing it. "Did you call the paramedics? Did you call the sheriff? Did you open the window and yell at Meredith to stop? No, you tried to think of a way to turn Robert's death into a profit and I almost gave you the opportunity when I told you that I suspected Trent of the murder. It's got to be upsetting knowing you were that close to almost a million bucks."

"Get off my land, you bastard. Go! Get out!"

"Gladly, because after I go and recover your precious Mourning Bear from a woman so lacking in conscience that she could be your clone, I'm heading home for a long hot shower. Being in the presence of someone as loathsome as you makes me feel soiled and I only hope we have enough soap to wash your stink from me." I released my hold on the door and was walking away when it slammed shut behind me.

Chapter 24

Pulling up in front of the Sheriff's Office, I parked next to a pair of gray State Police cruisers that had arrived some time while we were at the Ewell estate. I also noticed a cream-colored Ford Crown Vic sedan with county government license plates and suspected it belonged to the Commonwealth's Attorney. Tina had been busy during our absence.

We went inside the office and a deputy seated at the reception counter waved us on through, saying, "The Sheriff told me to send you right in."

A few seconds later, we stood in the doorway, obviously interrupting an intense discussion between Tina and an unhappy looking older man. I said, "Sheriff Barron? This is Meredith Audett and she's come in here voluntarily to tell you what happened to Robert Thayer."

"Mr. Emerson, this is Brad and Ashleigh Lyon, the folks I've been telling you about." Tina looked up at us and continued, "Mr. Emerson is our Commonwealth's Attorney and he's been telling me all about the political realities of Massanutten County."

"Which means he's trying to get you to drop the charges to protect himself and his cronies. God Almighty, I am *so* tired of dealing with slimy characters pretending to be good citizens." My leg was throbbing, I had a dull headache, and I didn't realize just how cranky I was until I turned to Emerson and said, "Look, you two-bit procurer, why don't you run home and lock yourself in a closet. That way you'll be ready for the experience of state prison, because you and I both know that Gene Holcombe is going to implicate you and a bunch of other 'servants of the people' in this graft ring."

"And although I'm not as diplomatic as Mr. Lyon, I agree with his assessment," said Tina. "Go home, Mr. Emerson. I'm calling the attorney general's office in Richmond to get a real prosecutor."

Emerson pushed past us, scowled at me, and stomped down the hall.

Tina stood up and pointed to the recently vacated chair. "Thanks for coming in, Ms. Audett. Why don't you sit down right here? I have to talk to the Lyons for a moment and then I'll be back."

Once Meredith was seated, Tina came out into the hall and shut the door behind her.

"What's wrong?" Ash asked.

"Poole's in the wind. His clothes closet was empty and his car was gone. It must have happened while we were tied up with the Holcombes. I put out a BOL."

"But it isn't likely you'll find him. He had to have been preparing for this day, so he probably has false ID and a bank account under the same alias. For that matter, he could have a cold car stashed someplace."

"I just feel awful. If we'd moved more quickly . . ."

"You mean, and not waited for a warrant? Don't kid yourself, Tina. He'd have posted bond and disappeared anyway. You did the best you could."

"Well, I'm glad he's gone. He'd spread so much 'charity' money around, he might have been acquitted if he'd stayed," said Ash. "Good riddance to bad rubbish."

"You're probably right, sweetheart. Now, on to other business." I nodded in the direction of the closed door. "Meredith confessed to killing Thayer and it sounded like a pretty valid 'heat of passion' situation. You'll want to get started on the interview immediately because if I'm any judge of Liz Ewell's character, she's going to hire Meredith a lawyer and he's going to come here and insist on seeing his client. After that, she'll invoke and there'll be no further opportunity to talk to her."

"Why would Ewell do that?"

"She still wants to pin the murder on Trent so that she can sue the county for an astronomical amount of money."

Tina shook her head and sighed. "People. You've got to love them. Are you going up to get the bear now?"

"Yeah. I'd like to take a deputy along just in case Cleland voluntarily comes outside the hotel room. That way, he can make a 'probable cause' arrest because she's out in public."

"You can take Deputy Bressler. He was at the front counter when you came in."

"Have you sworn out a warrant for Cleland's arrest?"

"Not yet."

"The arrest warrant will get you into her hotel room, but you'll also need a search warrant to recover any evidence that's not in plain sight."

"I know. I've got the state troopers working on that, but it's going to take some time."

"Don't worry. Once we're up there and the scene's been frozen, Cleland isn't going anywhere. Besides, it's been almost twenty minutes since I've spoken with a sociopath, so I'm really looking forward to chatting with her."

"Me too," Ash grimly added.

"I really want to thank you two for all the help," Tina said diffidently.

"It's a pleasure doing it for a friend . . . and someone we know will be a good and honest sheriff," I said.

On the way out, we paused in the lobby to brief Bressler on his new assignment. Then I grabbed a manila envelope from a stack on the counter.

"What's that for?" Ash asked.

"Camouflage. If we show up looking like this is police business, the hotel staff won't tell us what room she's in, claiming it violates their privacy policy."

"But how's an envelope going to help?"

"You'll see."

Soon, we were speeding down Coggins Spring Road toward Massanutten Mountain with Bressler in his patrol car behind us. The sun had already descended below the ridgeline by the time we turned onto the cobblestone lane leading up to the Massanutten Crest Lodge. A moment later, the ersatz castle came into view. I parked the truck in a handicapped slot near the entrance and we went into the hotel while Bressler waited outside for my telephone call.

With the huge stone fireplace in the corner and the maroon banners hanging on the walls, the lobby looked like a medieval feasting hall—so long as you could overlook the huge plasma television in the corner that was currently displaying a splashy commercial for adult diapers.

"Follow my lead," I whispered to Ash. Then, putting an idiotic grin on my face, I marched up to the young woman behind the registration counter and said, "Hi there! We're looking for Lorraine Cleland. Can you tell us what room she's in?"

"And you are?"

I waved the manila envelope as if it were a winning lottery ticket and did my best to sound jolly and just slightly demented. "Why we're the Lyons and we just want to return this contract we signed with Lorraine. She's going to make my wife's teddy bears and put them in toyshops. Do you like teddy bears?"

"I suppose."

"We love them. Our house is full of them."

"That's nice."

"Sometimes I pretend to make voices for them. You know, I make them talk."

"Oh."

Ash tugged my shirtsleeve. "Oh honey, do one of the voices for her. She'll love it!"

"That's all right. Really."

"So what room is Lorraine in? We want to drop off the paperwork and then go out and celebrate."

I could see the clerk weighing her options. The rules probably said she should call Cleland before releasing any information, but we looked harmless, and the girl seemed genuinely worried that I might give her a sample of one of my teddy bear voices. Finally, she said, "Room one-seventeen. Down that hall and to the left."

"Thank you, hon."

Ash waited until we were well down the hall before starting to laugh. "Oh my God, did you see the look on her face?"

"I thought she behaved very professionally, considering

she thought we were nuts." I took my wireless phone out and called Bressler. "We're in. Room one-seventeen on the ground floor. It'll be at the rear of the building. Let us know when you're back there and we'll make contact with Cleland."

We came to the end of the corridor and turned left. Room 117 was the third door on the right. A couple of minutes passed and then my phone rang. I answered on the first ring and heard Bressler say, "Okay, I'm in position."

"I'll call you back when I have some idea of what's going to happen." I disconnected from the call and used my cane to rap on the door.

"Who is it?" Cleland called from within.

"It's Ashleigh and Brad Lyon."

"Go away. I don't want to talk to you."

"Oh, but we want to talk to you and I'm perfectly happy yelling through the door so that your high-class neighbors can hear all about how you screwed a charity auction so that you could buy a stolen teddy bear."

"I don't know what you're talking about."

"Stick with that. The jury will love it."

"Go away!"

"Lorraine, it's in your best interest to open the door. Sheriff Holcombe is in jail and Reverend Poole has gone into hiding, but both of them were kind enough to tell us everything about your purchase of the Mourning Bear. Heck, we've even got your cashier's check and as we speak, two state troopers are hard at work getting a warrant for your arrest."

"What do you want?"

"We just want the bear back. Actually, that's not true. I also want to see you led out of this five-star hotel in handcuffs and put into the back seat of a police car just like any other grubby felon, but I'll settle for the bear."

The door opened and Cleland glared at us. "Come in and keep your voices down."

We went inside. Cleland was dressed in traveling clothes: khaki pants, a beige pullover shirt, and white deck shoes. An open suitcase lay upon the bed and a wooden box I was certain contained the Mourning Bear stood on the table.

"Going back to Boston?"

"Or just trying to get across the state line?" Ash added.

I perched myself on the edge of the dresser. "Lorraine, I just have to know. That damned bear represents the deaths of fifteen hundred people almost a century ago. This weekend, it was the cause of an armed robbery, followed by a murder, and it almost got Ash and me killed less than two hours ago. The idea of having it in my house gives me the creeps, so why do you want it so badly?"

"It's one of the rarest and most valuable stuffed animals in the world. You collect teddy bears. You ought to understand."

Ash looked puzzled and repelled. "We collect them because we enjoy them, not because of what they might be worth. There are some things that just can't be measured with a dollar sign, especially teddy bears."

When Cleland realized that Ash actually meant what she said and wasn't merely spouting empty platitudes, it was her turn to look perplexed. "That's sweet, Ashleigh, but what planet have you been living on?"

"Yeah, what could be sillier than thinking that the purpose of life ought to be something more than seeing how much expensive crap we can accumulate?" I said.

"I'm sorry, I didn't mean any offense," Cleland stumbled over the words. It was obvious she was becoming frightened. "Look, were you bluffing about the state troopers?"

"Not at all. They could get here any time."

"Can't we come to some sort of an agreement?"

"How do you mean?"

"You let me leave with the Mourning Bear and I promise to buy the rights to Ashleigh's teddy bears. There's stationery here, we could write up an informal contract right now. The deal could be worth a lot of money to you in the years to come."

"Boy, oh boy, that's a tempting offer, Ash," I said mockingly. "What do you think?"

"Yes, Ashleigh, I'd like to know what *you* think, since your husband seems to do all the talking for you."

Ash began advancing with a disquieting gleam in her eye that hinted at mayhem. Backing Cleland into a corner, she said, "You really want to know what I think? I *think* I'm going to punch your lights out for trying to bribe us. You can take your licensing contracts and put them where the sun doesn't shine because I wouldn't let someone as evil as you touch my bears—not for a million dollars."

Cleland bumped into the table and the wooden box began to totter. She grabbed at the box frantically and pushed it toward Ash, saying, "Here, take the damn thing! All I want is to get out of here!"

I put my hand on Ash's shoulder, gently restraining her. "Honey, let her go."

She turned and gave me an exasperated look. "Just one punch?"

"Sorry sweetheart, Lorraine is needed elsewhere."

"What do you mean?" Cleland demanded.

I hooked a thumb at the doorway, which was blocked by Deputy Bressler and two burly Virginia State Police officers. Bressler glanced at some sheets of paper in his hand, cleared his throat, and then said, "Lorraine Cleland, I have here a warrant for your arrest and another warrant permitting us to search these premises and all your possessions. You have the right to remain silent . . ."

Chapter 25

I sat on the bench in our front yard watching the moon-
light flicker and dance on the surface of the Shenandoah
River. It was late, but I wasn't tired. I sat there brooding.

I heard the front door open and close, and Ash sat
down next to me a moment later. She took my hand and
asked, "You've been out here for hours. Are you all right,
honey?"

"I don't know."

"You seem bothered."

"I am."

"Want to tell me?"

Keeping my eyes on the river, I said, "Sure. I feel like
a colossal failure. What did I really accomplish over the
past two days? Let's tally it up: Holcombe hasn't got a
job and his wife still has cancer and Meredith Audett is
going to state prison when she ought to be receiving a
community service award for single-handedly lowering

the property crime rate of Northern Virginia by killing Thayer."

"Brad?"

"Meanwhile, Poole has absconded with God only knows how much money generated by the sale of stolen goods and Cleland has already posted bond and she's got enough high-priced legal representation that they'll never extradite her back from Massachusetts. Trent is spinning elaborate lies to foist all the blame onto his father and Ewell is still planning on suing the county. St. Paul had it wrong . . . the wages of sin aren't death. In fact, sin pays pretty well."

"Brad?"

"And let's not forget that I managed to almost get us killed twice, and if we ever go up to the Massanutten Crest Lodge again for brunch, they're liable to call the cops and have us committed for psychiatric observation. Other than that, everything is just freaking peachy."

"Brad, *listen* to me."

"Sorry, sweetheart. Okay, I'm done ranting. What?"

"Good things happened too. Tina will be running unopposed in next month's election and that means we've got a new and honest county sheriff. The town is a better place because Poole is gone, and you got Trent off the streets and that probably saved someone a beating or maybe even prevented a murder. Finally, you did solve the case." She gently took my chin and turned my face until I was looking at her. "As far as the other stuff is concerned, you can't take responsibility for things that you don't have any control over."

"I know. It's just that during all those years of investigating murders I don't remember ever being so furious over all the deceit and backstabbing."

"You've changed."

"Could be."

"Darling, trust me, you've changed. The callous homicide inspector facade is fading and the kind, sweet man I love is becoming more and more visible. I like the change." Ash leaned her head against my shoulder. "You know, there's a teddy bear show up near Baltimore this spring. How would you like to design and make a bear for the show?"

"How about a sock puppet?"

"How about creating something you can be proud of— a handsome boy teddy bear? You'd have all winter to work on it."

"I'd need all winter and a lot of your help. You'll have to show me how to use your sewing machine."

"We'll work on it together and I'll give you lessons on the Bernina. It's easier that it looks."

"I hope so, because I'm afraid that if I touch the wrong button I'll accidentally start the countdown to Armageddon."

I suspected Ash was being a wee bit optimistic about how quickly I'd learn to use that sewing machine, yet I was warming to the idea of making a teddy bear and I could already envision him. He'd be made from curly brown mohair, have a black embroidered nose, friendly glass eyes, and maybe a white linen collar with a bowtie. And so Ash and I sat there in the dark, talking, laughing, and making plans for a future built around creating lovable teddy bears.

I'm looking forward to it.

Susan Arnot

In Chapter Seven, Ashleigh Lyon shows Deputy Tina Barron one of her favorite artisan teddy bears—one crafted by Susan Arnot and made from a recycled fur coat. Of course, Ash and Tina are fictional characters, but Susan is an actual teddy bear artisan who resides in Sacramento, California. My wife, Joyce, and I first encountered her unique and heartwarming "Under the Apple Tree" collection at a teddy bear show in San Diego, and one of her mink creations sits on our library shelf.

Like so many other artisans, Susan was originally a bear collector, but it wasn't long before her love of handicrafts and natural creativity pushed her into making bears and, soon afterwards, designing her own. That was twelve years ago and Susan still revels in creating new bears.

She said, "Sometimes it takes several 'drafts' to get just the look I have pictured in my mind. What I enjoy most is seeing the face and personality of the bear come alive in my hands."

In the beginning, Susan worked with plush and after that, mohair. Then, five years ago, a bear collector asked her if she could make a bear from an old fur coat. Susan said she'd give it a try and was thrilled with the results.

"The bear came out so cute and still had 'my look,' which is difficult to do sometimes because real fur is more challenging to work with than plush or mohair," Susan told me.

In the past, she used to produce about two hundred bears in a year but that number is going down due to the fact that working with real fur is also far more time-consuming than with other materials. Furthermore, most of her bears are either one-of-a-kind or part of a very small edition because there is only so much fur in a recycled coat.

As might be expected, Susan's bears have garnered widespread praise over the years and one of her bears was a nominee for the prestigious Golden Teddy prize in 1995. The Golden Teddy is an annual award sponsored by *Teddy Bear Review* magazine to recognize the finest artisans from around the globe. In addition, her bears have won first prize at the California State Fair on several occasions. Regrettably, the last time she won the State Fair, her winning bear was stolen and the episode was so heartbreaking that she stopped entering the competition. However, she still attends teddy bear shows and loves watching the sweet impact her creations have on collectors.

"The thing I enjoy most about bear shows is watching the faces of collectors as they fall in love with one of my bears," said Susan. "Most of the time I think it's the bears that choose who they want to go home with and talk to that person through their expression."

Susan is in the process of creating a web site, but in the meantime she can be contacted via e-mail at undertheappletree@msn.com. She invites readers to write her with any questions about her bears or to learn more about her schedule of appearances at future teddy bear shows.

One of the greatest pleasures of writing this series of mystery novels is the enormous privilege of associating with teddy bear artisans. So, I'd like to close by thanking Susan Arnot and all the other bear artisans whose creations make the world a kinder and happier place.

Afterword

Both Remmelkemp Mill and Thermopylae are imaginary communities, as is Massanutten County, which I created from portions of Rockingham, Page, and Augusta Counties of Virginia. Hence, there is no Massanutten County Sheriff's Department. However, the geographical landmarks mentioned, such as Massanutten Mountain, the South Fork of the Shenandoah River, and the Island Ford Bridge are genuine places.

The Steiff Mourning Bear is an actual teddy bear and the information in the story as to its history, manufacture, and value is accurate.

The scrapbooking mystery series from

Laura Childs

Carmela Bertrand owns a scrapbooking
store in New Orleans—and can't help but solve a
murder every once in a while.

Keepsake Crimes
0-425-19074-9

Photo Finished
0-425-19434-5

Bound for Murder
0-425-19923-1

FREE SCRAPBOOKING TIPS
IN EACH BOOK!

Available wherever books are sold or at
penguin.com